"What if I told you that last night my need was for you?"

Sam's words hung between them for what seemed like an eternity. Delaney's breath got caught somewhere between her chest and her throat.

What was he saying? Sam didn't see her as a woman. She was his buddy, nothing more.

Sam stepped forward again, within touching distance this time. Delaney watched with a strange, disconnected kind of astonishment as he reached out to wrap his hand around her forearm. His skin felt hot through the silk of her robe.

"I mean I couldn't stop thinking about you in bed. And it drove me crazy," he said.

His grip remained firm, and she felt her arm slide within her silk sleeve as she pulled away. A sudden coolness told her that her robe had slid off her shoulder before she looked down and confirmed it.

There was a sudden, electric silence as they both stared at her exposed breast.

Delaney heard the harsh intake of Sam's breath.

"Delaney," he said in a choked voice, "for what it's worth, I'm sorry." And then he put his hand on her.

Blaze™

Dear Reader,

For about as long as I can remember, I have loved romance stories about best friends where one of the partners is secretly in love with the other. There's something so poignant about an unrequited crush. All that anticipation and fantasizing, all the yearning—it stands to reason that if something actually happened, it would be pretty explosive. That was my starting point for *Anything for You,* and by the time I'd found Sam and Delaney and given them a business to run together, they pretty much grabbed the story and ran with it.

A quick word on Sam: I'm a big fan of inarticulate, loving men, and Sam just about takes the cake for being out of touch with his own emotions. I hope you enjoy his journey of self-discovery—I certainly enjoyed writing it!

I love hearing from readers, and you can contact me via my Web site at www.sarahmayberryauthor.com, or in care of Harlequin Books, 225 Duncan Mill Road, Don Mills, Ontario M3B 3K9, Canada.

Until next time, happy reading!

Sarah Mayberry

ANYTHING FOR YOU
Sarah Mayberry

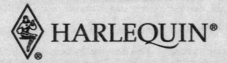

HARLEQUIN®

TORONTO • NEW YORK • LONDON
AMSTERDAM • PARIS • SYDNEY • HAMBURG
STOCKHOLM • ATHENS • TOKYO • MILAN • MADRID
PRAGUE • WARSAW • BUDAPEST • AUCKLAND

ISBN-13: 978-0-373-79282-5
ISBN-10:   0-373-79282-4

ANYTHING FOR YOU

ABOUT THE AUTHOR

Sarah Mayberry lives in Melbourne, Australia, with her partner of many years, Chris, who is also a writer. Before writing for Harlequin, she worked in publishing and as a scriptwriter/story person on television drama. When she's not writing, she fantasizes about living in a warehouse apartment, having longer legs and being able to surf.

Books by Sarah Mayberry

HARLEQUIN BLAZE

211—CAN'T GET ENOUGH
251—CRUISE CONTROL*

*It's All About Attitude

This one is especially for Chris. Thanks for
filling my life with love and laughter.

As usual, big thanks also to my reading buddies—
La La, Emma, Hanky Panky, Kirst, Caz and Satan.

And, of course, Wanda—
the best editor a girl could have.
Merci beaucoup!

1

SAM KIRK SAT BACK on his haunches and surveyed his hand-iwork. Not bad, even if he did say so himself. Smiling, he pushed himself to his feet and rubbed his hands on his jeans to clean the chalk dust off his fingers. The smile turned into an out-and-out grin as he admired the full result of his labors from a bird's-eye viewpoint.

Outlined on the navy industrial carpet in front of him was a classic crime-scene body outline depicting a form sprawled halfway across his business-partner-cum-best-friend's office. To add to the *CSI* look, he'd rifled through her filing cabinet, pulled a few books off her bookshelf and left all her desk drawers open. Highly satisfied with himself, he retreated to the doorway and began unrolling the police tape he'd wheedled from his mate in the force. Fixing one end to the doorframe, he stretched the tape to the opposite side and stuck it in place.

"Delaney is going to flip when she sees this," their receptionist, Debbie, said from behind him.

"I know. It's going to be great," Sam said with relish.

Debbie shot him a look designed to let him know she thought he was weird. She'd only been with their extreme sports magazine, *X-Pro,* for a month, so she wasn't up to speed yet on the office dynamic. When she'd been around a little longer, she'd understand that playing practical jokes on each other was just how he and Delaney operated. Every year when she went on holidays, he came up with some outrageous stunt to surprise her when she returned.

One year, it had been cajoling their printer to bind a single copy of the latest edition of the magazine inside out, then just casually leaving it on Delaney's desk on her first day back. She'd gone ballistic when she found it, and it had taken him twenty minutes to convince her that the full 60,000 editions of the magazine hadn't been mailed out to their subscribers in the same condition. Then there was the time he'd glued all her stationary accessories to her desk. Stapler, hole punch, computer mouse. Hell, he'd even stuck her wheelie chair to the carpet. Remembering the bewildered look on her face still brought a smile to his lips.

Stuffing the debris from his scene-setting into a carrier bag, Sam eyed his gathered staff of five.

"Remember, serious faces. She'll only buy this if no one laughs," he warned them.

"Sam, man, you're so deluded. She's going to know it was you the moment she sees it," their layout artist, Rudy, said.

"But she can't be sure. All I'm looking for is a moment of doubt," Sam said.

Checking his watch, he crossed to his office and looked out the window to see if Delaney had arrived yet. Her parking space was still empty, and he frowned. She lived in the apartment beneath him, and he hadn't heard her come home last night. But, he reminded himself, he didn't always hear her door open and close, and her car had definitely been in the space allocated to her apartment when he left early this morning, keen to get in and prepare his little surprise.

It wasn't like her to be late, especially on the first day back after two weeks off. Normally she was champing at the bit to get back in to it. That was one of the great things about owning their own business. Work wasn't a burden or a drag— it was something they enjoyed, even if sometimes it could be stressful or boring.

He was about to call her on her cell phone when he caught himself. Feeling a little foolish, he dropped into the chair behind his desk. He was carrying on like a dog who'd been locked inside all day, waiting for his master to come home. Delaney had only been away two weeks, but the truth was, he'd missed her like crazy.

His gaze fell on the photo occupying the one clear space on his desk. Two teenagers filled the frame—one a tall, chestnut-haired lout, the other a slim, brown-haired girl who was sporting a shiny black eye. Both wore Lycra rash vests and baggy board shorts, and their faces were tanned from long days at the beach. The boy was grinning hugely, his arm slung around the girl's shoulders, and the girl was looking furious and grumpy and determined. The picture had been taken when they were both sixteen, the summer he'd taught Delaney how to surf. She'd scored the black eye on the first day when her board flipped and clocked her in the face. She hadn't even cried, he remembered—just took a moment to get her breath before she started paddling again.

That was the thing with Delaney—when she wanted something, she bloody well went for it, both barrels blazing. Perhaps it was why they'd hit it off the moment her family moved onto his street when he was just twelve years old. The moving vans had barely started disgorging their contents before a scrappy, skinny girl had gravitated to the game of cricket he and his buddies had been playing in the street. She'd waited until the ball came her way before catching it deftly and asking if she could join in. The other neighborhood kids hadn't wanted to let her play, but she'd offered them a deal—if she could bowl them out, she was in. If not, she'd walk away without another word. She'd bowled a blindingly fast bouncer that almost took one kid's arm off before it hit the wicket, and all the others had hastily passed on their turns to bat, readily conceding that she could play.

It had been the beginning of a beautiful friendship, one that had survived every test thrown at it, from his insanely jealous girlfriend when he was in his early twenties, to the stress of starting a fledgling magazine on the smell of an oily rag. Delaney was the one constant in his life, the only person who got him—his jokes, his silences, his need to sometimes just get away and surf or skate or travel. Hell, she even shared the same address, since they'd bought warehouse apartments in the same building. She didn't constantly ask him what he was thinking or how he was feeling. She didn't need reassurance twenty times a day that she was an important part of his life. And she didn't play games and sulk if she didn't get her own way.

As though some all-knowing feminist deity had read his thoughts and decided to punish him, the phone on his desk buzzed.

"Sam, there's a Coco here to see you," Debbie said.

Sam groaned. "Could you tell her that—" he began to cajole, but Debbie cut him off.

"No, I couldn't. Delaney said when she hired me that under no circumstances was I to ever make excuses for you to one of your girlfriends. It's in my contract," Debbie said brightly.

Before he could counter this argument, the line went dead. A moment later, a wave of cloying floral scent preceded Coco as she minced her way to his office doorway.

"Hiya, bub," she said in her signature baby voice.

Sam barely controlled a cringe. How had he ever found that voice sexy? His eyes dropped to Coco's two best assets, clearly defined by the skin-tight white tank top she was wearing.

Right. Now he remembered.

Sadly, however, the sight of her generous D cups no longer sparked an ounce of interest from Little Sam, the man in charge of social activities. Perhaps it was the squeaky voice. Or the fact that Coco had a highly manicured white poodle that he'd caught her kissing on the mouth recently. Or the way she had of calling him *bub*. Or maybe it was all of the above, combined with the fact that he'd yet to have a single conversation with her that hadn't included the words "When I do a photo spread for your magazine." She seemed to think he was the man who was going to launch her modeling career, despite the fact that he'd told her over and over again that *X-Pro* wasn't that kind of publication. He'd been trying to ease his way out of their casual three-week relationship for the past few days, only returning every second call and manufacturing overtime at work to keep his nights unavailable. So far, so good—until now.

"Hey," he said, trying to inject a note of welcome into his voice. He might be a feckless love rat—as Delaney had told him many a time—but he wasn't a cruel, feckless love rat.

"Hey, yourself. I was just in the neighborhood, and I thought I would drop in and see if you were free for lunch." Coco pouted.

Sam frowned and flicked a glance at his watch. "Um, it's ten in the morning, Coco," he said.

"So? You're the boss, aren't you?" she said, eyes busy scanning the front covers of *X-Pro* that covered one of his office walls. Her wide blue eyes darted from image to image with increasing rapidity, taking in the skate boarders, snow boarders, BMX bike riders and surfers who had graced the magazine's cover over the past year.

"Is this the only magazine you publish?" she asked incredulously, the baby voice miraculously disappearing.

"Yep. Extreme sports, like I said," Sam said.

"*Triple X,* you said," Coco corrected him, eyes narrowing sharply.

Sam snorted his amusement. "*X-Pro,* Coco. I'm no Hugh Hefner. Although I wouldn't mind a visit to the Bunny Palace."

"But I thought…" Coco said, clearly disappointed.

"Like I said the other night—" the night he'd picked her up and she'd practically tongue-kissed her dog goodbye "—I'm more than happy to hook you up with a photographer friend of mine. I'm sure he could help you with your, um, ambitions."

Sam held his breath as Coco frowned, obviously thinking things over. Slowly.

"Can you call him now?" she asked after a *looooonnng* pause.

Sam smiled. "Sure I can. Hell, he might even be free for lunch," he added.

Without wasting another precious second of Coco's time, he reached for the phone. That was the thing Delaney didn't understand about his love life, Sam mused as he dialed. She thought he left a trail of brokenhearted women in his wake, but all the women he went out with were tailor-made for the kind of no-strings fun he specialized in.

As he waited for his photographer buddy to pick up, he registered that Delaney still hadn't shown up for work. Where the hell was she, anyway?

DELANEY MICHAELS sat in her parked car, staring blankly out the windshield. If she drove around the corner, she'd see the bright aqua street sign that announced the offices of Mirk Publications in the inner-city Melbourne district of Fitzroy. She'd find her reserved parking spot, along with an office full of people waiting for her return from holidays.

And, of course, Sam.

The thought of facing Sam was what had made her pull over nearly half an hour ago. She'd been doing really well until then, staying focused on her end goal, reminding herself over and over that she'd made the right decision—the only decision. And then she had flashed forward to how his face would look when she told him, the confused, hurt, baffled expression he would get in his eyes. That was when she'd had to swerve to the curb and take half a dozen deep, calming breaths to stop the panic tightening her chest.

She didn't think she could do this.

She *had* to do this.

Or she might as well sign up for the old spinsters club now and avoid the rush when she was sixty and grey and still ridiculously, besottedly, pathetically in love with Sam Kirk.

Gritting her teeth, Delaney scrunched her eyes shut and made an angry, frustrated growling sound in the back of her throat. She had been over and over and over this decision. The better part of the last week of her holiday had been spent facing the sad truth of her life and formulating a plan to change things. She wasn't a coward. She had never backed away from a challenge in her life. And she wouldn't back away from this. It was just…hard.

When a woman had been in love with the same handsome, ne'er-do-well, charming, funny, sensitive, generous, incorrigible rogue for the better part of her life, it was probably only natural for her to feel a little…shaky about how she was going to cope once she'd pruned him out of her world. But that was all it was—stage fright, pre-match jitters. Nothing would stop her from going through with her plan, because there was too much at stake.

If she hadn't decided to go on vacation with her sister's family, she might have let a few more years slip away before she made the vital break. Watching her sister's life from a prime, courtside seat, she'd had a cosmic revelation. She wanted a family. She wanted a husband and kids. She wanted snotty noses and tears for no reason and snuggling in bed with small, warm bodies. And she was never going to get any of it while she was in love with Sam.

How was she ever supposed to find someone she liked enough to marry while Sam filled her whole world? Even the fact that she thought in terms of *liking* someone, not *loving* them, was testament to how long Sam had been her everything.

It was pathetic. Especially since the big dope didn't have a clue. Even when she'd been a doe-eyed teen, mooning around after him, he'd never gotten wise. Thank God. She'd swiftly learned what happened to the love interests in Sam's life—a few blissful, heady moments in the warm sunshine of his attention, then a lifetime of exile in the land of shadows once he'd moved on. She'd soon worked out that it was far better to be his ever-present buddy and sidekick than to risk all for a few fleeting moments of perfection. And it was a compromise she'd been happy with the bulk of her adult life.

It wasn't like she wasn't getting any action of her own. She had needs, after all. And there were only so many Sam-fueled fantasy sessions a girl could host in the privacy of her lonely bedroom. She'd had lovers, off and on, over the years. None of them had so much as put a dent in her love for Sam, of course. And she'd hurt some of them, she knew, with her emotional unavailability. But she hadn't been celibate, pining in a tower somewhere over her unrequited love.

In all honesty, she'd thought she had it worked out. Sex when she needed it, and Sam in her life forever. Perfect. Right?

Except now it was time to grow up and face the facts: if she wanted children and a husband, she had to get Sam out of her head and heart.

She knew herself well enough to know that that meant excising Sam from her life. Just the thought of it made tears well up in her eyes as she stared bleakly out her windshield. She couldn't imagine her life without Sam in it. He was her best friend. Her business partner. The one who finished her sentences. He could always make her smile, and he could infuriate her like no one else on the planet. It would be like losing an arm or a leg.

Or a heart.

But there were no half measures with this thing, she could see that. She'd be cheating her future husband if she remained friends with Sam. She had to at least be open to the possibility of loving someone else.

She felt sick to her stomach. Their lives were impossibly intertwined. She lived beneath him, for Pete's sake. She worked with him. No, not just worked—she owned half the business, he owned the other half. It really *would* be like lopping off a limb.

But she didn't see that she had much choice. It wasn't as though her love for Sam would just curl up and die of its own accord one day. It had been nearly sixteen years and it showed no signs of waning. So, she was faced with a choice—Sam, or a family of her own.

Sitting in her car, Delaney felt the panic rising again. She forced herself to think practically and push the panic away.

It was nearly a quarter past ten. She needed to get in to work. At the very least, there would be a big pile of paperwork in her in-tray that needed to be dealt with.

Starting her car, she drove the remaining short distance to the office and parked in her spot. Taking a deep breath, she exited the car and beeped it shut. For the first time ever, the sight of her red-and-white MINI Cooper didn't bring a smile to her face.

"That bad, huh?" she asked herself wryly as she turned toward the entrance to the building.

She blinked as a startling vision almost plowed in to her.

"Careful!" the woman said, pursing hot pink lips. Delaney's gaze swept from the woman's honey-blond mane of tangled hair past impossibly blue eyes, cute little ski-jump nose and neon mouth, only to come to a grinding halt on the woman's truly spectacular breasts. Whoa! They were so large and so tightly outlined by a white tank top that Delaney could barely pull her gaze away. And she was a woman! She felt a small stab of pity for the male of species. Against breasts like these, most men were powerless.

"Sorry," she muttered, stepping aside to let the other woman pass.

Jessica Rabbit flashed a tight little smile before strutting away, ass wiggling in her high stiletto heels and short leather miniskirt, despite the fact that there was no one but Delaney to notice.

A true professional, Delaney thought, *always committed to the cause.*

She couldn't imagine what it would be like to look like that and walk like that and behave like that. She and Jessica Rabbit might as well come from different planets. Delaney glanced down at her own slim, boyish figure. If the bra manufacturer was on the generous side with their measures, she was a B cup. But more often than not she was an A. And where the other woman's waist swerved in and out again like the corner of a racetrack, her own body sort of ran straight down, side-stepping the need for such womanly accoutrements as an hourglass waist or childbearing hips. Narrowing her eyes, Delaney decided that she might rival the other woman in the legs department, however. She had a good four inches in height on Jessica, and much of that was leg. And she'd been told she had a nice ass, firm and small.

She sighed and pushed her bangs off her forehead. Why was she standing on the threshold of her business taking stock of herself like this?

Because you know what that woman was doing in this building, she told herself. *Or, more accurately,* who.

Steeling herself, Delaney pushed open the door and strode into the reception area of their small offices. Debbie looked up from her computer screen and broke into a welcoming smile.

"Hey, Delaney! Thank God you're here—Sam has been driving us crazy, asking if anyone's heard from you," Debbie said.

Delaney's treacherous heart leaped in her chest, but she barely gave it the time of day. She was used to the damned thing lurching around inside her whenever Sam was in the vicinity. Occupational hazard of having an unrequited crush on her best friend.

"He's highly excitable," she said, and Debbie blushed a little.

Delaney gave Debbie an intent look. Yep, all the signs were there—Debbie had a crush on Sam. The poor fool.

Great. Another receptionist bites the dust.

Delaney wondered how long it would take before Sam had to deliver the "I don't dip my pen in the office ink" speech to

Debbie, leading their receptionist to quit so he could go out with her. Judging by the depth of Debbie's glow-on, not long.

"Your messages are in your office. Sam handled most things, but a few clients only wanted to speak to you and they said they would wait until you got back," Debbie said.

Delaney nodded her acceptance of this. She was largely responsible for the advertising sales side of the business, while Sam supervised and wrote for the editorial half of the magazine. While he could step into her shoes on occasion and schmooze with the best of them, it wasn't his natural element.

"About time, lazybones," a deep male voice said from behind her, and all the small hairs on her forearms stood on end.

"Sam," she said, bracing herself for the first sight of him after two weeks away.

As usual, absence *had* made the heart grow fonder. He looked taller, broader, sexier than ever in his worn, faded denims, crumpled T-shirt and scruffy skate shoes. His skin was always tanned thanks to his weekly surfing sessions, and he was still sporting the ridiculously clichéd dreadlocks that he'd been cultivating for the past year. A mixture of his natural chestnut and sun-bleached blond, they hung to his shoulders in thick, matted ropes. On any other thirty-year-old man dreadlocks might look like a pathetic attempt to cling to their youth, but Sam pulled it off with ease.

Bright blue eyes sparkling with pleasure, he stepped forward.

"Laney!" he said, scooping her into his embrace.

For a few heady seconds she was held tight against his hard, hot chest, and his smell swamped her—a mixture of sun and pine forest and spice. Probably soap and laundry detergent, knowing Sam. He famously decried aftershave as being "one step too close to being a she-male" for his tastes, and any scent he had was all his own.

If Calvin Klein bottled it, he could buy himself the World Bank, she figured.

"Sorry I'm late. I had some stuff to take care of," she said evasively as she extracted herself from his embrace. She swallowed a lump of lust and forced a smile.

"How're things? No problems while I was gone?" she asked.

"Nothing I couldn't handle," Sam said.

He was wired about something, she noticed, studying him. A bit too perky, a little too shiny-eyed.

"Okay, what have you done this time?" she asked resignedly. She pretended to hate the practical jokes he played on her, but she secretly loved the trouble he took to amuse and annoy her.

"Nothing. Although there *was* an unfortunate incident while you were away...." Sam said, doing his best to sound solemn as he steered her toward her office.

She registered the Crime Scene, Do Not Cross tape across her door with a blink. Then she saw the chalk outline on the carpet, and her paperwork strewn all over her desk.

"We're not sure how they got in, but it appears there was a falling-out between thieves, and there was a bit of a struggle...." Sam said with admirable composure.

Delaney rolled her eyes. "*Puh-lease.* As if you wouldn't have called me on my cell phone if someone had bitten the big one in my office. And you're tidying up my desk, mister," she said, poking a finger into his chest.

He grinned, clearly proud of himself.

"Admit it—had you going for just a second," he said.

She shook her head. "You're too transparent, Kirk. I can read you like a billboard."

He shrugged a shoulder. "Just like I can read you, Michaels—and when you saw that police tape, you had your doubts," he said.

She quirked an eyebrow at him as she unceremoniously tugged the crime-scene tape loose and let it flop to the floor. Entering her office, she dumped her briefcase and turned to face him, propping her butt on the edge of her desk. He hooked his hands over the top of the door frame and grinned at her. God, it was good to see him. Unable to help herself, she fished to confirm her guess about the woman outside.

"So who was the pneumatic blonde?" she asked, careful to keep her tone light and disinterested. She had a Ph.D. in light and disinterested. It was almost an art form for her.

"Coco," he said, waving a hand dismissively.

And that, thought Delaney, *is the end of that.* She almost pitied Coco, but the other woman hadn't looked heartbroken in the least.

"How long this time? A week? Two weeks?" she asked.

"Three. With time out for bad behavior," he said.

"Bad behavior?"

"Yeah. Caught her kissing her dog on the lips," Sam explained with a grimace. "Had to wait for the cooties to settle."

"Ew. That's just plain wrong, as well as giving the dog false hope," Delaney said.

Sam threw back his head and let out a crack of laughter, and she felt a warm surge of pleasure that she'd amused him.

She realized she was staring at the strong column of his throat, her eyes caressing the firm, muscled planes of his chest and shoulders, nicely defined by the soft material of his T-shirt and his hanging-off-the-doorframe posture. She could feel her nipples tightening, and she crossed her arms over her chest. Occupational hazard number two: unruly body parts that always seemed to be on the verge of betraying her.

But not for much longer, she promised herself.

"Coco wanted us to feature her in the magazine," Sam said.

Delaney blinked. "Does she skate or something?" she asked, her mind boggling at the effect those D-cups would have on the boys down at the skate ramp.

"Not exactly. She must have misheard me when I told her the name of the magazine. She thought it was *Triple X,*" Sam said, deadpan.

Delaney's mouth dropped open. "As in…?"

"Yep."

Delaney broke into giggles. "That's why she was looking so pissed off outside," she said.

"Was she?" Sam looked a little piqued. "It's not as though we didn't have some fun. What is it with women these days? Multiple orgasms not enough anymore?"

Delaney suddenly got very interested in tidying up her desk. Multiple orgasms with Sam Kirk. It was enough to set her underwear on fire.

"How was the holiday? Did those horrible brats of Claire's drive you around the bend?" Sam asked, dropping onto the visitors' couch.

"The holiday was great. And they weren't brats. They were…perfect," she said, her voice softening as she remembered all the special little moments from the last two weeks: Travis's pencil drawing to say goodbye, Callum's nightly insistence that she be the one to read his bedtime story, Alana's repeated intrusion into her suitcase to play dress-up—a high compliment, her sister assured her.

"You catch any waves? Heard Gunnamatta was going off," Sam said, naming a famous surf beach a few minutes drive from where they'd been staying.

"Not really. Just paddled around on the bay with the boys. Travis wants to learn how to surf," she reported.

"Excellent. Another little grommet to clog up the water-ways," Sam said wryly.

"You were a grommet once. A particularly annoying one, as I recall, always dropping in on other surfer's waves," she reminded him.

"I was precocious. Oozing natural talent," he said.

"Oozing something, that's for sure."

Sam just grinned at her. "Missed you, Laney," he said, sliding a hand casually beneath his T-shirt to scratch his stomach.

She was treated to a flash of taut, muscled belly, the tanned skin sprinkled with crisp, caramel-colored curls that tapered down toward the waistband of his favorite jeans.

She snatched her eyes away and took a deep breath. *Do it now,* she told herself. *Before you spend too much time with him and lose your nerve.*

"Um, I need to speak to you sometime, too," she forced herself to say, eyes fixed on the stack of papers she was shuffling together.

"Sure. What's up?" Sam asked.

"I didn't mean now," Delaney said, panicking.

"No time like the present," Sam said easily.

He was right, even if he didn't know exactly how right. *Suck it up, Michaels,* she told herself.

Crossing to the door, she kicked it shut. Sam raised an eyebrow.

"A closed door conversation. My, my—I must have been really naughty this time," he said lightly.

Delaney moved back to her desk and sank into her chair. Then she just stared at him for a moment, her eyes lovingly cataloguing his handsome, open face. This would be the last time she saw him without anger or confusion or resentment clouding their relationship. The last time that he would be her old, much-loved friend, no strings attached, no issues between them.

The lines around his eyes crinkled as he smiled nervously. "Okay, you're freaking me out now. What's going on?" he asked. He leaned forward, elbows on his knees. "Talk to me, Laney," he said.

Delaney closed her eyes for a moment. She took a deep breath, then opened them.

"I want to sell you my half of the business," she said in a rush.

Sam shook his head in confusion. "Sorry? Do you need money or something, Laney? Because you should have said—"

It was her turn to shake her head.

"No. I want out. I want out from the magazine, Sam."

2

SAM FELT AS THOUGH he'd been punched in the gut. Delaney wanted to sell her half of the magazine? It just didn't make sense to him. He shook his head again, frowning.

"I don't get it. What's changed all of a sudden?" he asked.

She was staring at the carpet, but she lifted her eyes to meet his before she spoke.

"I've had enough. I realized while I was away that I wanted to do something different. Maybe travel. I don't know," she said.

She was lying. He knew her better than he knew himself, and there was something she wasn't telling him.

"Bull. Tell me what's really going on," he demanded, starting to feel angry and a little threatened.

Delaney couldn't just walk out on him. They were a team, a tight little duo. He'd barely survived her annual two-week vacation with his sanity intact, for Pete's sake.

"Sam," she said, then she sighed heavily and put her head in her hands.

After a shocked second he saw that she was crying. Delaney never cried. Ever.

"Hey," he said, shooting to his feet and moving to stand by her chair. Wrapping an arm around her shoulders, he held her tight. "Whatever it is, we'll work it out," he said.

He felt her body stiffen under his arm, and she sat up

straighter. He got the message—she didn't want his comfort. Feeling doubly rejected, he returned to the couch.

There was a long silence as they stared at each other across the small space that separated them. He studied her closely, trying to find some clue as to what was really going on. But she looked the same as ever—her long mid-brown hair pulled back into a ponytail, the fringe sitting straight across her brow. Her hazel eyes were clear and bright, not a skerrick of makeup in sight, as usual. Her nose was a little red on the end, true, but that was from the crying, he guessed. And she was biting her lower lip, her teeth nibbling at the full curve. She had a small mouth, but her lips were full, the lower one particularly so. A Cupid's bow, Delaney's mother always called it, to which Delaney inevitably rolled her eyes.

She looked the same as she always had—like Laney. His best friend.

"Come on, spill," he said softly.

She sniffed inelegantly and he leaned over to grab the box of tissues off her bookshelf.

She waited until she'd blown her nose before speaking.

"I want children, Sam. I want a husband. A family," she said, shrugging one shoulder.

Sam frowned. Laney never talked about her love life. He was always a little bit surprised when he caught sight of a guy leaving her apartment. He could count on the fingers of one hand the times he'd been introduced to a man she was dating. She'd always been very private about it, and he'd respected that. Truth was, he didn't really want to know, he suddenly acknowledged. Probably that made him a selfish bastard for not wanting her to be happy. Deep down inside he'd always feared that if she met Mr. Right, their friendship would change irrevocably. Sam would be number two in her life.

And when children came, he'd be shuffled even further down the food chain. It didn't say much for his nobility as a human being that the thought of Delaney with a family made him feel scared and lonely and threatened. But there it was.

Struggling to contain his messed-up emotions, Sam smoothed his hands down his thighs, then clasped his knees, bracing himself to be a grown-up.

"Of course you want kids," he finally managed to say.

Delaney laughed, a watery, reluctant chuckle.

"You are the worst actor in the world, Kirk," she said.

He shrugged sheepishly. "Okay," he conceded. "You know I'll be jealous as hell when you get married and have kids," he admitted.

She looked startled. "Jealous?"

"You know—'cause things won't be the same anymore," he explained awkwardly.

Delaney's eyes dropped to the carpet and she hunched a shoulder. "No, they won't."

"But I don't see what any of that has to do with leaving the business," Sam said. He might be about to lose most of Delaney, but he would cling to what little he had left. If she stayed in the business, she would always be a part of his life, no matter what.

"It's too all-consuming, Sam," she said. "We live for this place. How am I ever supposed to meet someone when all I do is eat, sleep, breathe Mirk Publications?"

"Then we'll get a sales assistant. You can do half days. Whatever it takes," he countered.

"No. It wouldn't work. I'm a control freak, you know I am. And it's thinking about the business when I'm not here that's part of it, as well. I'd still be doing that if I owned half of it. I need a complete break," she said.

There was a determination in her tone, a firmness that he recognized. Delaney had made her decision. Without talking it over with him. Without consulting him in any way. She'd simply gone away, and come back determined to do her own thing.

He started to get angry. "And where does that leave me?" he asked. He hated the fact that he sounded like a sulky kid, but that was how he felt, so he might as well own up to it.

"Sam, you can easily afford to buy me out. You know you can. Or you can get in another partner. Or go into partnership with another small publisher. God knows, we've had enough of them sniffing around over the years," she said.

Sam stared at her. She was serious about this. Completely serious. He wanted to yell at her. To tell her in no uncertain terms how stupid and selfish and wrong all this was. But he didn't. He bit his tongue and fought for control.

"When do you want out?" he managed to ask.

"As soon as possible," she said baldly.

Unbelievably, in light of their conversation to date, her words still stung. He rocketed to his feet.

"I'll talk to the bank," he said, and then he pulled her office door open, slamming it behind him as he exited. Their entire staff turned his way, but he ignored them all, crossing next door to his own office and slamming that door, too.

Then he threw himself into his office chair and dropped his head into his hands.

What in the world was he going to do without her?

DELANEY TOOK A LONG, shuddery breath and then let it out. She'd just had the hardest conversation of her life, hands down. Swiveling in her chair, she leaned forward and rested her forehead on her desk.

The look in Sam's eyes. The hurt. The lack of comprehension. She hated causing him pain, but she had no choice.

Unless she was prepared to tell him the real reason she had to go.

Which was never going to happen.

Which left her back at square one. Although, technically, she was at square two now. She'd delivered the big blow. Now she just had to live through the next little while before she could walk away from the business. And Sam.

Her heart wrenched painfully in her chest at the thought. But she had to face up to it. One day soon, in a month or two's time, she would walk out the double doors of this building and out of Sam's life forever.

She lifted her head off the desk, then dropped it down again, banging her forehead. It felt like an appropriate punishment for the mess she'd created, and she did it several more times—bang, bang, bang, bang—until it suddenly occurred to her that she might bruise her forehead. Good luck explaining that one to sane, ordinary people—I'd just screwed up my entire life, so I thought I'd add brain damage to the mix.

Lifting her head, she stared blindly at the wall planner in front of her. Absolute honesty time—there had been a part of her that had hoped that when Sam heard her big news he'd break down and say something to give her hope. She figured that the exact same part of her twisted female psyche was responsible for believing in unicorns when she was five and Santa Claus until she was eight, but it didn't make the realization any easier to bear. How sad could she get? Even at the eleventh hour, she was hoping for a reprieve, that he'd tell her he was mad about her, he couldn't stand the thought of life without her. As if Sam wouldn't have found some time over the past, say, sixteen years to recognize that his brotherly affection was actually repressed lust for her slim, boyish body, if that were actually the case.

A knock sounded on the door behind her.

"Yes?" she called out.

The door opened a crack and their desktop artist, Rudy, poked his head in. "You okay?" he asked cautiously. With his flamboyant red-and-blue-dyed hair and multiple piercings, coupled with his tendency to dress in brightly colored rave club wear, Rudy looked like a demented elf.

Delaney summoned a smile for him. "I'm fine," she lied.

"Right. I've been with you guys for five years, Delaney. You and Sam have never slammed doors before," Rudy said.

"Sam slammed the door," Delaney pointed out.

Rudy rolled his eyes as if to say it was the same difference. "Is everything all right?" he asked.

Delaney opened her mouth to offer up another soothing platitude, but she realized that she might as well just tell him the truth. The sooner it became an accepted fact, the sooner she could move on.

"I've asked Sam to buy out my share of the magazine," she said. "I'm leaving the business."

Rudy's eyes almost bugged out of his head. "No way!" he said.

Delaney just held his eye until the incredulous expression faded from his face.

"But you and Sam are like bread and butter. Or strawberries and cream. Or…or…peanuts and bananas. You *never* have one without the other," Rudy said.

"Peanuts and bananas, Rudy?" she queried.

"Try it sometime," he said. Then he stared at Delaney as if he were a lost puppy.

She tried her best to be reassuring.

"It's not going to change anything for you guys. Sam will still be here. The magazine will be exactly the same," she said.

"No, it won't. It's not the same without you around. If you'd been here for the past two weeks you'd know that. Sam can't do all the things you do. Just like you can't do all the things he does. That's why you make a great team. Like peanuts—"

"And bananas. I got it," Delaney said. "I'm sorry, Rudy, but it's just the way it is. It'll all work out okay, you'll see."

If only she could believe her own advice. Shooting her one last bewildered look, Rudy slipped back out into the main office. Within seconds, their remaining four employees would be up to speed, Delaney guessed. Which would save her having to conduct the same difficult, uncomfortable conversation four more times.

Working on autopilot, she turned her computer on and began to organize her desk. Sam's practical joke had left her normally neat and tidy work surface a mess of disordered paper. She spent the next twenty minutes mindlessly filing and straightening things, then she worked her way through her phone messages. By the time she'd dealt with the more urgent ones, it was lunchtime.

She usually ate lunch with Sam. They'd walk to a local café, or jump in the car and go somewhere farther afield, just to clear their heads. Once or twice a year, when the weather was too damned irresistible and the surf report was too enticing, they'd bail on work completely for the whole afternoon and take off for the nearest surf beach.

She could just imagine his expression if she sauntered next door and suggested they grab a bite. She hadn't heard a peep from him since he'd barreled out of her office and into his own—no low murmur of phone conversation, no chatting with the other employees. Like her, Sam was probably staying put in his office, reeling from her announcement.

For a second she was gripped with a wild impulse to tell him it had all been a big, stupid joke. That she'd just been yanking his chain, the ultimate practical gag.

The urge was so strong she forced herself to scoop up her car keys and purse before she could give in to it. Striding to the front door, she told Debbie that she'd be back in an hour.

The mall was probably not the best place to go when she was feeling down, but somehow she wound up there. Fluorescent lighting, neon signs, crowds of dull-eyed shoppers— she fit right in as she walked around aimlessly, staring blankly at clothes racks, sorting pointlessly through sales bins. It wasn't until she caught herself burrowing furiously through a bargain bin, trying to find a complete set of Christmas-themed napkin rings, that she snapped out of it.

Not only did she not own napkins, she hated knick-knacky home decor items with a passion. Dropping the offending objects like hot potatoes, she exited the store and sat on the nearest bench. Pulling a notebook from her handbag, she forced herself to focus.

Yes, she was a little off balance after making such a life-changing decision and then following through on it by telling Sam her intentions, but it was no excuse to wig out completely. She had to keep moving toward her end goal—find a husband, build a family.

She wrote both things down in her notebook, then groaned and tore the page out, throwing it into the nearby bin. Who was she kidding? She didn't need a to-do list—she knew what had to be done.

First, she had to stop comparing every man she met to Sam Kirk. Second, she had to actually start taking more men up on their offers to take her to dinner/the movies/bed. With Sam out of her life, hopefully the rest would simply fall into place.

Wig-out over, she stood and smoothed the creases from her tailored slim-line trousers. Her hands stilled on her thighs as she stared down at her sensible, businesslike outfit. She always wore pants to work. And she almost always wore a shirt, or some other kind of sensible, tailored top. She wasn't a fussy, frills-and-flowers kind of woman, never had been. But still…

Scanning the mall, her eye was drawn to the glint of a mirror, and she crossed to stand in front of it. The woman staring back at her was plain-looking, with long straight mid-brown hair pulled back into a ponytail. She was wearing navy linen pants and a cream cotton shirt, and while both were of good quality and well-cut, there was no escaping the fact that she looked a little like a military nurse. Or a postal worker.

Her mind flashed to the eye-popping blonde she'd encountered outside the office that morning. No one would ever mistake Coco for a postal worker, that was for sure. And while Delaney knew she could never even begin to play in the same league as the epically endowed Coco, there was no reason why she shouldn't make the best of her assets.

That's what it was all about, after all, wasn't it? Using what you had to attract the opposite sex. Then it was down to personality and compatibility and chemistry.

Once again she scanned the mall, this time looking for a hair salon. There were three to choose from, all situated close to one another. She spent a few minutes analyzing the cuts of the hairstylists in each establishment, as well as those of their clients, then she simply picked the one that looked the most expensive. She hadn't had a haircut in months. Normally she tidied up her own bangs with the kitchen scissors, and just had the spilt ends cut off the back every now and then.

Approaching the counter, she smiled nervously at the receptionist.

"Hi. I'd like to get a haircut," she said.

"Of course. We actually have an opening now, if you're interested," the girl said smoothly. "Someone canceled at the last minute." She flicked a strand of perfect hair over her shoulder, and Delaney found herself following the silky fall of the woman's multihued locks. Eyes narrowing, she assessed the receptionist's haircut: shorter at the front, it gradually became longer toward the back, just skimming her shoulders. The choppy texture of the cut was emphasized by a mixture of brown streaks, ranging from darkest chocolate to cinnamon to a golden bronze. It was sexy hair, alluring hair. Nothing postal or military about it at all.

"Do you think they could cut my hair like that?" Delaney asked impulsively.

The receptionist tilted her head to one side and considered her. "Absolutely. Let me get Volker. He's the expert," she said.

Delaney found herself being ushered into a seat by a lanky hairstylist with a pronounced German accent.

"Oh, yes, we can do something with this," he said approvingly as he freed her hair from its tie.

"It needs to be like hers," Delaney said, pointing toward the receptionist who had once again resumed her station at the front of the store.

"It will be better," Volker announced, no hint of ego or boasting in his voice—he was simply stating a fact.

Two hours later, Delaney decided he was right on the money. The woman staring back from the salon mirror was a stranger. Gone was her straight, no-nonsense fringe. Now her hair swept gracefully to one side of her face to fall in graduated layers onto her shoulders. Each layer was made up of a myriad of colors—russet, chocolate, ginger—so that when she ran her hand through it or shook it, her hair shimmered with light and movement.

"Wow," the receptionist said when Delaney stepped up to the counter to pay her bill. The girl's gaze flicked doubtfully to her own reflection in a nearby mirror and Delaney felt a dart of feminine pride. She had hair that other women envied! How good was that!

Her euphoria lasted for all of the five seconds it took for her mind to default to wondering what Sam would think of her new cut.

Stupid stupid stupid, she told herself, but it didn't make any difference. He had been the sun her world orbited around for so long, it was going to take time to wean herself away from using him as her touchstone.

The realization drove her into the nearest David Jones department store, her step determined.

Another hour and a half later, she stuffed a dozen rustling shopping bags into the back seat of the MINI. She'd gone berserk. There was no other word for it. Julia Roberts in *Pretty Woman* had nothing on Delaney. She'd practically handed her credit card over to the sympathetic sales assistant and told her to go crazy. New makeup, perfume and underwear, six pairs of shoes, a pair of boots, three pairs of figure-hugging jeans in black, red and dark denim, and a host of skirts, dresses, tank tops, T-shirts... She honestly had no idea exactly what she'd bought. But it was all fitted. Tight, even. The skirts were either short and flirty, or short and figure-hugging. The dresses were triumphs of design, with minuscule straps and cinching belts and draping skirts that made her look willowy and elegant and mysterious. And the bras... Who would have thought that a bra could make such a difference?

She refused to wear a padded bra, but the underwire balconette bra the saleswoman had shown her actually gave her cleavage. And the colors! She had a rainbow of silk and lace in her shopping bags. She'd *oohed* and *ahhed* so much she was sure the saleswoman must have thought she'd just escaped from behind the Iron Curtain. But the truth was, Delaney hadn't spent this much time thinking about her appearance since she was a teenager and she'd made a single pathetic, misguided attempt to make Sam look at her as a woman. He'd laughed at her too-bright lipstick and her sister's clothes and asked if she was going to a fancy dress, and she'd gone home and scrubbed at her face until it was red raw.

Since she'd long ago given up on Sam loving her, she'd relegated the art of allure and seduction to the dustbin. If a man was interested in plain old Delaney, she'd give him a whirl. But she had never gone out of her way to be sexy before. And this new wardrobe of hers was undeniably provocative.

Good, she told herself firmly. She was thirty years old. She only had a limited amount of time to meet a decent man, fall in love and start making babies.

She'd called Debbie from the hair salon to explain her long absence, and she stopped at the other woman's desk to collect her messages on the way in to her office.

"Just three calls. Everyone still thinks you're on holiday," Debbie said absently, passing the chits over without looking up from her computer monitor.

"Thanks," Delaney said, turning away.

"Get out of town!" Debbie suddenly squealed from behind her. "Delaney, what have you done?"

Delaney felt a stab of apprehension. She'd changed into the black jeans at the shop, matching them with a bright aqua tank top that made the most of her newly upthrust bosom. It was just like the time she'd dressed up for Sam—clearly she'd got it all wrong again. She closed her eyes for a second, then braced herself and turned back to face Debbie.

"Not good, huh?" she asked flatly.

"Are you kidding?! You look amazing. Astonishing. Stunning!" Debbie babbled. "Rudy, come and check Delaney out!"

Of course, that meant everyone else came as well, Amanda and Justin and Sukie trailing Rudy out into the reception area. They all circled around her oohing and ahhing.

"Your hair is so gorgeous. I want to eat it," Rudy said worryingly.

"Those jeans, Delaney. Wow," Justin said admiringly. Delaney noticed he was having a hard time taking his eyes off her ass.

Sukie was staring at Delaney's chest, and she winked knowingly. "Mademoiselle FiFi," she said, naming the brand of Delaney's new bra. Sukie patted her own perky chest with satisfaction. "I love her work."

It was all salve for her ego, and she felt her confidence blooming. She should have done this ages ago. She'd always taken the line that what people saw with her was what they got, but she realized now she'd been missing out on a lot of fun. She'd liked putting on lipstick and a touch of mascara and eye shadow with the expert guidance of the woman in the beauty section of the department store. And testing the perfumes had been a hoot. It was nice to feel desirable and attractive for a change.

Her gaze kept flicking toward Sam's closed door, but Debbie answered her unspoken question before she had to ask it.

"Sam left not long after you," the receptionist said.

Delaney stomped on the absurd sense of disappointment she felt at Sam not being there to see her transformation. This was not about Sam Kirk! She had to get that through her thick head.

She registered that everyone had sobered. She guessed they were thinking about the news she'd given Rudy before lunch.

"Don't worry, your jobs are all safe," she said quickly. "No one's going anywhere."

Except for her, of course. But she was sure they weren't worried about her.

"But it won't be the same," Sukie said, echoing Rudy's earlier remark. "We like working for you and Sam. It will be weird without you."

"You'll get used to it. And it's not like I'm going straight away," Delaney said, moved by her employees' sincerity. Maybe they *were* a little worried about her.

"Are you—are you getting married or something?" Justin blurted out.

Delaney blinked. "No!"

Justin turned beet-red. "I just thought maybe you'd fallen in love with some jerk who didn't want you to work and maybe we could go around and break his kneecaps or something."

Delaney was touched all over again. "There's no guy, trust me. I just want to do something different with my life," she assured them.

Offering up one last smile, she crossed to her office.

The smile faded when she saw the note Sam had left on her desk.

Gone to talk to lawyers. Will have answer for you by p.m.

Wow. He'd moved quickly.

She sat with a thump. Soon, it seemed, she'd get what she wanted.

So why wasn't she feeling relieved or happy?

Because you're a besotted idiot, she told herself. Determined to change that, she grabbed her phone messages and focused on work.

She had to be strong now, or suffer the consequences later. There was no other way.

SAM WAS SO WORKED UP when he got home from the lawyer's office that he had to play five rounds of *Grand Theft Auto* on PlayStation before his stress levels were manageable. When he'd finally maxed out his personal best score, he shut the unit off and grabbed himself a beer from the fridge. Heading out onto the balcony, he gazed across the crowded inner-city suburb of Richmond as he sucked down some much-needed liquid calm.

The evening breeze was cool, and the sky was a faded apricot color by the time he lifted himself out of his lounger and padded back into the house.

He'd been so angry with Delaney earlier that he could barely think, but now a semblance of rational thought had reasserted itself. For some reason, Delaney's biological clock had suddenly exploded. Personally, he blamed Claire and her three offspring. Clearly the kids—evil geniuses that they were—had implanted some kind of hormonal device in Delaney's brain while she was on holidays and Claire was making hay while the sun shined. Women always wanted other women to have children. They were constantly encouraging each other to procreate—a maternal conspiracy.

So. Delaney wanted kids of her own. It wasn't the end of the world. But it didn't mean she had to get out of the business. When he'd been discussing things with his lawyer this afternoon, a number of options had been floated. The one that appealed the most was keeping Delaney in the business as a silent partner, and bringing in an advertising sales manager to handle Delaney's role. That way Delaney was still a part of the business—still connected to his life—but she could go off and find Mr. Perfect at the same time. Everyone was a winner.

It was such a great idea, Sam decided he should just go sell it to Delaney on the spot. Plus, he'd never stayed angry at her for this long before, and it felt weird. And, of course, there was dinner to be considered. He couldn't cook, Delaney could…. Again everyone was a winner.

Grabbing the remaining two beers from his fridge, he snagged his house keys and made his way downstairs to Delaney's apartment. Her door was red where his was blue, but the layouts inside were identical. They'd bought the empty warehouse shells at the same time, and shared the cost of an architect to fit out both spaces. There were small, idiosyncratic differences, of course—Delaney's bathroom was all white where his was dark grey. And her kitchen had a lot more stainless-steel equipment than his. But apart from that, the apartments were a matched pair. Like him and Delaney.

She took her sweet time answering his knock, and he was beginning to frown with impatience when the door swung open.

"Sam!" she said, clearly surprised to see him. He was too busy doing a double take to register the fact, however.

What on earth had she done to herself?

"What on earth have you done to yourself?" he demanded, eyeing her freaky new haircut uncertainly.

Since when did Delaney have soft layers of honey and toffee-colored hair gently framing her face? His stunned gaze moved from her new hair to her face itself as he realized that that looked different, too. Eyes bigger and smokier, mouth redder and poutier. She was wearing makeup! His Delaney was wearing makeup!

Then his eyes dropped below her neckline and he nearly had a heart attack. What had happened to Delaney's signature crisp cotton shirt? Or the man-sized surf T-shirts she wore around the house? The tiny, teeny aqua thing she had on barely justified the words *tank top*. It was like the ghost of a tank top, an imprint that might be left behind when a tank top passed over to the other side.

For a full, mind-bending five seconds he found himself focusing on the twin stars of Delaney's new purchase—two of the perkiest, prettiest breasts he'd seen in a long time. Thrusting up toward the low neckline of her top, they positively begged for a man to reach out and see if they felt as delectable and firm as they looked. Wrenching his eyes away, he continued on his downward spiral into madness as he caught sight of the jeans she was wearing. *Painted-on* was the term that came to mind. Darkest black, and so tight that if she was a man he'd know what religion she was. But she wasn't a man. *Oh boy, she* so *wasn't a man.*

"Shit!" was all he could think to say.

Delaney flinched and her eyes flashed at him.

"Thanks a lot. That's all you can say? *What have you done,* and *shit?* Nice," she said.

Then she turned her back on him and walked away and, for the first time in his life, Little Sam reared up in his boxers and saluted his best friend. Since when did Delaney have such a delectable butt? Heaven. Pure heaven. Round and high and so grabable that when he looked down he saw his fingers had actually curled in anticipation.

Suddenly Sam registered what he was doing, and the fact that he now had an embarrassing, incredibly inappropriate, illicit boner making itself at home in his jeans.

Had the world fallen off its axis? What in the name of all that was good was going on here? Where on earth did he get off *cracking a woody* over his best friend?

He never had sexual thoughts about Delaney. She was a complete no-go zone where that kind of stuff was concerned. She meant too much to him for him to stuff it up with some stupid sex thing. A long time ago, he'd made a decision—Delaney was out of bounds. And it had worked. It really had. He'd never even peeked when they changed out of their wetsuits at the beach. She was his *friend,* damn it. You didn't check out your best friend.

So why was there now a hard-on making its presence felt in his underwear?

Sam shook his head to clear it.

It was surprise, that was all. Delaney's new look had taken him unawares, made him look at her in a different way before he could get his defenses up. That was all it was.

And he'd offended her with his shocked reaction.

"Shit," he said again, but under his breath this time. Depositing the beers on Delaney's recycled Oregon dining table, he followed her into her bedroom.

She was pulling clothes out of the jumble of shopping bags on her big king-size bed. By the looks of it, she'd cleaned out the whole women's department at David Jones.

"You've been *shopping?*" he asked stupidly, reeling from yet another blow to his perception of the world.

Delaney hated shopping almost as much as she hated makeup and...*perfume?* He sniffed the air suspiciously, becoming aware that a sweet, light fragrance had wrapped itself around him. It was the odor equivalent of crack cocaine—once he'd had one sniff, he couldn't seem to get enough.

"What's that smell?" he demanded.

Delaney threw her hands in the air. "It's Dolce and Gabbana Light Blue. What's wrong? Does it smell like horse manure? Is that what you're going to tell me next?"

Sam blinked at her anger, then admitted to himself that it might be a little justified. The problem was, he was in free fall here, staggering from one shocking revelation to another. But he probably could be a little more diplomatic about what was coming out of his mouth.

"No, it's nice," he said.

Delaney went back to clearing out her shopping bags, her movements tight with anger.

"I'm sorry," he said, painfully aware that he'd hurt her feelings with his insensitive reaction. Although it had been more oversensitive, if he were being pedantic about it.

In fact, her hair looked great, not freaky at all. Silky and touchable. A perfect frame for her sweet face. Which wasn't quite so sweet anymore, thanks to Mr. Max Factor and friends. More…sultry. Promising.

Sam swallowed and shook his head. It was so not his place to be thinking any of these things about Delaney. She would completely flip out if she had even an inkling that he'd gotten aroused over the sight of her ass in her tight new jeans. Even as he thought it, Delaney turned and bent to pick up something off the ground. He thrust his hands into his pockets to counteract the ass-grabbing urge that once again rocked him, and wrenched his eyes away.

"So, um, I went to the lawyers this afternoon," he said, trying to get a grip on himself.

"Uh-huh," Delaney murmured, hanging dress after dress

in the wardrobe. He frowned when he saw how short they were. Maybe they were tops, not dresses? If he was to have any chance of keeping his sanity and conquering this sudden, aberrant bout of hyper-awareness where she was concerned, they'd better be.

"He floated another idea, something we hadn't considered. We get someone in to take over your role, and you stay in the business as a silent partner. Maybe just give advice whenever required, that kind of thing," Sam said, leaning against the wall.

Delaney shook her head, her newly streaked hair dancing around her face hypnotically.

"But I told you, Sam. I want out. I don't want to be connected to the business at all."

Sam should have been more worried about what she was saying, he knew he should, but she'd just emptied out a shopping bag full of lacy, silky scraps. He watched, fascinated, as she sorted through the rainbow-hued mass, matching bras to panties or thongs. *Thongs!* Delaney in a thong. Delaney's perfect, ripe peach of a butt in a thong.

Little Sam once again made a determined effort to join proceedings, and Sam fisted his hands in his pockets, dreading the thought that Delaney might look up and see his erection and get completely the wrong idea.

He was not turned on by her new underwear. He was not turned on by her. He was just freaking out over the fact that she wanted out from the business. That was all. His body's response was just a weird offshoot of his reaction.

Belatedly he realized that Delaney had stopped packing things away to stare at him, waiting for his response.

"Um, right," he said.

She sat on the bed, offering him an untrammeled view down the neck of her new top.

"Sam, I know this has been a bolt from the blue, and it's going to take you some time to adjust, but it's what I want," she said firmly.

Her breasts rose and fell with each breath she took, straining upward as though they wanted to escape the confines of her clothing. He licked his lips, wondering what color her nipples were.

It was such a basic, primal thought that Sam actually turned toward the door, ready to flat-out run from his own animal instincts.

"What's wrong?" Delaney demanded. She stood again, and Sam heaved a sigh of relief that he could no longer see down her top. The pressure in his boxers eased a notch, but he didn't dare pull his hands from his pockets.

"Nothing. Just a bit of…gas," he said lamely when nothing else came to mind.

"Not in my bedroom," Delaney said instantly, pointing toward the door. "And you need to get out anyway. My date will be here soon and I need to start getting ready."

Sam froze. "Date? What date?"

Delaney lifted a shoulder negligently. He just managed to keep his eyes above her neckline.

"Jake dropped by this afternoon. He asked me out to dinner tonight," she said.

Sam stared at her. "Jake the printing rep? That Jake?"

"Do we know any others?" she asked.

"But he's a complete sleaze, Delaney. He's always checking out chicks, and every time I see him out somewhere he's with a new woman," Sam said indignantly.

"So? Maybe he just hasn't met the right woman yet," Delaney said.

Before he could tell her how wrong she was, what sort of trouble she was inviting, she shoved him out of her bedroom and shut the door in his face.

3

CRACKING OPEN ONE of the beers he'd brought down, Sam paced back and forth across Delaney's jarrah wood floor, sucking in beer and trying to breathe out tension and frustration. He was supposed to go back upstairs to his own apartment—the way Delaney had yelled through her closed bedroom door that she'd see him at work tomorrow had been something of a giveaway in that direction. But he wasn't going anywhere. He was worried about Delaney going out with a bona fide lady's man like Jake. The guy was six foot, solidly built, and Sam knew from listening to the girls in the office that they thought he was dreamy. Delaney wouldn't stand a chance against a practiced make-out artist like that.

He could hear the sound of the shower as Delaney got ready for her date, and he tried to keep himself from imagining what she was doing in there. What she looked like naked, those perky, high breasts of hers slick, the nipples pebbled from the water's warm touch, how she might slide her hands down over her hips and round over that perfect butt...

What was wrong with him? Why was he suddenly having these intimate, crazy-making thoughts about Delaney? She was like his sister. He wasn't supposed to care that she was a woman. It just wasn't a factor in their relationship. At least, it never had been. But all of a sudden, it was as though someone had ripped down an invisible force field that had been between them and he was seeing her for the first time.

And Delaney was definitely a woman. A beautiful, desirable woman.

And Jake the sales rep was going to take her out tonight and do his best to get inside the tiny, lacy scraps of silk he'd seen Delaney sorting through earlier.

It made Sam so angry that he almost threw his beer bottle at the wall. The tempo of his pacing increased. She couldn't go out with Jake. It was a simple as that. Once she got out of the shower, he'd talk sense to her, and she could call Jake and give the guy the brush-off. Then Sam would take her out for burgers or something. They'd have a few beers together, and get things back on their old, solid footing.

The clock in Delaney's open-plan kitchen read just five minutes shy of eight by the time she emerged from her bedroom. She came wrapped in a cloud of perfume and precious little else from what he could see.

The dress she was wearing was the color of autumn leaves—a dark, burnished orange—and it set off Delaney's tan perfectly. It had tiny spaghetti straps and a tight bodice that hugged her breasts, then it swooped down over her hips to end a bare few inches below her butt.

"You cannot be serious," Sam said before he could help himself. He'd planned on staying calm, being the voice of reason. But Delaney could not go out in public in that dress. For starters, it almost certainly violated several decency codes. And it would definitely pose a medical risk for elderly males. Surely she didn't want to be responsible for giving some randy octogenarian a fatal heart attack?

"Sam, if you haven't got something nice to say, go home," Delaney said wearily.

He'd hurt her feelings. Again. Determined to get this right, he crossed to her and put both hands on her shoulders. She tried to twitch out of his grasp, but he just held her more firmly.

"Laney, you look amazing. Hot. Too hot, in fact. There is no way Jake will be able to keep his hands off you," Sam explained honestly.

"Did it ever occur to you that I might not want him to?" Delaney said, pushing his hands away.

"Well…no. Why on earth would you let a guy like Jake take advantage of you? He's not good husband material, Delaney, if that's what you're thinking."

"Because you're such a great judge of that, right?" she challenged him.

Sam pulled his dreadlocks off his forehead, frustrated that he couldn't seem to get through to her.

"He's going to look at you in that dress, and all he's going to think about is sex," he finally said. There, he couldn't be more blatant than that.

"Good," she replied.

"What?"

"I said good. I *have* had sex before you know, Sam. I do know what goes where. I have needs, too," she said defiantly.

She pushed her hair behind her ear, and he saw that she was wearing slinky silver drop earrings that drew attention to her long, slim neck. She was so fine and sleek and strong. She was way too good for Jake the rep.

"I don't know what to say to you," Sam said after a long silence. "If you're willing to just put yourself out there like that…I can't protect you."

"I didn't ask you to! I'm a grown woman, I can take care of myself," Delaney all but shouted back at him. Her cheekbones colored up nicely, and her breasts seemed in imminent danger of popping out over the top of her dress.

While he was giving himself a mental bitch-slap for looking in the first place, Delaney crossed to the door and opened it wide.

"Out. Now," she said unequivocally.

Sam opened his mouth to deliver one last warning, but she glared at him and he closed his jaw with an audible click.

Feeling distinctly hard done by, he moved past her and out into the hall.

"I just hope you know what you're doing," Sam said.

"Hey there, Sam," a voice said from behind him, and he turned to see Jake approaching down the corridor.

The cheesy schemer was dressed like Mr. Slick from a fashion catalogue, and he was even carrying a bunch of flowers. Sam felt his lip curl as he eyed the other man.

"Jake," he managed to bite out. Jake offered his hand, and Sam stared at it for a beat before reluctantly shaking hands. He made sure he squeezed the other guy's knuckles good and hard, though, just so Jake would know who he'd be dealing with if he got out of line with Delaney.

"Sam was just leaving," Delaney said meaningfully.

Sam twitched, but he knew he had no choice. She was right—she was a grown woman. A fully grown, fully adult woman. With needs, she'd said.

Great.

"Delaney—you look sensational," Jake said, bending to kiss her hello.

Sam felt the lip curl make a return appearance as Jake's arms slid around her, his hands lingering way too long on her lower back. Sam knew exactly what the other guy was thinking: *how much small talk do I have to fake before I can get my hands on that amazing caboose?*

If he stayed any longer, Sam knew he was going to do something really, really dumb.

"Have a great night," he said sourly.

Then he turned and walked away.

DELANEY TOOK A DRINK from her wineglass. Across the table, Jake's lips were moving, but she had no idea what was coming out of them. She gave herself a mental shake. She had to focus on Jake instead of constantly slipping back to her earlier conversation with Sam. It was pointless to go over and over what had passed between them. As if she'd needed yet another reminder that her feelings for him were unrequited, Sam's attitude could not have shouted indifference more clearly. Although perhaps she was being unfair. He hadn't been indifferent. He'd been…brotherly. As he always was. A concerned friend. It was enough to make her want to scream.

"Should we get another bottle?" Jake asked, and Delaney realized that she'd drained her glass in one long gulp.

"Um, sure," she said.

Jake signaled for the waiter, and Delaney forced herself to concentrate. It wasn't as though Jake wasn't attractive or fun to be with. Normally she really enjoyed exchanging banter with him when he came into the office. And there was no denying his masculine appeal—he was the epitome of tall, dark and handsome. So why wasn't she sitting here hoping that he'd kiss her when he took her home tonight? Instead, she was wondering how she could head him off at the pass. Would it be unforgivably rude to get a taxi home on her own at the end of their meal? Or should she just go the whole hog and fake an appendicitis attack right now?

Damn Sam Kirk, and damn herself for letting him ruin her for any other man.

"You know, I've wanted to ask you out for a while," Jake said as the waiter moved off.

Delaney blinked. "Really?"

"Yep. But I always kind of got the feeling you weren't available," Jake said.

It made her wonder if that was the way other men had seen her, too—unavailable. Was it possible that she subconsciously sent out "keep off" signals because her feelings for Sam were so strong?

"Well, I'm single, always have been," Delaney shrugged, not quite sure what to say. If she flirted with Jake, she felt as though she'd be doing so under false pretences.

"When I saw you this afternoon I hoped maybe my luck had changed."

"What do you mean?" Delaney asked.

"New hair, new clothes—the classic relationship break-up makeover," Jake said.

Delaney stared at him for a beat. In a way, he was right. She *was* breaking up with Sam. He just didn't know it.

"It was time for a change," she said feebly.

"Speaking of which, I still can't believe you're leaving Mirk," Jake said, shaking his head.

"Well, I *have* been there since the beginning. Nearly eight years now," Delaney said.

"Why the big move, if you don't mind me asking? Don't tell me you got poached by one of the big guys? I know a ton of publishers who'd love to have you on their sales staff," Jake said.

She tried to find a way to answer without lying. She was doing enough of that with Sam.

"I'm thirty," she shrugged, opting for brutal honesty. "I realized that I could spend the rest of my life working like a dog...or I could start thinking about the other things in life."

"Like…?" Jake asked, his dark eyes intent on her.

"You know. A husband, kids. It sounds kind of clichéd when you say it out loud," Delaney said self-consciously.

"If it's a cliché, it's only because most single people in their thirties start looking around, wondering if there are any lifeboats left. No one wants to stay too long on the dance floor and get stuck when the Titanic goes down," Jake said, smiling self-deprecatingly at his own analogy.

"Especially if you can't swim," Delaney added wryly.

"I don't think you need to worry about not being able to swim," Jake said warmly. "I bet there will always be some guy willing to share his life raft with you."

It was a compliment, she knew. And she should probably feel flattered. But she didn't. Instead, she felt mildly uncomfortable and completely transparent. Surely he could tell she wasn't interested? A part of her was tempted to confess all to him, apologize for wasting his time and offer to pay for his meal.

She should have waited until she'd expunged Sam from her life before trying to date. She was just perpetuating the same problem she'd always had while Sam was on the scene: no man ever measured up.

Sure, Jake was good-looking. But his brown eyes weren't half as engaging as Sam's bright blue ones, and his smile not nearly as sincere and fun-loving. And while Jake was witty and clever—he'd read all the latest books and seen all the coolest movies—he didn't make her laugh nearly as much as Sam. He also didn't make her blood fizz in her veins, or her heart shimmy in her chest, and she wasn't sitting on the edge of her seat, hoping for an accidental brush of his fingers against hers, or the feel of his knee nudging hers beneath the table.

He just…wasn't Sam. It was as small and as sad as that. Reaching for her wineglass, Delaney took another big gulp. Surely taking a taxi home wouldn't be *that* bad form…?

SAM FELT LIKE A CAGED TIGER with a bad case of hives. It was ten o'clock. Delaney had been out with Jake for two whole hours. In all likelihood, they were still at dinner, trying to decide whether or not to have dessert, talking about politics over coffee, hoping the weather would be a little cooler next week….

Or old smoothie Jake had already finagled Delaney back to his pad and was even now peeling her clothes off. Sam ground his teeth together at the thought of Jake sleazing his way beneath Delaney's defenses.

Sam ground his teeth even harder when it occurred to him that maybe Delaney didn't have any defenses to sleaze beneath. Maybe *she* was the one grabbing Jake by the crotch and throwing him onto the bed. If Delaney tackled sex the way she tackled everything else in her life, she'd be a force to be reckoned with in the bedroom.

She was fit and tanned from all their surfing. She'd be limber, lithe. And she *had needs.* Jake would probably think all his Christmases had come at once.

Sam paced some more and worked on reducing his molars to dust.

What exactly did *having needs* mean, while he was on the subject? That Delaney needed to have sex? That she craved an orgasm? And if that were the case, why couldn't she just take care of the matter on her own in the privacy of her home without putting him through all this torture? Anything was preferable to the thought of her being with Jake.

Instantly an image of Delaney pleasuring herself popped into his mind's eye. Her head was thrown back, and one hand cupped a pert, high breast. Her other hand was busy between her wide-spread thighs, stroking her own wet heat with gentle fingers—

Sam swore explosively. When had he turned into such a Grade A creep? This was Delaney he was thinking about, imagining naked. Getting the world's largest, most persistent boner over.

Delaney. The girl next door. His old street-cricket buddy. His business partner. His best friend in all the world. Delaney was *not* about sex and desire and urges. Delaney was about loyalty, and intimacy and knowing someone would always be there for him, no matter what.

There was no way he was going to screw all that up by suddenly turning into Mr. Horndog around her. Hell, it wasn't as though he was deprived in the female companionship area. Coco's hideous perfume was still fading from his apartment. He wasn't exactly hard up.

By midnight, he'd given up on the pacing and gone to bed. With one ear cocked for the sound of Delaney's apartment door closing, he pretended to read the latest surf mag from the U.S. until he finally admitted to himself that he'd been staring at the same page for ten minutes.

Switching the light off, he told himself he was going to sleep. What Delaney did with Jake was none of his business. Sam knew he should be far more concerned about this bee she had in her bonnet about selling him her half of the magazine. Why wasn't he lying there, unable to sleep, worrying about that instead of obsessing over her love life?

Plus, she'd slept with other guys before, he knew she had. It wasn't as though she was a virgin or anything. Although that would solve a lot of his current problems, he decided as forty minutes went by and there were still no telltale noises from downstairs or any indication that he would be getting some shut-eye anytime soon.

Turning onto his stomach, he pushed his prickly dreadlocks out of the way, irritated by the feel of his ropey hair against his face. The sheets felt itchy and scratchy, too, even though he'd just changed them yesterday. Restless, he rolled over again, this time trying his side.

Maybe he should just wait out this thing that was going on with Delaney and the business. She was freaking over her biological clock, that much was obvious. Perhaps if he let her settle a little, she'd ease back on the idea of bailing on the magazine.

Because try as he might, he just couldn't get his head around the idea of doing it all without her. She was so fundamentally essential to the way the magazine worked, to the way he worked.

Sighing heavily, he changed sides, making an impatient noise as his hair scratched his face and neck again. His feet got tangled in the bedsheets, too, and he kicked at them viciously until they came loose.

Why couldn't he get to sleep? All he wanted was to stop thinking about all this crap and have a little bit of peace and quiet. Was that too much to ask?

But everything was annoying all of a sudden—his hair felt like pipe cleaners on his head, his sheets might as well have been made from sandpaper and his whole body felt too hot. After another few minutes of tossing and turning, he bounded from the bed and strode purposefully into the bathroom. Flicking on the light, he found the scissors in the bathroom drawer and grabbed a handful of dreadlocks. Impatient, he hacked away until they came loose in his hand and he could dump them in the bin. Within minutes he'd cut the whole lot off, plugged his hair clippers in and set the blade to number two. It didn't take long to trim his remaining hair to a short, sharp buzz cut. Before he'd grown the dreads, he'd kept his hair like this for years. Satisfied that he'd done a decent job, he rinsed off briefly in the shower, then returned to the bedroom.

Throwing himself onto the bed, he ran a hand over his newly clippered hair. Better. Much better. His brain even felt cooler, less frenzied, if that were possible. Maybe *now* he could get some sleep.

Curling onto his side, he closed his eyes—just as the dull thunk of Delaney's door shutting sounded below. His whole body was instantly on the alert. He held his breath, ears pricked.

Was Jake with her?

Sam couldn't hear anything. Scrambling to the side of the bed, he craned his head toward the floor, knowing that Delaney's bedroom was directly under his own. Surely if they were in there, doing…*it,* he'd hear them, right?

He felt faintly nauseous. And still he couldn't hear anything. Sliding out of bed completely, he knelt on all fours and pressed his ear to the floorboards.

He was self-aware enough to be ashamed of his own actions—but not enough to stop them. Straining to hear, he held his breath until black spots floated in front of his eyes.

Still nothing. It wasn't as though either Jake or Delaney were trained ninjas—he should be able to hear *something.*

Swearing repeatedly under his breath, he padded naked out into his living area and crossed to the sliding doors that opened onto his balcony. Creeping outside, he got down on his hands and knees again and peered through the cracks in the decking that made up the floor of his balcony.

He couldn't see anything. And his bollocks were shrinking to the size of marbles in the cold night air.

Realizing at last how ridiculous and pathetic he must look, he went back inside.

Delaney was home. He suspected without Jake, but he wasn't sure. It didn't really mean anything if she were alone, anyway, since it was nearly one-thirty and she could have had several bouts of energetic, need-fulfilling sex at Jake's place before coming home to her own bed.

Furious for no good reason, Sam punched his pillow into submission and threw himself back onto his bed.

Sleep seemed like a far-off oasis, never to be attained.

At around three, he groaned into his pillow. It wasn't enough that his brain was feeling well and truly fried from all the back-and-forth bullshit he'd been indulging in all night, but he had a persistent, throbbing erection that would not quit. He was practically drilling a hole to China, the thing was so hard.

Rolling over, he got a grip on the situation. With a bit of luck, a quick bout of hand relief would also do the trick for his insomnia—in his book, an orgasm was nature's most effective sleeping pill.

Closing his eyes, he gave himself up to the slow build of sensation as his hand stroked up and down. Images flashed in front of his mind's eye as he trawled his own personal X-Files for inspiration: a pair of lean, hungry thighs, spread wide. A peachy backside arched high in the air. Small, pert breasts pouting for his tongue and his touch.

Sam grunted, building his tempo as the images began to coalesce into one sexy, hot woman. She was beneath him, her long legs wrapped around his torso as he hammered into her. Her back arched, her nipples demanding his mouth and her head tossed from side to side as she panted her pleasure.

"Oh, yeah, baby," he encouraged in the privacy of his fantasy.

Then the woman opened her eyes, and he realized he was

staring into Delaney's pleasure-clouded face, and that he was riding her body, his erection buried deep inside her.

He swore angrily and jerked his hand away from his penis as though he'd just been electrocuted.

Wrong. So wrong, on so many levels.

But he'd been so close. So damned, temptingly close.

Lying in the dark, panting, Sam made a decision and slid his hand back onto his hard shaft. He could control his own fantasies, couldn't he? For the sake of a bit of fulfillment? Squeezing his eyes shut tight, he concentrated on calling another woman to mind. Coco. Or that cheeky brunette... Sandra, that was her name. Or Mandy, with her sexy little laugh.

But it was no good. The only woman his subconscious wanted to have sex with was Delaney, and she kept snaking her long legs around him and panting in his ear.

After an unequal struggle, he gave up all resistance. He was so close, and too greedy for release. *It's just a fantasy,* he told himself as he imagined burying his face in Delaney's breasts. *It doesn't mean anything. And, more importantly, she never needs to know.*

In seconds he was shuddering out his orgasm, Delaney's name on his lips, her image in his mind. Afterward, he wallowed in unaccustomed guilt. He hadn't felt this bad about a bit of harmless self-gratification since early puberty.

What a sterling day, he thought as he at last drifted off to sleep. *Absolutely sterling.*

DOWNSTAIRS, DELANEY TOSSED and turned for hours after Jake dropped her off and she'd crawled into bed. Jake had wanted to come in, but she hadn't felt up to the pretense. It had been exhausting enough making it through dinner.

She felt bad about letting him kiss her, though. She hadn't really wanted to, and she'd had no intention of following through. He must have thought he was in with a good chance when she let him press her up against her door and thrust his body against hers. But she'd only done it out of a sort of morbid curiosity, just to confirm how big a hopeless case she was.

Pretty big, was the answer. Not a single zing from Jake's very practised kiss. Nothing but a realization that mouth-to-mouth contact was really kind of disgusting if you didn't want to jump someone's bones.

At six in the morning, she got sick of pretending she was ever going to sleep. Throwing off the covers, she strode into the bathroom and ran herself a bath. When it was foamy and full, she dimmed the lights and sank into the steaming water. If she couldn't sleep, she could at least try to unwind a little. Yesterday had been a trying day, between breaking her big news to Sam, getting a makeover, and going out on her first date in over six months.

Easing her head back against the rim of the bath, Delaney closed her eyes. The water was warm and soothing, sweetly scented with her favorite mango bath gel. Slowly she felt the tension ease from her limbs.

She'd spent the night agonizing over whether she was doing the right thing or not and mourning the loss of her friendship with Sam. Because that was inevitable. Once he learned the next stage in her plan—that she was going to sell her apartment—he would understand what she was doing: cutting him out of her life. And then things would really get ugly.

No one liked to be rejected, least of all by the person they trusted more than anyone else in all the world—and she knew she was that person for Sam, just as he was for her. She was going to hurt him so much. But she felt as though she was fighting the battle of her life—and if she lost, she would have to give up on having a full and complete existence and resign herself to remaining Sam's faithful, reliable sidekick for the rest of her days.

She really didn't know if she had the strength to go through with it all, though. That was the troubling part. As soon as she'd seen Sam yesterday, her thighs had gone weak. How could she get so turned on just by being in the same room with him, yet he was completely indifferent to her?

Even though she knew it was a refined form of torture, Delaney let herself remember how he'd looked when she first saw him yesterday. Strong and tanned, his eyes sparkling with energy, his hard body relaxed. She shifted minutely in the bath as she remembered the flash of belly she'd seen when he'd scratched his chest. He had a great stomach, ribbed with muscle and sprinkled with exactly the right amount of hair. She'd seen it so many times when they were out surfing that it should have been about as sexy as a foot or an ear or an elbow to her. But it never failed to excite her.

She realized her thighs had spread apart in the water, and that her hand had found its way to the nest of curls at the juncture of her thighs. Biting her lip, she slid a finger between her own folds. Her clitoris was swollen, already aroused by her thoughts, and she slid her finger over and over it gently, imagining it was Sam's hand between her legs, Sam about to bring her to climax.

Panting, Delaney let her head drop back and gave herself up to the building tension between her thighs. Her free hand slid onto her breasts, sliding from one soap-slicked mound to the other, plucking at her nipples with increasing firmness.

"Oh, Sam," she sighed, completely lost in her fantasy.

Only to have the mood abruptly shattered by the sound of someone pounding on her front door. She shot bolt upright in the tub, water sloshing around her as she wondered who on earth would be on her doorstep so early in the morning.

She guessed who it was at the same time that Sam called out for her to let him in.

"Come on, Delaney—we need to talk," he bellowed from behind the door.

Climbing from the tub, Delaney hastily towelled herself dry and dragged on her silk robe. It was ridiculous to feel caught out, but she did. She'd been indulging her sexual fantasies about Sam for years, and it had always been hard to look him in the eye the next time she saw him. Now she felt as though she'd been busted in the act.

"Delaney, come on!" Sam bellowed, pounding on the door again.

"Hold your horses," she called as she made her way across the living room.

Swinging the door open, she gasped with surprise when she saw that he'd shaved his dreadlocks off. He looked younger, oddly, without his now-familiar dreads, and the planes and angles of his handsome face were thrown into sharper relief. She resisted the urge to curve a hand into his cheek, touched by the vulnerable boy she could see in his man's face all of a sudden.

"You cut your hair," she said stupidly as he pushed past her into her apartment.

Sam shrugged. "Yeah, well, I had some spare time on my hands last night," he said sulkily.

"What's that supposed to mean?" she asked.

Sam shook his newly shorn head. "Nothing." Striding into the center of her living space, he propped his hands on his hips and scanned the apartment.

"So, is he still here?" he asked.

There was a definite note of belligerence in his tone, and Delaney bristled.

"Sam, I don't know what exactly has crawled up your butt this morning, but take it back to your place and deal with it, okay?" she said shortly.

"What's the big problem? We're both adults. I'm just asking an adult question," Sam said.

He was angry, agitated, she could see, and she guessed this was about her pulling out of the business.

"I know you're pissed about me wanting to sell out of the magazine, but there's nothing you can do about it," she said with determination. "I've made my decision."

"Did he stay the night or not, Laney?" Sam asked.

She stared at him. "Why do you suddenly care so much about my love life?" she demanded, utterly bewildered. What was really going on here?

Sam avoided her eye as he ran a hand over his short-cropped hair. "I don't want you to get hurt."

"Fine, here I am, unhurt. Can you please go now?"

Sam's eyes flashed with suspicion as they ran over her. She was painfully aware of her flushed face, of what she'd been doing when he pounded on the door.

"He *is* still here, isn't he? That's why you're so hot and bothered."

He made a move toward her bedroom, almost as though he was going to barge in there and inspect it. Delaney couldn't believe the way he was behaving.

"I just had a bath, Sam! If you must know."

Sam stopped in his tracks, and they eyed each other for a moment. "Oh," he said.

For some reason, she had the horrible feeling he'd just guessed exactly what she'd been doing in the bath.

"The water was hot," Delaney heard herself say a little defensively. Sam's gaze dropped below her face, and she crossed her arms over her chest just in case her nipples were doing their usual "Hey, Sam, look at us" routine.

"So you didn't sleep with him?" Sam asked.

Delaney let out a heavy sigh. "No. Are you happy now? Is that what you wanted to hear? I'm still the same hard-up singleton I was last night."

Sam ran a hand over his head again, the movement drawing his T-shirt tight across his chest. Why did he have to be so fatally attractive to her? It was cruel, perverse and unfair.

"Back to the needs thing again, huh?" he asked.

"Whatever. Sam, I really think you should go. I had a crappy night's sleep, and I'm really grumpy, and this conversation is just too weird for me right now."

"It's just you've never told me you have…needs before," Sam said.

Delaney felt herself flush. "Well, I'm human. You like sex, don't you?"

"Yeah."

"Well, there you go. You have needs, too."

Sam took a step toward her, his body jerky, uncoordinated. It almost looked as though it were moving against his will, and the look on his face was deeply uncertain and tortured.

"What if I told you that last night my need was for you?" he said suddenly.

The words hung between them for what seemed like an eternity. Delaney's breath got caught somewhere between her chest and her throat. She felt her pulse beating thick and slow in her belly.

What was he saying? That he was jealous of Jake? Surely not. Sam didn't see her as a woman. She was his buddy, nothing more.

His blue eyes were intent on her, his body tense.

"I don't know what you mean," she finally whispered.

Sam stepped forward again, within touching distance this time. Delaney watched with a strange, disconnected kind of astonishment as he reached out to wrap his hand around her forearm. His skin felt hot through the silk of her robe.

"I mean I couldn't stop thinking about you and Jake in bed. And it drove me crazy," he said.

So he *was* jealous of Jake. That *had* been what he was saying. Which meant…which meant that Sam desired her himself. Didn't it?

It was so close to her most cherished dream that Delaney flinched away from him, jerking her arm from his grasp. Whatever was going on with Sam, he hadn't suddenly fallen in love with her. She would be the biggest fool in the world if she believed that.

Sam's grip remained firm, however, and she felt her arm slide within her silk sleeve as she pulled away. A sudden coolness across her right breast told her that her robe had slid off her shoulder before she looked down and confirmed it.

There was a sudden, electric silence as they both stared at her exposed breast. As though her nipple knew it was the connoisseur of all eyes, it darkened and puckered, begging to be touched.

Delaney heard the harsh intake of Sam's breath.

"Delaney," he said in a choked voice, "for what it's worth, I'm sorry."

And then he put his hand on her breast.

4

A SHAFT OF PURE DESIRE rocketed through Delaney's body. A low moan sounded in her throat as she watched Sam's thumb slide over her nipple, then back again. A tidal wave of lust threatened to swamp her—sixteen years of fantasizing, imagining and wanting, banked up and ready to explode.

"Sam," she whispered brokenly, trying to warn him. "Do you have any idea what you're doing?"

Sam's face was flushed, his eyes fixed on her straining breast.

"Tell me to stop, and I will," he said.

Stop? She couldn't tell him to stop if her life depended on it. Even as he said the words the tidal wave hit, and she was gripped by desire, a passion so strong, so all-consuming that she knew that nothing was going to stop her from having Sam Kirk right there and then on the hard boards of her living room floor.

"You have no idea," she said, and then she grabbed him by the neck of his T-shirt and hauled him close, her mouth angling up to meet his, her hips straining forward.

Sam needed no further encouragement. His mouth was hot and urgent on hers, and their tongues danced madly, feverishly, as their hands clutched at each other's bodies. Delaney gasped with need as Sam pushed her silk robe off her other shoulder, both hands on her breasts now, his fingers plucking and caressing and teasing her nipples.

"Oh, yes," she said, sliding her hands down Sam's back to grab his butt and drag his hips tighter against hers. His erection felt thick and long and so promising that she ground her hips against it instinctively.

He was wearing too much clothing. They both were, and she grabbed at his T-shirt to wrench it over his head. Sam was on the same wavelength, his fingers hauling at the sash keeping her robe cinched around her waist. She felt the slide of silk against her bare legs and then Sam was groaning with approval and running his hands down the length of her torso and down onto her hips and butt.

"Perfect," he muttered against her mouth, his big hands cupping her butt as though he owned her.

Delaney fumbled with the waistband on his jeans, dragging the zipper down and reaching greedily inside for the heat of him. His erection was strong and proud, and achingly hard. She eyed it hungrily, then gripped it firmly and slid her hand up and down his shaft. Sam's breath caught in his throat and the next thing she knew she was on her back, and Sam had shucked his jeans to lie naked on top of her, her nipple undergoing exquisite torture in his mouth.

"Yes! Yes!" she heard herself cry too loudly, but she was beyond caring. Her hips bucked wildly, and she clutched at his head to ensure he didn't stop.

Even as the feel of his mouth on her breasts almost sent her over the edge, Sam smoothed a hand down her belly and into the wet heat between her legs.

"Oh, Laney," he whispered, his voice breaking as he discovered for himself how ready she was for him.

Her muscles tightened as he slicked a finger across her clitoris, back and forth, back and forth. She spread her thighs wide to invite him in and he took her up on the invitation, sliding a finger inside her. Delaney closed her eyes and almost died on the spot. It was so good, almost too good—but also not enough.

Unable to wait any longer, she twisted beneath him and rolled so that she was now on top, her thighs astride his, her breasts rasping against his chest. Sam's blue eyes glinted up at her as she reached for him, guiding his erection to the heart of her. Biting her lip, Delaney savored the first nudge of his hardness against her softness. Swiveling her hips, she teased herself and Sam with the almost-penetration, anticipation driving her wild. Sam's face was taut with desire, and she felt his hips tense as he prepared to thrust up into her to complete the act. Preempting him, she slid down onto his erection with a single graceful tilt of her hips.

He filled her utterly, perfectly, completely, and she threw back her head and reveled in the moment.

"Yesssss," she sighed.

It was…beyond words. Primal. Needful. Demanding. Gripped with the need to complete the ride, she tilted her hips and began to slide against him. He was everything she'd ever imagined and more. Long and thick, his tanned, taut body flexing beneath her, his hands eager on her breasts, his mouth hot and hard on hers. It was all too much, too overwhelming. Inevitably she felt the tightening of desire inside her as she rode him.

"Yes, Laney," he encouraged her, and she closed her eyes as her body stiffened with release, her internal muscles pulsating around Sam as she shuddered out her orgasm. It seemed to go on and on, and her cries were primitive and mindless. Beneath her, she felt Sam's body tense also, his hands clutching at her hips and desire twisting his face as he came after her, his hips thrusting up into her powerfully.

Delaney collapsed onto his chest, her breath rasping in her throat as though she'd just run the hundred-yard dash. Perspiration slid down between her breasts, and she could feel the hot steaminess of Sam's body against her own. His chest was rising and falling rapidly beneath her cheek as he struggled to catch his breath, also, and for a short while, the only sound in her apartment was the harsh sound of their breathing.

The inevitable fear and anxiety didn't take long to make themselves felt in the pit of Delaney's stomach.

What on earth had she just done?

She was such a fool. She had just exposed herself to Sam in the most blatant, damning way. She'd practically ravished the guy, riding him like some demented porn starlet. There was no way he wasn't lying there in full knowledge of the fact that she was desperately in love with him.

Awkward where before she had been graceful, Delaney rolled to one side and slid away from him. Not daring to even glance at his face, she pushed herself to her feet and retreated to the bathroom.

SAM STARED AT THE CEILING high above him for what seemed like ages, his mind a complete blank. Vaguely he was aware of Delaney standing and walking away, but he was so blown away, so stunned by what had just happened between them, that his rational self was down for the count.

Slowly, by small increments, he came back down to earth. First, he registered that the floor was cool and hard beneath him, and that he was lying on the bunched-up mass of his jeans, the lump uncomfortable against his back. Then he heard the sound of traffic passing by outside, and realized that the door to the balcony was slightly ajar. Finally, full, brutal awareness returned, and he closed his eyes and swore under his breath.

He'd just had the most spectacular sex of his life with his best friend. He'd grabbed her breast, for Pete's sake, then jumped her bones like an oversexed dog. What was wrong with him? What kind of an idiot was he, to risk the only worthwhile relationship in his life because parts of him had been standing to attention? Was his penis so damned important to him? Did he have no impulse control whatsoever?

A low groan sounded in the room, and after a beat he realized that it had come from him. He pressed his hands hard on his closed eyes, wishing the pressure could eradicate the last few minutes from existence.

Recognizing that he couldn't just lie there and pretend nothing had happened, Sam rolled to one side and dragged his jeans out from beneath himself. He stood and pulled them on, then ran a hand over his head and blew out a breath.

Delaney. He had to say something to Delaney. Something along the lines of "I'm sorry, I don't know what happened. If I could take it back I would."

His penis stirred as he tacked on the last remark. Sam shook his head at his own lack of moral fiber. Okay, maybe he wouldn't take it back if he could. It had been pretty sensational, after all. Intense, hot, wild. Delaney had been…

Too late Sam registered that he had an erection again, the denim of his jeans bulging out aggressively.

He stared down at himself. Was he really no better than this?

Sadly, he didn't think he was. The sound of water starting up in the bathroom caught his attention. Delaney was in the shower. He should probably go and talk to her. Deal with this head on, right now. Before a crazy one-off solidified into the death knell for their friendship.

He took a step toward the bathroom, then another. Then he imagined walking in on Delaney in the shower, and stopped in his tracks. That was never going to happen. Just because they'd had sex with each other didn't mean he had a free pass to walk in while she was showering. His penis twitched again as he thought of Delaney's lean, sexy body all wet and soapy and slippery and naked. Another good reason not to go in. He didn't relish the notion of trying to have a rational, mature discussion with an erection making a tepee in his jeans.

Which left just one alternative. Feeling like the love-rat Delaney often accused him of being, Sam slunk out the door.

He found no relief in the silence and space of his own apartment. He kept flashing back to those moments with Delaney—the look in her eyes as she lowered herself onto him, the way she'd thrown her head back as though having him inside her was the best, most fulfilling feeling in the world. Or the way she'd asked him if he knew what he was doing when he couldn't help but touch her breast. She'd been quivering with passion, he realized. Quivering with wanting him. Just as he'd been agonizing over wanting her all night long.

All of which got him nowhere except painfully erect and ready for a round two that was never going to eventuate. A cold shower—the age-old cure for unwanted activity down south—did nothing but leave him shivering and wet with a persistent, resilient hard-on. He stared down at himself— just his luck to at last find a cold-water-proof stimulant in the form of his best friend. Just damned dandy.

As he was toweling himself dry, the phone rang, and he automatically crossed to answer it. He hesitated before picking up, however, his hand hovering over the receiver. What if it was Delaney? What was he going to say to her? The phone rang on and on as his better and lesser selves battled it out, and then the decision was taken out of his hands as the phone clicked over to the answering machine. There was a long pause, then finally Delaney spoke.

"Sam, you chickenshit," was all she said, then she slammed down the phone.

Sam stared at the now-silent phone. She was right. He was a chickenshit.

Suddenly filled with rage at himself and the world, Sam dragged on a pair of long skater shorts, grabbed a T-shirt and his beat-up Van street shoes, and snagged his skateboard as he headed out the door.

The Prahran ramp was just a ten-minute drive away, and the moment he got there he launched into a series of hand-plants, shooting up the steep curve of one side of the ramp and planting one hand on the upper lip before flipping his body and board in the air, rotating 180 degrees, then coming back down and doing exactly the same thing on the opposite side. It took a few minutes for the knot of tension in his belly to loosen, but eventually the speed and discipline of managing balance and momentum did its work. When he'd pummeled his anger down to manageable proportions, he let up, allowing gravity to take him to the lowest point in the center of the U-shaped ramp. A group of kids watching from the sidelines gave him a small cheer as he used the hem of his T-shirt to wipe the sweat off his face.

"Shouldn't you kids be in school?" he asked them testily.

One of the kids, a pint-sized little demon with his trucking cap on backwards, flipped Sam the finger. "Shouldn't you be at work?" the kid asked smartly.

Sam opened his mouth to give him a piece of his mind, but stopped when he realized the kid was right—he *should* be at work. It was probably around nine by now, despite his early start knocking on Delaney's apartment door. He was no better than these kids, ditching school because they thought they had better things to do. He was thirty. He should be able to have a minor crisis in his life without reverting to the stratagems of a thirteen-year-old. The number of times he'd taken his anger and fear out on the skate park when he was a kid… And here he was, a supposed adult, ostensibly in charge of his world, turning to the same old solace.

Worse still, he knew that the acknowledgement that he was being juvenile wasn't going to stop him from spending another hour or so on the ramp. The thought of going in to work and looking Delaney in the eye… He just couldn't do it.

That made him a coward and a cad and probably a whole bunch of other things, he knew. Climbing the stairs to the top of the skate ramp, he placed the board in preparation to do a drop-in.

The problem was, he'd ruined everything—everything. And he had no idea how he was going to make it right again.

DELANEY SLID HER CAR into her parking spot outside Mirk and tried to think of a reason—any reason—why she didn't have to go in there right now. She kept flashing back to the moment when she'd grabbed Sam's T-shirt and kissed him. How had all the self-control she'd learned over sixteen years fallen by the wayside like that? One minute she was ordinary old Delaney Michaels, frustrated, unrequited lover of her best friend, and the next she was some kind of sexual Valkyrie, straddling Sam like a rodeo queen and glorying in her conquest.

Then she'd made things worse by spending half an hour in the shower, trying to get her courage up to go face Sam, only to find him gone. She winced every time she remembered calling him chickenshit over the phone. In her defence, she'd been pretty overwrought at the time, having searched her apartment from top to bottom, unable to believe he could bail on her like that. The sinking feeling in her belly had swiftly given way to anger, and the next thing she'd known, she'd had the phone in her hand and was breathing brimstone down the receiver.

But rational thought had not taken long to return. So, Sam had gone back to his apartment to try and get his head together. Was that any more or less shocking than her retreating to the bathroom and hiding under the shower for half an hour? How long had he hung around for, waiting for her to come out and talk to him? What must he have been thinking when she rolled away from him and hightailed it out of there?

It was hard to admit she'd behaved poorly, but she knew she wasn't exactly standing on a pedestal in this situation. And that was before she even took in to account the fact that she was the one who'd instigated the whole thing in the first place. Granted, he had put his hand on her breast. And rubbed her nipple with his thumb. But she was the one who'd turned into a tigress and ripped his clothes off. And grabbed his erection like a joystick, refusing to let go. And raced ahead to the finish line thanks to years of pent-up fantasy and anticipation.

So, really, they were kind of at a draw in the self-recrimination and blame stakes.

Which only left the small, insignificant task of how she was supposed to face him again. Because he must know. Her reaction had been such a giveaway. How could he not know?

Forcing herself to get out of her car, Delaney decided to give herself a small break. Probably she wasn't going to come up with a world-class solution to any of her major problems right now, with her body still humming from Sam's expert touch. The one really, really important, vital thing that had to happen was that she and Sam talk about what they'd done, get things out in the open and deal with the resulting issues. Even though she was in the process of edging him out of her life, she wasn't ready to lose him just yet. Not like this. She refused to let a few minutes of sexual heaven destroy a friendship that had survived all other obstacles.

Her heart in her mouth, Delaney pushed open the door to their offices and tried to look normal. Whatever the hell that was anymore.

"Hey, Delaney, you dirty dog," Debbie said meaningfully as Delaney paused to collect her mail.

A bone-deep heat rushed up Delaney's chest and shoulders and into her face. Debbie knew. How did she know? Had Sam told her? Why would he do that?

"Wh-what?" Delaney managed to stammer.

"Look at you—I guess Jake must be as good as all the rumors say," Debbie said, eyebrows wiggling salaciously.

Delaney blinked. What in the hell was the other woman talking about? Jake? Who was Jake?

In a flash, her brain caught up. Debbie was talking about Jake, the printing rep. The man she'd had dinner with last night. The man with the take-no-prisoners tongue. *Riiiiiiight.*

"So how was it? Did you go somewhere nice?" Debbie asked, all avid interest.

"Um, yes. Dinner was just….fine," Delaney said, momentarily stumped for a way to deflect the other woman's curiosity. But maybe it wasn't such a bad thing if the office staff thought she had something going on with Jake. It might stop them from taking one look at her and realizing that she'd shagged Sam senseless that very morning.

Summoning a strained little smile, she flicked her eyes across to Sam's office. To her relief, it was clearly empty. He hadn't arrived yet. Good. She had some time to get herself together, put her game face on. When he asked her what was going on, why she'd thrown him to the ground and had her way with him, she was going to need all her hard-won sang-froid where he was concerned to convince him that the reason she'd jumped him had been hormonal. Or astrological. Or political—whatever worked, in fact. Anything but that she was in love with him, and had been all her adult life.

Her relief at his absence lasted about an hour. Then she began to feel uneasy. Was he not coming in at all? Had she scared him so much that he was now too terrified to set foot in his own workplace?

Just before lunch time, Sam hobbled in, a graze on his left cheekbone, his knee a bloody mess of scraped skin. Delaney sat in her office, her heart pounding at about a million miles an hour as she watched Debbie cross to the kitchenette to collect the first-aid kit. Taking a deep breath, Delaney pushed herself out of her chair and intercepted the receptionist as she returned to Sam's side.

"I'll do it," she said, relieving Debbie of the kit. She'd cleaned Sam's cuts and grazes so often that she practically had a medical degree, and it was good to have something to break the ice before they discussed what had happened.

Indicating Sam should head for his office, Delaney followed him in and waited while he propped himself on his desk. Both of them were very careful to avoid eye contact, looking anywhere but at each other.

"What happened?" Delaney asked as she knelt to inspect his knee. It looked a lot worse than it was, she judged.

"Got slammed doing a boardslide grind." Sam shrugged.

Delaney knew this meant Sam had been trying to slide his skateboard down the handrail on a flight of stairs. It was highly dangerous, but a spectacular stunt if pulled off. Unfortunately, most of the time it ended in a spill.

"Hmm," she said, tipping some antiseptic onto a square of sterile gauze.

"What's that supposed to mean?" Sam asked.

"Nothing. Except that you could have killed yourself," she said, pressing the soaked gauze onto his wound.

"Ow!" Sam howled, flinching away.

"Don't be such a sook. I have to clean it up so I can see where the gravel is," Delaney said matter-of-factly.

Despite everything that had happened between them, it felt good to wrap her hand around his calf and return his foot to its resting place on her bent thigh. His skin was warm and his muscles firm. She'd wondered for so many years what it would be like to sleep with Sam. She'd imagined his hands on her body, tried to envisage the length and breadth of his erection, what it would feel like inside her. Nothing had prepared her for the reality. He had been…perfect. Everything she'd ever fantasized about and more.

Belatedly she became aware that she was panting. Swallowing loudly, she concentrated on dabbing at the blood on Sam's knee. She was playing nurse, for Pete's sake—how could anyone get turned on with a bloodied, dirt-encrusted knee in their face?

Get a grip, Delaney, she told herself. She was supposed to be doing damage control, not revealing even more of the tragic inner workings of her warped mind.

Using the tweezers from the first-aid kit, she began picking small bits of dirt and gravel from the wound.

"Thanks for doing this," Sam said after the silence had stretched for an uncomfortably long time.

"Part of the deal, isn't it?" Delaney said. "You bang yourself up, I pick up the pieces."

The tension in the room stretched even tighter. Why had

she said that? It was so loaded! And why use the word *bang,* of all the possible alternatives available in the English language?

She covered her unease by pouring more antiseptic onto the gauze.

"This is going to sting again," she said.

Sam flinched as she cleaned the last of the dirt away.

"Why does that stuff have to hurt? Can't they come up with something that cleans *and* takes the pain away?" he complained.

"Am I going to have to get you a lollypop?" Delaney asked, and Sam cracked a smile.

For a second their eyes clashed and held.

Here it comes, thought Delaney, taking a deep breath. Brushing her hands down the front of her thighs, she pushed herself to her feet. She wanted to be standing when they had this conversation, for some reason. Perhaps in case she needed to bolt for the door.

"Well," Sam said, standing also. Then he glanced down at his knee, bending it a few times. "Feels good, thanks."

He reached out a hand toward her, hesitated a second, then completed the move, patting her on the shoulder in an awkward, avuncular gesture of thanks. Then he walked around his desk, slid into his chair and flicked his computer on.

Delaney stood frozen for a moment, not quite comprehending what had just occurred. One second they'd been on the brink of discussing what had happened that morning in her apartment, and the next Sam was acting as though it was just business as usual.

And perhaps, for him, it was.

She had a sudden out-of-body flash of how they must look, Sam staring determinedly at his computer screen, her standing, stunned, in front of his desk.

We're never going to talk about it. Delaney suddenly understood. *He wants to just pretend it never happened.*

Operating on automatic pilot, she gathered the debris from her Florence Nightingale routine and exited his office. Dumping the gauze in the bin and returning the first-aid kit to its place under the kitchen sink, she walked, zombielike, across to her office.

She couldn't believe they weren't going to talk about it. They'd been friends for sixteen years, and they'd just had wild, impetuous, animal sex on the floor of her apartment. And apparently that didn't even rate a mention, not even a few bare words to sign it off or wrap it up or explain it away in some way.

She sank into her office chair and stared at the blank scribble pad on her desk.

For a strange, vertiginous second she wondered if the whole thing had simply been a figment of her crazed imagination. Maybe in her stress and anxiety over separating her life from Sam's she'd concocted an elaborate delusion that she'd had sex with him, while in the real world, Sam had simply gotten up, eaten his breakfast and gone to the skate ramp.

Yeah, right.

Her body was still tingling from his touch. If she crossed her legs and squeezed her thighs together, she could almost feel him inside her. It had been real. It had been the best damn sex of her life.

But in Sam's world it didn't even rate a mention.

IN HIS OFFICE, Sam stopped pretending to read his computer screen and put his head in his hands. He should have said something. The words had been there, right on the tip of his tongue. *Sorry,* and other humble, peace-making words. But he just hadn't been able to force himself to the point. He'd given her plenty of opportunity to jump in, though. After all, it had taken two to tango. Delaney could just as well have brought it up. But she hadn't, and that had to mean that she didn't want to talk about it, too, right? Because Delaney was pretty up front about most things. She always let him know when there was something on her mind. She'd have said something if she was worried or anything, definitely.

Sam winced at his own willful cowardice and stupidity. Who was he kidding? There was no way Delaney was okay with what had happened between them. They'd had sex. Great, amazing, terrifying sex. It wasn't something they could brush under the carpet. The earth had practically shifted on its axis.

But she'd walked out of his office without saying anything. So what did that mean? The only conclusion he could draw was that she didn't want to talk about it. Or that she'd been waiting for him to take the initiative. But Delaney was no shrinking violet—she always said what she was thinking. Which brought him back to square one—she didn't want to talk about it. Which meant he was off the hook.

He should have been ashamed of the surge of relief he felt at this realization. After years of *Oprah* and *Donahue* and *Sally Jessie Raphael,* he knew he was supposed to want to talk and emote and cry and be sensitive and understanding. It was the modern, reconstructed male thing to do. But, frankly, he'd rather wrestle with a two-hundred-pound alligator than start trying to explain the complex, messed-up stuff that had been going on in his head when he reached for Delaney's breast. He didn't understand it himself—how could he expect her to?

The best course was the one they were taking—ignore it, and it would go away. Sure, it would be awkward for a few days, but, after all, it had been a freakish one-off, an aberration. Soon the memories would fade and it would become one of those things that he'd begin to think maybe he'd imagined.

A vision of Delaney's passion-filled face flashed across his mind. His hands twitched as they remembered the shape of her perfect behind, the smooth curve of her perky breasts.

He was a deluded fool. A desperate, terrified, deluded fool. But it was all he had, and he was clinging to it.

5

SAM HAD ONLY BEEN HOME for a matter of minutes that evening when a knock sounded on his front door. His pulse kicked up. Delaney. It had to be Delaney.

He opened the door to find his mother standing on the doorstep. As he took in her stiffly styled blond hair and her face set in its habitual expression of tense resignation, he decided that the cosmos really was, indeed, out to get him. If there was anyone he didn't have the energy or inclination to deal with right now, it was his mother. Even having to face the music with Delaney would be better.

"Sam. How are you? I was in the neighborhood, and I thought I should drop by since it's been so long since you called," she said. Her eyes were reproachful, a study in suburban martyrdom.

"Nancy. Come in," he said.

His parents had been Jim and Nancy to him since he was about ten. Around the same time that he'd given up on them ever acting like the moms and dads his friends seemed to have. As an adult, he didn't have a close relationship with either of them, something that suited him just fine. His mother and father had spent too many years either ignoring him or trying to use him as a weapon to hurt each other for Sam to feel any great sentiment where they were concerned. Sure, they were his folks, his blood. That went without saying. If they needed anything, he'd be there for them. But he didn't crave their counsel, or think of them in times of crisis. They weren't his friends. They weren't anything, really—just two people who had lived in the same house with him when he was a kid.

"You've bought new furniture, I see," his mother said, eyeing his couches.

"No. Same stuff as last time you were here," Sam said neutrally. That had been over a year ago, when Delaney had helped him cook dinner for his mother's birthday.

"Something looks different," she said, frowning.

Sam shrugged, suddenly impatient to have the pretense over and done with. His mother hadn't just "popped in" to see how he was doing. They didn't have a pop-in kind of relationship. She had an agenda.

"Anything up?" he asked, crossing his arms over his chest.

"Why does anything need to be up for me to visit my son?"

Sam bit back a sigh. They were going to do this the long, circuitous way, obviously. "Do you want a drink? I've got some wine in the fridge."

"A chardonnay would be nice if you have one," Nancy said. She slid her handbag off her shoulder and dropped it on the kitchen counter. Sam resigned himself to a couple of hours of emotional dodgeball as he dragged the fridge door open.

"How is the magazine going?" she asked.

Sam grit his teeth. He wasn't sure how she did it, but whenever she mentioned *X-Pro,* his mother managed to imply that the business was teetering on the brink of bankruptcy.

"The magazine's doing fine," he said. He'd long since given up on the need to prove himself to her.

She sniffed. He wasn't sure what he was supposed to take from that, but he let it ride.

"What about you? How's the garden?" he asked. Nancy had been retired from her job as a secretary for several years now, and the one passion in her life was her garden.

"Oh, fine, I guess. The back fence is practically falling down. The neighbors are being stingy about fixing it." She took a swallow from her wineglass.

"If you need help, I'm happy to come over and take a shot at it. Or if you need help getting someone out to fix it…?" he offered.

His mother's lips tightened briefly; he'd touched a raw nerve.

"I don't need your money, Sam. I'm not your responsibility. You've got enough on your plate, funding this lifestyle of yours." She cast a disapproving look around the apartment. "We both know that any financial problems I experience can only be laid at one person's door."

Sam stared at the floor for a beat. He didn't have to be a Mensa candidate to guess where this was going. His parents' bone-of-contention du jour was a parcel of shares his father had received in the divorce settlement nearly fifteen years ago. They'd been valued as worthless at the time, and to Sam's knowledge, nothing had changed over the years. Only in his mother's mind had the shares suddenly become hot property.

"My lawyer has drawn up some papers," Nancy said, rustling around in her handbag until she'd extracted an official-looking envelope.

"What sort of papers?" he asked warily.

"I need to get a court order to force your father to hand his financial records over," his mother said. "This just says that he's talked to you about getting dividends from the shares."

"You want me to sign a statutory declaration so you can take my father to court?" Sam asked flatly.

He felt the familiar weight of anger and helplessness

descend on him. No matter what he did, he could never stem the tide of his parents' mutual acrimony. As a kid, he'd tried everything, from keeping his room superneat to getting perfect marks at school, to simply not being there. Nothing had ever stopped them from wanting to hurt each other. Just the memory of their furious slinging matches was enough to make his belly tense. It had been years, and still they persisted in taking shots at each other through him.

"Nancy, I've told you a million times. I am not getting involved between the two of you," he said as calmly as possible.

His mother puffed her cheeks out, the picture of outrage. "Jim has stolen from me, Sam. He declared those shares valueless at our divorce, but I know he's been receiving dividends. That money is half mine. I deserve it, after all the years of misery I put up with."

"We're talking a few bucks here. Your handbag cost more, for Pete's sake," he said, trying the rational approach.

He should have known better.

"It's the principal of the thing, and if you don't understand that, you're more your father's son than I knew," she said angrily.

Words crowded his throat. He wanted to tell her to shut up, to leave, to never come near him again if the only thing she was going to bring to his door was more unhappiness and anger. But he'd heard his parents yelling at one another too many times to give in to his temper. It wasn't the way he chose to solve his problems or live his life.

"You need to talk to Jim about this, not me," he said firmly instead.

"I will not let you wash your hands of this the way he has," his mother said shrilly.

Sam reached for his beer, his hand clenching around the

cool glass. He would not lose it with his mother. If it killed him, he wouldn't.

But it was going to be a very long night.

WHEN DELANEY HEARD the woman's voice filtering down from Sam's apartment, her mouth filled with bile. He had one of his women up there. Just hours after he'd driven her mad with desire, he was wining and dining some other stupid, self-destructive woman.

She glared down at the vegetables she'd been chopping for a stir-fry. She'd always known it would be like this, hadn't she? If by some miracle Sam had actually found her attractive and taken her to bed, she'd known she wouldn't stand a chance against his determination to remain single. There was absolutely no reason under the sun for her to expect him to treat her any differently than he'd ever treated one of his other easy lays. No reason at all.

Crossing to the stereo, she intended to crank up the volume, resolutely ignoring the acid burning in her stomach. *This is your just desserts for your moment of weakness,* she told herself.

Before she could hit the volume, however, she recognized the shrill, throbbing note of his mother's voice in high-drama mode. She stared up at the ceiling, listening to the ebb and flow of Nancy Kirk's voice as she harangued her son. He didn't have another of his women up there, after all. The knot in her belly eased. So. He wasn't that much of an asshole. She felt inordinately relieved, and she shook her head at her own foolishness. It didn't mean anything. If not tonight, then tomorrow night, or the next night, there would be a perky blonde or brunette warming his bed. It was inevitable.

Upstairs, Nancy's voice shrilled into a crescendo of nagging acrimony. Delaney shot another look at the ceiling.

It reminded her of all the times she'd heard the muffled sounds of his parents fighting when she was a kid. Every evening, like clockwork, the Kirks' misery had leaked over the fence in fits of raised voices and crashes of furniture as they gave vent to their unhappiness and anger. Her parents had made a habit of playing music to try to drown out their fighting, especially if Sam was over to visit.

Even the memory of it made her feel a little sick. She could just imagine how Sam was handling his mother's current attack. She'd seen him around his parents enough over the years to know exactly how he would be. Even though Jim's and Nancy's determination to drag their son into their unhappiness was enough to try the patience of a saint, Sam never raised his voice or laid down the law. In all other areas of his life he was assert-ive, even aggressive. But when it came to his parents, he refused to become part of the family act. And if that meant simply enduring one of their diatribes without saying a word, he'd do it. She'd seen him do it a number of times, too, and afterward she'd invariably urge him to just let rip and give his father or mother both barrels when they next came calling, trying to make trouble. But Sam wouldn't. Or couldn't. The lessons of his childhood were burned too deeply into his psyche.

She didn't have to work hard to picture the withdrawn, distant look Sam would have on his face. She'd seen it so often through their teen years. He'd be there, but not there, his feelings locked away as he retreated inside himself.

She was moving before she'd consciously decided what she was doing. She was angry with Sam, yes. Confused, hurt, bewildered. But she would not let that hyena of a woman feed off him. She had to go protect him.

Swiftly she crossed to the bathroom, swiping some mascara on and following up with lipstick. As soon as she was satisfied that she looked suitably professional, she grabbed her new denim jacket and her purse and house keys and headed for the door.

Sam answered the door on her second knock, and her heart wrung in her chest as she saw the frozen expression in his eyes.

"Hi," she said brightly. "You ready to go?"

Sam stared at her blankly, and Delaney widened her eyes at him meaningfully.

Play along, idiot, she semaphored with her eyebrows.

"Laney," he said, the single word sounding flat and forced.

"You've forgotten, haven't you?" she said, shaking her head. Breezing past him, she pretended surprise at seeing Nancy Kirk propped at the kitchen counter, a glass of wine clenched in her hand.

"Oh, Mrs. Kirk. I didn't realize you were here," she said cheerily. Striding forward, she planted a dutiful kiss on the older woman's cheek, even though she really wanted to grab her by the ear and demand to know why she persisted in inflicting her miserable life outlook on her son.

"I just popped in to see Sam," Nancy said.

Delaney marveled at the way the woman could get a whiny note into such an innocuous phrase.

"Well, I'm afraid I'm going to have to steal him off you," Delaney said. She turned to Sam. "We've got that trade night with triple-fin surfboards, remember?"

Sam had had more than enough time to put his game face on.

"Man, I'm sorry. I completely forgot. Give me five minutes to change my shirt," he said. He looked as though he were about to rush off and do just that, but he hesitated, then turned back to his mother.

"Sorry about this, Nancy," he said. He didn't sound that

sorry, but Delaney didn't think any less of him for being a bad liar.

Nancy Kirk nudged her half-finished wine aside and picked up her handbag.

"I didn't realize I was intruding. I suppose I should have called ahead to let you know, since you're so busy," she said.

Delaney ground her teeth together. Could the woman be any more passive-aggressive?

She channeled her anger into looking at her watch and tapping it pointedly.

"Better shake a leg, Sam. Sorry, Mrs. Kirk," she said. She guessed she probably sounded about as sincere as Sam had, but she didn't care.

"I'll just leave these papers here for you, Sam," Nancy said, placing an envelope on the countertop.

Delaney saw a muscle flex in Sam's jaw. "They'll go straight in the bin, but it's your call," he said.

Nancy looked as though she was about to burst into speech again, but her eyes shot to Delaney and she bit her tongue.

Good, Delaney thought. Nancy had never liked the idea of having a public audience, despite the fact that the whole neighborhood could hear her and Jim screaming at each other day and night. As long as the curtains were closed, it was private business in her book.

Lips pinched, Nancy slid the contentious envelope into her handbag. Within moments, she'd kissed Sam goodbye, and the door was closing behind her.

Sam instantly let out a gusting sigh and ran a hand across his head.

"Jesus. Thank you, Laney. I was seriously afraid I was going to lose it when she dragged out that envelope," he said.

Delaney ached to soothe the lines from his face, to hold

him until the desolate look had faded from his eyes. "Maybe I should have waited a little longer then. She needs a come-uppance, in my humble opinion," she said instead.

"There's nothing humble about your opinion," Sam said wryly.

He moved toward the fridge and pulled out a bottle of wine.

"She was on about those shares again. I swear, if Jim's getting a cent from them I'd be amazed. But he loves cranking her up. He keeps hinting at things every time she makes contact. It's like a hobby for him," Sam said, shaking his head in disgust.

He poured two glasses of wine, sliding one toward her before leaning back and sipping from the other. Delaney stared at her wineglass as reality crashed in.

"I—I can't stay, Sam," she said. Whatever impulse had brought her to his door had dissipated now, and all she could think about was what had happened between them—and how he hadn't even acknowledged it.

"Oh. Right."

A dull blush colored his cheekbones, and he fumbled the glass as he poured the wine down the sink. Suddenly, con-straint was like a third presence in the room.

Delaney stared intently at him, willing him to say some-thing. Earlier, at the office, she'd dreaded their inevitable confrontation, fearful that he might have guessed her true feelings. But not talking about it was worse. Far worse.

Sam didn't pick up on her cue. Instead, he avoided eye contact and tucked his hands into his pockets. "Thanks for coming to my rescue, anyway."

She bit her lip. If he wasn't going to say anything, it was up to her. She was part of this, too. She opened her mouth.

"It was no biggy," she said. Not quite the brave words she'd framed in her mind. Not even close, in fact.

"Yeah, it was."

Sam glanced up at last, locking eyes with hers. She saw gratitude and friendship and warm, fraternal love in his gaze, and her courage failed.

She wanted him to be the one to bring it up, she realized. She'd pined for him for years. Obsessed over him, fantasized over him. She was sure that her true feelings had been more than obvious as they thrashed around on her living room floor—what woman ravished her best friend that way without being secretly in love with him? It just didn't happen. She'd already exposed herself enough. She needed him to take a single, small step in her direction.

And he wasn't going to take it. Because Sam saw her as a friend. Just a friend.

While she stood in front of him, quivering with the need to touch him, to have him touch her, to have him inside her again.

Hurt and humiliation and regret welled up inside her, and she said the first thing that came to her mind.

"Have you spoken to the bank about buying me out?" she asked abruptly.

Sam's face stiffened.

"No. Not yet."

"Do you want me to set up a meeting?"

"I can do it," Sam said tersely. "I said I'd do it."

"I'm free most mornings for the rest of the week. I'd really like to get the ball rolling," she said, pushing. She needed to get this done fast, try to minimize the pain.

Sam's eyes flickered with anger. "Fine. I'll set it up."

Delaney nodded tensely, then turned for the door. He didn't say another word, and she kept her back stiff until she heard the door close behind her. Her shoulders instantly sagged and she closed her eyes for a long moment. One breath…two, three.

Then she opened her eyes again, straightened her shoulders and went back downstairs to her solo dinner.

SAM CHECKED HIS WATCH for the fifth time.

"She should be here soon," he told their bank manager, a stiff-backed, balding man named John.

"Perhaps we could discuss the preliminaries?" John said, opening up the thick folder in front of him on the conference room table.

Sam forced his concern at Delaney's no-show to one side. It was Friday morning, four days since he'd slept with her. He'd put a call through to the bank the first thing Wednesday morning, and arranged for John to come out ASAP. That was what Delaney wanted, right? So he was giving it to her.

Why had he jumped his best friend? It was the burning question that occupied all his waking hours. The way she'd run interference for him with his mother had driven home to him just how much he stood to lose if he let sex come between them. They had barely spoken all week, and already he missed their dinners, their banter, their comfortable silences. She was the last person he could afford to screw with—literally and figuratively. She meant too much to him, and God only knows, as soon as sex entered the equation where he was concerned, Disasterville was just around the corner. It was in the blood, as inevitable as death and taxes. He *had* to get things back to the way they'd always been, with Delaney as his best, uncomplicated, platonic buddy.

He was still convinced that his original decision to forge on with business as usual was the best move he could make. The awkward post-mistake stage he'd anticipated was stretching out a little longer than he would have liked, true, but he and Delaney had years of friendship to fall back on. One stupid, misguided roll in the hay couldn't wipe all that out. Could it?

"Sorry I'm late."

Sam's head shot up as Delaney spoke from the conference room doorway. She was wearing a neatly tailored white shirt and a just-above-the-knee skirt, and she looked harried, her hair tousled, her cheeks a little flushed. Not unlike a certain morning just a few days ago, when she'd climbed on top of him and taken them on the ride of a lifetime….

Sam clenched his jaw. This was the problem. In his mind, when he thought about his relationship with Delaney, getting things back on track seemed easy. Natural. Then she walked into the room, and all he seemed to be able to think about was sex.

Which just went to show what a swamp-dwelling lowlife he really was. No wonder he'd blanked out the fact that she was a woman all these years.

"I had a flat tire," Delaney said as she pulled up a seat. "Have I missed out on much?"

"Why didn't you call me?" Sam said. "I would have taken care of it."

Four days ago, she wouldn't have hesitated, he knew. Now she just shrugged and avoided his eyes.

"I handled it okay."

Signaling that the issue was closed, she focused on John and smiled encouragingly.

"Where do you want to start?" she said.

"I thought we could take a look at the general health of the business before we start talking about valuations and equity," John said.

Sam took a deep breath and willed himself to concentrate

on the matter at hand. Which meant not noticing Delaney's alluring new perfume, or the fact that she'd tucked her hair behind one perfect, shell-shaped ear to reveal the elegant, sensual curve of her neck.

She's your friend, jerk, he reminded himself. *Start acting like one.*

"I've taken a look at these profit projections you've put forward. They're pretty ambitious," John said.

"Not when you consider that the extreme sports industry has grown in double figures for the past four years, with predictions suggesting that we've barely seen the tip of the iceberg," Delaney said, smoothly clicking into business mode. "Our readership has increased more than ten percent every year for the past three years, and our advertising sales have grown proportionately."

She shot a look at Sam. With the ease of long experience, he fielded her pass.

"Take skateboarding, for example. It's not just a fad for boys anymore," he said. "It's an industry. At present, there are several hundred men and women around the world who make a good living from doing nothing but skating in comps and exhibitions. The big names are millionaires several times over. We don't think we're being too optimistic in anticipating our slice of the pie. *X-Pro* has been there since the beginning of the wave in Australia. It's well-respected, credible. Our readers value our opinion, they trust us."

Sam shot his eyes to Delaney, signaling for her to take the lead once more. She stepped in without hesitation, as always. He felt the adrenaline buzz he always got when a meeting was going well.

"Have a look at these results from a recent reader survey we did," Delaney said, sliding a document toward John. "We rated above all the other competition in every area. Even above the more specialized surfing mags out of the U.S."

While John ran his eye over the figures, Delaney flicked Sam a quick look, the confident lift of her eyebrow telling him that she thought they were kicking goals left, right and center, too.

A warm glow started in Sam's belly as he realized that the tension that had sat between them since The Incident had dissolved. The old teamwork was once more in play—the Sam and Delaney show was back in town.

His shoulders relaxed. He'd just found the key to resolving things with his best friend. Meetings. Lots and lots of meetings. Once the initial awkwardness was gone between them, it was just like old times. He should have forced more interaction between the two of them earlier—they'd both been avoiding one another so much this week that this was the longest time they'd spent in the same room for days. But now Sam saw that the more time they spent together, the more relaxed and comfortable they both became. They were a team. He simply had to remind Delaney of that, and the rest of it would melt away. A wave of relief washed over him. It was going to be okay. He felt almost euphoric.

A few more meetings like this, and they could consign those mad moments in Delaney's flat to the dustbin of history—memories to be locked away and sealed and buried deep, never to see the light of day again.

Balancing back on his chair, Sam put his feet on the table, a goofy smile on his lips as he watched Delaney talk with John. In light of all that he'd almost lost, Delaney wanting out from the business didn't seem like the insurmountable barrier that it had on Monday. At the end of the day, if it made her happy to stretch her wings and try something else, he was happy. Their friendship was the important thing. And who was to say, anyway, how long this bug about leaving the business would last? If he kept reminding her of how good they were together, there was every chance she'd change her mind about that, too.

"Man, I need some caffeine, bad," Delaney suddenly announced, pushing her chair back and standing in one smooth, athletic movement. "You want a coffee, John?"

"Black with one, thanks, Delaney," John confirmed.

She cut her eyes across to Sam. "I won't even bother asking you, since you're just a big caffeine pig," she said wryly.

"Oink, oink," Sam agreed. "Actually, make it a triple oink—I missed my morning hit."

Delaney shook her head at him as she crossed to where the espresso machine sat on the sideboard near the window.

"You're looking at a man who can single-handedly chew through a catering-sized bag of coffee in a week, John," she teased as she hit the button to grind the beans.

Sam opened his mouth to respond in kind just as Delaney stepped into the streaming sunlight pouring through the window. Instantly her newly tinted hair caught fire, and her white shirt became virtually translucent. He nearly choked on his tongue as he stared at the perfectly outlined contours of her breasts in a lacy white bra. All rational thought fled his brain as the bulk of his blood supply rushed south. He closed his eyes for a long, long beat, powerless to stop the unwanted images flashing across his closed eyelids—Delaney's breasts puckering under his hands, the arch of her back as she asked for more, the unfocused passion in her face.

He opened his eyes and blinked, but nothing had changed. He couldn't tear his eyes away from her breasts, even though he knew he should. Was that really a hint of nipple darkness he could discern through the layers of shirt and bra? He got

harder just thinking about it, and he bit back a groan of despair.
The guy from the bank was sitting opposite him, for Pete's
sake! It didn't get less sexy than that, as far as Sam was concerned. Yet there he was, practically howling at the moon.

"Sam? Did you hear what I was saying?" Delaney asked.
Sam swallowed and realized that Delaney had been talking
to him. Possibly for some time.

"Um. Sorry," he said, rocketing his feet. "I, ah, I just remembered something."

And then he bolted for the door. Feeling like a complete
and utter loser, he slammed his way into the washroom and
braced himself against the sink. This had to stop. Delaney was
not up for grabs. She was not one of his bed buddies, an easy
shag he could blow off at will. She was his lifelong friend.
And he knew that unless he could keep his sudden aberrant
lust for her under control, he was going to lose her forever.

Lifting his head, Sam stared at himself in the mirror. He
was crap with women—fine in the bedroom, but useless at
anything else. Always had been, always would be. But
Delaney was sacred, special. Unique.

"Don't stuff it up," Sam warned the man in the mirror.
Problem was, he wasn't sure if the guy was even listening.

AT FOUR O'CLOCK, Delaney looked at the clock and willed the
last few hours of the working week to pass. She wanted to go
home, lock herself in her apartment and mourn the loss of her
old life. No matter how many times she told herself she was
making the right decision, she still felt vertiginous every time
she thought about walking away from *X-Pro* and her friendship with Sam. Since the meeting with the bank that morning,
she'd been experiencing odd, jolting lurches of anxiety as she
contemplated the fact that in a few weeks' time, she would

be free to step out the doors off their small office and never return.

Shuffling papers on her desk, she sighed heavily. She hated being angry with Sam all the time. It was such an alien emotion in their relationship—it made her feel more heart-sick than all her unrequited longing ever had. She was the one who'd stuffed things up, after all. Sam just wanted to be her friend—and who could blame him for that?

It wasn't as if he'd ever had much incentive to explore anything more meaningful. Her recent encounter with Nancy Kirk had reinforced for her that Sam had every reason to avoid committed relationships like the plague. Why should he believe in love and respect and forever when he'd only ever seen how miserable two people could make each other?

The ring of the telephone startled Delaney out of her dark thoughts and she reached for the receiver with a sense of relief. Anything to distract her from her own tortured musings.

But the frown creasing her forehead only deepened as she recognized the voice of one of her most lucrative advertisers. Within seconds, she'd learned that he was calling to pull two double-page spreads due to problems at his end. She didn't need to check the calendar to know they were right on dead-line—the files were supposed to be with the printer tonight.

Taking a set of rapid notes, she asked for a few minutes to consult Sam before she offered a response. She hung up the phone and ran her fingers through her hair. Distraction was one thing, but an out-and-out crisis was definitely overkill.

She found Sam making himself a milk shake in the kitchen-ette, staring at the blender as it buzzed angrily. In no mood to yell her bad tidings over the sound of the machine, she propped herself against the wall to wait until the blender stopped its awful whirring. As soon as the shake was frothing at the top of the glass jug, Sam hit the stop button and pulled the lid off. He was just holding the jug up to his mouth when she spoke.

"Brace yourself, we have a problem," she said.

Sam started violently, and chocolate shake slopped over the front of his T-shirt and down onto the floor as he struggled to stop the jug from slipping from his hands. Delaney winced, belatedly realizing that he'd had no idea she'd been standing there.

For a second they eyed each other as chocolate shake dripped from his T-shirt and down onto the tiles.

"Sorry," Delaney said.

"Never sneak up on a man while he's drinking a shake," Sam said.

Then, to Delaney's consternation, he peeled his soaked T-shirt over his head and mopped the bunched up fabric across his chest to clean away the remainder of the milk. Delaney stared at the golden brown expanse of his chest, her eyes taking an explicit, no-holds-barred tour of every inch of sculpted muscle on display. He was beautiful. So sexy. Every inch a man. Of their own accord, her eyes dipped toward the waistband of his jeans as she thought about those other, vital inches hidden by the worn denim.

Oh, yeah.

She was staring—ogling, really—and gave herself a mental slap, and stern instructions to tear her eyes away from his perfect, irresistible body.

"So, what's the problem?" Sam said he reached for the kitchen sponge to clean up the tiled floor.

"Um. We, um, we just lost two double-page spreads," she said, trying not to notice the way his muscles flexed so beguilingly as he crouched to wipe the floor.

His skin looked so warm and firm and touchable. Her fingers flexed, aching to caress him again.

"But we're right on deadline," Sam said, staring up at her.

Delaney forced herself to process what he was saying. Unfortunately, most of her brain was concentrating on not drooling. She figured she'd have to compromise essential body functions, like breathing, if she wanted to actually talk and make sense.

"Yeah. Something went wrong," she finally managed to say.

Sam straightened, tossing the sponge into the sink.

"Wrong? What does that mean?"

Delaney made the mistake of giving in to her need for one last peek at the sexy ridges of his abdominal muscles before answering.

"It means— It means that someone made a mistake," she heard herself say.

Sam was frowning, confusion warring with irritation in his eyes. Delaney forced herself to wrench her eyes away from his body, fixing them on a point over his shoulder.

"The ads were supposed to be on their way to us by courier. Except the client was using a one-man advertising agency, and apparently the guy has flipped out and trashed his office. Everything's gone."

"Shit."

"They've asked us to wait until Monday for the material, or go without them."

Sam rubbed a hand absently across his belly. With a valiant effort, Delaney managed to limit herself to just a quick peek.

"Monday's too late. We'll miss our slot at the mail house," Sam said.

"And the billings will be off, not to mention we guaranteed Brash Bikes that the issue would be out in time for their new product launch," Delaney added, squinting her eyes so she could block his chest out of her peripheral vision.

"Have you got something in your eye?" Sam asked, leaning toward her.

Delaney tilted backward, fully aware that if her bare skin touched his she would not be responsible for the consequences.

"No. Just thinking," she bluffed.

He gave her a searching look, but she just raised her eyebrows and tried to look like a professional instead of a lust-crazed woman on the verge of a nervous breakdown.

"What do you want to do? I told them I'd call back with an answer once we'd spoken," she said.

"We could drop the ads and fill the space with editorial. I've got a couple of emergency articles in the bottom drawer."

"Great. Except we just handed the bank a bunch of profit projections for the next six months. Losing two double-page spreads takes twenty thousand off the bottom line," Delaney reminded him.

Sam leaned against the cupboard, arms braced behind him on the countertop. Delaney almost whimpered when she saw the way it made his pecs flex. *Dear God, have mercy,* she begged mentally. *I'm only human!*

Sam's eyes had darkened and lost focus, and she knew from long experience that his brain was working at light speed as he tried to find a solution.

"Okay," he said suddenly, straightening from his position. Even though she was sure his abdominal muscles would have put on a stellar performance as he straightened, she kept her gaze fixed determinedly on his face.

Score one for Team Self-Control. At last.

"We'll do the creative for them. We've got Rudy to throw the images together. I can write the copy. We just need a brief from the advertiser. If we push hard, we can get it together and still get the files to the printer by midnight," Sam said decisively.

From long experience, they both knew they could stall their printer a few hours before they lost their slot to another job. Her mind still numb with lust, Delaney spoke without thinking.

"Maybe I should have put out for Jake the other night after all," she muttered, thinking of the tap dancing she'd have to undertake to sweet-talk their printing rep around.

Sam's mouth tightened, and Delaney felt heat rush up her neck and into her face. For a long moment neither of them said anything.

"I'll go see if Rudy can stay late," Sam said.

Delaney jerked backward as he moved past her.

"Maybe you should put something on," she blurted.

Sam flicked a look at her, then glanced down at his bare chest. "It's not like I'm wandering around in my Y-fronts," he said dismissively.

Delaney had a mental image of Sam walking around with a bare chest all evening. She knew without a doubt that she wouldn't be able to survive the experience a sane woman.

"It's not professional. The girls might be offended," she said.

Sam squinted at his pecs. "Because they can see my nipples?" he asked disbelievingly.

Like iron filings to a magnet, Delaney's eyes flew to the flat, brown circles of his nipples. She swallowed noisily.

"You never know," she squeaked. "Might be risky. Sexual harassments laws and all that."

Sam shrugged. "I think I've got an old sweater in my office."

Then he was gone. Delaney sagged against the wall and touched a hand to her forehead. As she suspected, it was damp.

And it wasn't the only part of her anatomy that was feeling a little…steamy as a result of Sam's impromptu strip show.

"You going to call them back and get a brief for those ads?"

Delaney almost jumped out of her skin as Sam ducked his head back around the corner,

"Yep. Right on it," she said, heading back to her office.

If only she had a spare brain hidden in there—one that was impervious to crazy female hormones—she'd be fine.

"OKAY, I'M DONE," Rudy said, hitting the save button and flopping back in his chair with a loud sigh.

Delaney stared at the double-page ad on Rudy's supersized computer monitor.

"Rudy, my man, you are a god," Sam said, clapping a hand onto the other man's shoulder.

Delaney leaned forward, checking that Rudy had made the last changes that the client had requested as part of their sign-off.

"It's a beautiful thing," she agreed. "Now, you get your skinny behind out of here and go and have a weekend."

"I still need to print out a proof, and compile the files," Rudy said.

"It's fine. Sam and I will handle it. It's been a while since we did all this stuff ourselves, but I think we remember how it's done," Delaney said. Rudy looked beat, and she and Sam really could manage without him.

"Okay. Thanks, guys," Rudy said. "See you Monday."

Delaney slid into his empty chair as Rudy grabbed his backpack and headed for the exit. The front door thunked shut behind him, and silence crept over the office. Delaney shifted a little, suddenly very self-conscious. Another great side-benefit to having had sex with Sam—now she no longer felt comfortable with her best friend. It just got better and better.

The sound of Sam's stomach growling was a welcome intrusion.

"I need food," he announced.

"No kidding," Delaney said. She had the feeling he welcomed the diversion as much as she did.

"I'll go grab a pizza. What do you want?" He slid off his perch on top of Rudy's desk return, patting his pockets to check for money.

"Suit yourself. You know what I like," Delaney said, forcing herself to concentrate on the screen in front of her. The sooner she compiled the files for the printer, the sooner she could get out of there.

There was a short pause before Sam turned away, and Delaney felt the sting of yet another blush climbing into her cheeks as she replayed her words inside her head. *You know what I like.* Why did she keep saying such suggestive things around him? And then blushing over them like some stupid teen girl?

For the next ten minutes she buried herself in compiling the files for the printer. She'd almost finished when Sam arrived back with a large pizza box in hand. She saw the logo of her favorite pizza place on the lid, and inhaled deeply.

"That smells fantastic," she murmured as she saved the last file to disk. The proofs of their newly created ads were sitting on the color printer, and she braced her legs against the floor and pushed herself off so that Rudy's wheelie chair whizzed along the carpet to the printer station. Sam busied himself calling a late-night courier while she put the proofs into a large envelope with the other hard copy for the magazine, sliding in the vital layout files last of all.

"Done!" she said with satisfaction.

"Guy said he was just around the corner," Sam said, and

even as he spoke, someone tapped on the front door. Sam scooped up the package, grinning at Delaney.

"Have to get lucky sometime."

Delaney rubbed her sore neck muscles as Sam dealt quickly with the courier, locking the door behind him and dropping the after-hours blinds in place.

"Man, that was a long day," he said. Delaney checked the time on the corner of Rudy's computer and saw that it was past one.

"Just like the old days," she said, pushing her chair back toward the pizza box.

"Yeah." Sam's smile faded. "Guess I'll have to get used to doing it on my own from now on."

Even though her heart lurched in her chest, Delaney didn't look at him as she flipped the box open. "I'm sure one of the others will stay late with you, if you ask nicely." Then she saw the pizza. "What the hell is this?"

She stared down at the family-size pizza in front of her.

"A pizza, last time I looked," Sam said.

"No, I mean this," Delaney said, poking her finger at the offending item. Yellow and cubed, it made her nose wrinkle just thinking about it finding a home on her pizza.

"Pineapple. You said suit yourself, so I got a super Hawaiian," Sam said.

"But I hate pineapple. You know I hate pineapple," Delaney said, glaring at him.

"No, you don't," Sam said defensively. "You hate anchovies. You love pineapple."

"I think I know what I do and do not like, thank you. And I do not like pineapple. Especially tinned pineapple. It tastes like a can," she said.

"Then you should have said. When I asked, what do you

want, you should have said no pineapple. But you didn't. You said, and I quote, *suit yourself.* Am I wrong?"

They locked eyes over the pizza, and Delaney felt her pulse pick up. Even with a five o'clock shadow and a ratty old sweater he'd dug up from his desk drawer, Sam looked good enough to eat.

"I also said you know what I like," she said. "Sure got that wrong."

Sam's eyes narrowed. "Are we still talking about food here or something else?"

Delaney looked away from his intent gaze. "I was referring to the pineapple."

"That's what I thought," he said a little smugly.

Delaney felt another killer blush stealing its way into her cheeks. How dare he refer to her off-the-scale response to his lovemaking! Trying to save what little dignity remained to her, she launched herself out of Rudy's chair.

"Where are you going?" Sam wanted to know.

"Home."

"What about the pizza?"

"I don't like Hawaiian, Sam," she said through gritted teeth.

"Fine. Look, see—I'll pick the pineapple bits off. Happy?" Sam said, picking lumps of pineapple off a section of pizza.

"I'm not hungry."

She just wanted to get out of here. Surely some sleep and some privacy would make her life seem more bearable.

"Right. Something else that's changed," Sam said.

Delaney swung on her heel, hands automatically finding her hips. She knew she should grab her bag and walk away, but for some reason she found herself squaring up to Sam, spoiling for a really good, loud, vocal fight.

"What's that supposed to mean?" she demanded.

"It means that I don't know what you want anymore. One second I've got a business partner, then you're feeding me some bull about needing to concentrate on building a family. Next you want a pizza, then you don't."

"A pizza. You're comparing my desire to start a family, to have children of my own, with not wanting to eat a stupid pineapple-covered pizza?" Delaney asked incredulously.

Vaguely she realized that she and Sam had moved closer together, the better to yell at each other with no distractions.

"Why not? At least you told me you wanted a pizza in advance. I had a little warning on that one, before you changed your mind," Sam yelled.

"You are unbelievable! All week you've barely been able to look me in the eye after what happened in my apartment, and now you're accusing *me* of not talking!" she yelled back.

"*Me?* You're the one who didn't bring it up! What am I supposed to do, force you to talk about something that you obviously deeply regret?" Sam demanded.

"At least you got one thing right," Delaney snapped back at him, in full fight-to-win mode now. "If I could take back one thing in my life, that would be it—gone, in a second," she said, snapping her fingers to indicate how quickly she'd make the decision.

"Ditto, baby, don't worry," Sam said, right in her face now, blue eyes glittering fiercely.

They stared at each other for a beat, both panting from the exertion of being so angry with one another. Then the next thing she knew, Sam had hauled her close and was kissing her like there was no tomorrow.

6

SAM COULDN'T BELIEVE how good she tasted. Sweet and hot, her tongue dancing with his as he pressed himself against her.

"Oh, Laney," he groaned. He knew it was wrong, knew that he should have had the willpower to resist the need to touch her, to have her again. But he didn't. She'd looked so hot, standing there glaring at him, her breasts heaving and her cheeks flushed. Desire had gripped him, and before he knew it she was in his arms, and his tongue was in her mouth.

He deepened the kiss, and her hands slid down his back to clutch at his butt, pulling him closer. He was already fully erect, his hard-on pushing against his jeans, but when she ground herself against him he nearly lost it. Growling low in his throat, he slid his hands up to capture her breasts, kneading them firmly.

"Yes," she gasped, thrusting her hips against him even harder.

Sam felt her nipples harden under his thumbs as her breasts swelled in his hands. Operating on pure animal instinct, he tugged at the neckline of her shirt. He needed more, now. Her buttons popped off and without hesitation he buried his face in her cleavage, laving the curve of one breast, and then the other, with his tongue. Impatient, he shoved the lace of her bra away and suckled a nipple deep into his mouth. Delaney's hands clutched at his head, holding him in place as he played his tongue across her nipple. If he could have talked, he would have reassured her—he wasn't going anywhere. He'd been thinking about her breasts, about having them in his mouth again, all week. With one hand, he unhooked the catch on her bra, and slid it off her shoulders altogether. Her breasts fell into his hands, nipples pouting for his attention—and he was more than happy to oblige.

Switching focus to Delaney's other breast, he slid his hands down her back to cup her butt. Someone made a deeply satisfied noise, and he realized it was him—her ass was so good, he couldn't get enough of it. Aware that she was panting, her hands grabbing at him impatiently, he slid his hands farther down her skirt. Within seconds he was underneath, hands sliding up her silk-stocking-covered thighs, his imagination rampaging ahead of him as he remembered how hot and wet she'd been last time they were together.

Then his hand slid from stockinged thigh to bare flesh, and he stilled. *Please, please, please be wearing garters and stockings,* he willed as he reached down to tug her skirt up around her waist so he could see properly.

He bit his lip at the sight that met his eyes—Delaney's long, lean legs clad in black silk stay-up stockings, the lacy tops stopping just south of the part of her he was most eager to touch.

"Do you have any idea…?" He panted, staring down at her.

Delaney just reached for the waistband of his jeans. "Get these off," she demanded.

She reached for the tab on his zipper, but Sam batted her hand away. Not this time. This time, he was running the show, and he wasn't finished with her yet. When she opened her mouth to protest, he silenced her with a kiss and drove her back against the wall, simultaneously sliding a hand between her legs to cup her silk-covered mound. She quivered, her stance widening as she welcomed his touch. Peppering kisses across the arc of her cheekbone toward her ear, Sam ran a teasing finger along the edge of her panties. Her whole body shook and Sam smiled as he pulled the sensitive lobe of her ear into his mouth. Then he slid a finger beneath her underwear and into the wet heat of her. She moaned helplessly as he found her clitoris, slicking his finger backward and forward across the tightened bud.

"Do you like that?" he whispered in her ear.

"You know I do," she said.

"What about this?" Sam asked, his gaze intent on hers as he slid his finger deep inside her. Her eyelids flicked down and she bit her lower lip, her face suffusing with need. Between her legs, her muscles pulsed around his finger.

"Sam," she begged, reaching for his waistband again.

This time he didn't stop her. Any self-control he'd laid claim to was rapidly slipping through his fingers. She was so desirable, so hot. He needed to make her his. Even if it was just for a few moments.

She pulled his jeans down over his hips, and he found the closure on her skirt and returned the favor. Sacrificing skin contact for practicality's sake, he stepped away from her to kick his jeans off, and she did the same, stepping out of her skirt and underwear and tossing them to one side.

"And this. I want to see all of you," Delaney insisted, tugging at the waistband of his sweater.

Sam obliged in record time, then pulled her close to revel in the sensual feel of skin on skin.

"So good," he murmured as he slid his hands down onto her butt and pulled her tight against his aching erection. She ground her mound against him, her own hands clutching his butt. Sam slid his hand lower, caressing the lower curve of her bottom and dipping his fingers between her thighs.

"Sam, I need you," she whispered in his ear, her voice breaking as he toyed with her.

"Yes," he said.

Grabbing her hips, he lifted her, and she came willingly, wrapping her legs around his waist. His hard-on twitched as it made first contact with her intimate heat, and he lost no time in taking the four or five steps needed to bring him inside his office. Keeping hold of her weight with one arm, he swept his desk clear with the other, then slid her onto its surface. Delaney lay back on the polished wood, her breasts perky as hell, her eyelids at half-mast, her thighs still firm around his waist. Sam felt his erection swell even farther, if that were possible. He was shaking as he positioned himself between her thighs.

Then he could wait no longer, and he was sliding into her tight, slick heat, his muscles tensing as he registered how good she felt.

He groaned, smoothing his hands up across her belly to find her breasts again. Delaney closed her eyes and dropped her head back as he began thrusting into her, his hands busy on her breasts.

He was torn in two, wanting it to last forever, yet greedy for completion. Ducking his head, he pulled her nipple into his mouth and gave himself over to the tension building inside him.

DELANEY THOUGHT she was going to die. She'd never been so turned on in her entire life. Every touch of Sam's hands was like a brand on her skin. He seemed to know exactly where to touch her, when, and how often. Each thrust brought her closer to the edge, and she tossed her head from side to side, every nerve ending craving release.

He looked so amazing, poised above her, his body tensing with each thrust. His face was intent, his mouth slightly open as he buried himself again and again inside her. She could tell he was close, and watching the desire build in him only turned her on even more.

Then he bent his head to her breasts again, sucking her nipple so firmly that it almost hurt. She clenched her thighs more tightly around him, reaching for the edge of the desk. She was close, so close….

As if he sensed this, Sam slid a hand across her hip and into the nest of curls between her legs. With each thrust, he flicked his thumb across her clitoris, and Delaney let out a low, desperate moan.

"Feels so good," she heard herself pant. And then Sam picked up the tempo, his thumb massaging her clitoris more firmly now as he thrust faster and faster inside her. Closing her eyes, Delaney lost all sense of the world as her body reached its peak. Clutching at Sam's hips, she rode out her orgasm, only vaguely aware that he was coming, too. Tiny aftershocks raced through her body as he shuddered against her, fingers curled into her waist. His head dropped down, masking his expression from her, and Delaney dropped her own head back to stare at the ceiling and try to catch her breath. Like something she could almost see in her peripheral vision, regret lurked, but she refused to acknowledge it just yet. For these few precious seconds, she wanted to revel in the fact that once again she'd had her heart's desire—Sam, inside her, wanting no one else but her.

Then she felt Sam's body tense, and she knew that her moment of reprieve was over. He stepped away from her, and she was instantly aware of how naked and exposed she was, lying spread-eagled across his desk. Abruptly she sat up and closed her legs. Sam ran a hand over his head. She could see the confusion and regret in his face, and she felt weak with hurt and despair.

There had been a moment there, when he'd pulled her close and started kissing her when she'd had a tiny shred of self-control left. The sensible part of her brain had sent out a last, desperate warning—*pull back now, or forever hold your peace.* But she'd wanted him so badly, she'd deliberately pushed the thought of consequences away. How could something that felt so right possibly have a downside?

Sam backed up a few more steps, then sank into one of his guest chairs. Leaning forward, he put his head in his hands. Something twisted in Delaney's belly as she saw his shoulders tense. Could this get any worse?

"I'm sorry. I don't know why that happened," he said after a long silence. He sounded choked, smothered.

Delaney stared at him, all her self-consciousness taking a backseat as she registered his words.

"You don't know why we just had sex?" she repeated, wanting to make sure that he'd really just said what she thought he'd said.

"I just—I don't know what's gotten into me," Sam said, shaking his head.

Delaney's hands curled into fists. First, he made love to her like Casanova and Don Juan rolled into one, then he sat there looking as though someone had just told him he had twenty-four hours to live. And now he was telling her he had no idea why he'd done it all in the first place?

"You... You...idiot!" she said. She was so angry, she kicked his chair, not caring that the action set her boobs to jiggling and almost made her fall over.

He was impossible. *Impossible.* She couldn't believe that

two minutes ago, he'd been inside her, and it had been the most transcendent experience of her life. She needed to have her head read, even letting him lay a hand on her. He'd never had a long-term relationship in his life—she knew this about him, just as she knew that he had a scar on his back from when he'd fallen off his bike when he was a kid, and that he would do almost anything to avoid an injection. Yet she'd indulged her need, her craving for him. And gotten what she deserved.

A black wave of despair welled up inside her. Tears gathered at the back of her eyes, but she was *not* going to cry in front of him, not after what had just happened. Her body stiff with tension, she scooped together her clothes. Giving him one last, searing look, she stalked past him and off toward the bathroom. There was nothing more to say.

SAM HEARD THE BATHROOM DOOR slam and dug his fingers hard into his scalp. What had he done? He'd just taken Delaney across his desk, like some desperado with no style or finesse. She must think he was an animal. Or some kind of sex-obsessed creep. This was the second time he'd hit on her in a week. And it hadn't escaped his notice that the strange compulsion to jump her bones had come hard on the heels of her declaration that she wanted to leave the business.

Was that what this was all about—some pathetic attempt by his subconscious to keep her close? *You conceited jerk,* he told himself. *As if a couple of shags with you is going to make the difference.*

Sam shook his head, instinctively rejecting his own hypothesis. He hadn't had sex with Delaney because he was trying to manipulate her into doing what he wanted. He'd had sex with her because he hadn't been able to keep his hands off her. And then he'd promptly insulted and hurt her—all before his heart rate had returned to normal. A new world record for insensitivity.

The front door slammed shut, and he winced as he heard Delaney start her car with an overzealous rev of the engine. She was so angry with him—and, underneath that, probably hurt and disgusted. She didn't sleep around—he knew that about her, even if he had always kind of looked the other way when it had come to her love life. He'd taken advantage of her. He remembered what she'd said when they were fighting: if she could take one thing back, it would be what had happened between them at her apartment.

Sam scrubbed his face with his hands. She was right—he was an idiot. What kind of a jerk didn't have the common decency to keep his grabby hands to himself when it came to his best friend?

Slowly he became aware that he was still buck naked, hunched over on one of the visitor's chairs. Sighing, he straightened his shoulders and lifted his head. It was done. He couldn't take it back. He just had to think of some way of making it up to Delaney.

His gaze fell on his desk, and he saw that her bra was strewn across the photo of the two of them on the beach. She must have missed it when she collected her other clothes. Standing, he lifted the lacy scrap, staring down at it, so fine and delicate in his hands. It was still curved into the shape of her breasts, and he rubbed his fingers against the fabric, savoring the texture of silk and lace. It was a sexy, fragile, beautiful thing—just like Delaney. He put the bra down, exchanging it for the photograph of the two of them from that long ago summer.

Even back then, Delaney had been beautiful. Had he really never noticed the lithe sexuality of her lean body? Or the compelling depth of her toffee-colored eyes? Even with a walloping shiner, they glowed with life and passion.

At sixteen, she'd stared down the barrel of the camera as though she was daring the world to take a shot at her. The adult Delaney wasn't much different—she was still a doer, a darer. She'd taken on every challenge he'd ever thrown at her, from snow-boarding to scuba-diving to martial arts training. And now she'd risen to meet his passion, matching him kiss for kiss, thrust for thrust, touch for touch. And he had nothing to offer her in return.

Putting the photo down, Sam slowly pulled his clothes on, tucking Delaney's bra into his back pocket to return to her later. He felt sick and scared. Because he knew he was dangerously close to making Delaney hate him.

Feeling suddenly claustrophobic, he scooped up his car keys and strode toward the door. Pausing only to set the alarm and lock up after himself, he jumped into his SUV and pulled out into the quiet streets of early morning Fitzroy. He needed to clear his head, and this time half measures wouldn't cut it.

Turning his car toward the freeway, he put his foot down and drove. By the time dawn was lightening the rim of the world, he was pulling into the gravel driveway of his mate's beach house on Philip Island, south of Melbourne. Sam had an open invitation to treat the place as his own, and he knew Charlie was in the U.S. at present on a business trip. It was the perfect place to make peace with himself and work out how to make it up to Delaney.

Fortunately, he always traveled with a surfboard in the back of the car, and there was bound to be an array of cast-off clothes lurking there, also. Enough to see him through, anyway.

It took only moments to locate the spare key in its hiding spot in the garden, and he let himself into the house and flicked on some lights. Ensuring that he'd switched on the electric hot water service, he trailed his way through to the spare bedroom. It was furnished with two saggy single beds, remnants from Charlie's childhood. Uncaring, Sam threw himself onto one and closed his eyes. For now, he wanted some sleep. In a few hours, he would wake up and go find some waves. Only after he'd immersed himself in sea and spray for several hours would he let himself think about Delaney again.

And then he'd find a way to make things right.

DELANEY HAD the whole weekend to examine her folly from every angle. She'd called Sam an idiot, but she was just as stupid. Why had she listened to her slathering hormones and not her common sense? When were hormones *ever* right? And now she'd compounded the disaster of Tuesday morning by adding a big cherry on top of it in the form of Friday night's little debacle. Or, if she were being technically correct, *big* debacle, given the quality of the orgasm she'd experienced.

Pacing the balcony of her apartment on Sunday evening, Delaney took a big mouthful of wine from the glass she was holding and admitted to herself that she was well and truly screwed up. In love with her best friend, about to throw away a great career and rapidly on the way to becoming sexually obsessed.

Why, by all that was good in the world, did Sam have to be so great in bed? Or on a desk, or a living room floor, for that matter. The man was a sensual master. A sexual genius. A Mozart of the bedroom. He had plucked and stroked and sucked and teased her into the most heightened state of arousal she'd ever experienced in her life.

And then pulled the afterglow right out from under her by

immediately proclaiming himself sorry for all of the above. It was too, too humiliating.

Delaney took another sip from her wineglass and leaned on the balcony railing. Around her, thousands of lights twinkled in the night, the sprawl of inner-city Melbourne stretching off into the distance.

Briefly her mind wandered to the apartment above. She hadn't heard Sam moving around all weekend. It didn't surprise her. He'd probably done a runner for a few days. He'd never been big on dealing with difficult situations. How pleasant to find herself filed under that heading in his life.

Turning back toward her apartment, she caught sight of her reflection in the darkened glass door. It wasn't a very attractive sight. She'd been moping around all weekend sulking about what could have been or what should have been, and she hadn't washed her hair for two days in a row. Now it was scrunched up on the back of her neck in a rubber band, a very unsleek, unsophisticated mess. Then there was her clothing. Baggy sports pants, baggy T-shirt, no bra, floppy socks. The inside of her didn't feel any better, either. Her teeth were fuzzy from eating too much chocolate, and she had a cramp in her eyebrows from scowling all weekend.

"Get over yourself, Delaney," she told herself.

So she was in love with a man who didn't return her feelings. It wasn't going to kill her, was it? There were worse things in life. Right?

For a second her mind was a complete blank as she tried to come up with a worse scenario.

"Pathetic," she muttered to herself, tossing off the last of the wine. Then she marched back inside her apartment and went straight to the bathroom.

A long hot shower later, she combed out her newly washed and conditioned hair and sat down with the real estate section of the newspaper.

The only thing to do was to keep moving forward with her plan. Soon she would be out of the business, and the next step would be removing herself from the temptation of living beneath Sam.

She shot a wistful look around her apartment. She'd put a lot of herself into this place. But hanging on to it would just be an excuse to hang on to Sam. And he'd made it abundantly, brutally clear that there was nothing to hang on to.

Her shoulders sagged as she at last acknowledged the most galling aspect of her recent encounter with Sam. As he'd reached for her, his eyes hungry, his body needing hers, she'd been on fire with hope. Because he wouldn't have grabbed her like that if he didn't feel something, right?

And then he'd said those fateful words. *I don't know why that happened.*

But what had she been expecting him to say? *Delaney, I love you? Please don't leave me, I can't imagine my life without you?*

Really? Did her folly really extend that far?

Delaney stared sightlessly down at the newspaper spread across her lap.

Yes. She was that foolish. She had hoped, even after all these years. Even after the way he'd behaved after the last time they'd slept with each other. Which was why Sam's words had hurt so much. Would she never learn her lesson where he was concerned?

You know what to do, she berated herself. *Just do it.*

Picking up a pen, Delaney refocused on the real estate ads. *Coming up, one new Sam-free life. Stat.*

SAM SLAMMED the back of his car shut and reached for his surfboard. Tucking it under one arm, he strode out onto the sand, angling up toward the peak of the dunes that stood between him and the beach. There was an easier way to the water, cutting through the dunes rather than over them, but the view from the top was spectacular. And he needed every bit of inspiration that Mother Nature had on offer at the moment.

After four days of surfing, eating and sleeping, he was finally beginning to see a way forward through the mess he'd made of his relationship with Delaney.

For starters, the sex had to stop. It was amazing, mind-blowing, addictive. But it was also the fastest route to losing her. For perhaps the first time in his life, he would have to exercise some self-restraint and keep his hands out of the cookie jar.

It was about more than just keeping his mitts off her, however. Straddling his bobbing board out past the break early one morning, Sam had had an epiphany. Delaney was his friend—his dearest, most loyal, most beloved friend. And she had told him that she wanted to have a family. She wanted to meet someone special, fall in love, make babies. Build a life, in short.

If he were a true friend, her goal would be his goal. It was so clear to him out there on the ocean, the salt spray fresh in his face. He had to help Delaney find a man worthy of her. He had to help her find new challenges.

He'd grown more and more certain about his decision over the ensuing days. Now, he crested the top of the dune and paused to take in the view, his board propped beside him in the sand. Below him, golden sand stretched down to a private, untouched cove. Waves licked the beach, their peaks foaming as they curled into the sand. The blue-grey ocean seemed to stretch on forever.

The wind stirred his hair and he squinted his eyes against the glare of the mid-afternoon sun. Inside his chest, there was a hollow place that had been there ever since he'd made his big decision. The ugly truth was that he wanted Delancy all to himself. He didn't want to watch her fall in love with Mr. Two-Point-Five-Kids. He didn't even want to play favorite uncle to her children, to teach them how to surf and skate and get in trouble. He was that much of a selfish bastard. The thought of her building a life for herself that didn't include him in a major role was almost unthinkable.

But it was what she wanted. And he was determined that Delaney would get it.

Slinging his board under his arm again, Sam made his way down to the water. Splashing into the shallows, he stopped to secure his leg rope around his ankle, then waded in deep enough to launch himself onto his board. Paddling surely and strongly, he made his way out past the break.

For the next hour, he surfed hard, his mind a complete blank. Delaney, the magazine, everything receded into the distance. It was all still ticking over somewhere down deep, but he'd won himself some valuable breathing room. By the time he stepped back onto the beach, he felt crystal clear and very calm.

He was going to come clean to Delaney, tell her that he was threatened by what was going on with their friendship. He didn't relish the conversation, emotional chitchat not being his strong point, but he would make the effort for her. Then he would offer her his services as a matchmaker. It was the least he could do, he figured, to make it up to her after shamelessly taking advantage of her the way he had. After all, who knew her better than him? He knew all her habits, good and bad. He knew she was always grumpy in the morning, and that she adored Turkish delight, and that she was compulsive about sleeping only on one-hundred-percent cotton sheets.

Plus, he knew a lot of guys. Surfing mates, skating mates, drinking mates, partying mates. Some of them even fell into all categories. Somewhere in his rich and varied catalogue of friends there must be a man worthy of Delaney.

Making his way back to the car by the easy route this time, Sam turned the matter over and over in his mind. The first candidate who sprang to mind was Macca. Short for Scott McCarthy, a friend of both his and Delaney's for years. Which was good, for starters—no weird vibe about Macca not wanting Sam and Delaney to continue their friendship. And Macca earned a sweet living running his own construction company. He was a good mate, talked about his sister's kids a lot and wasn't a bastard with women. Three ticks. On the down side, he didn't have much of a sense of humor. And he was pretty passive, usually backing down in an argument.

Sliding his board into his car, Sam dried himself roughly with a towel as he mentally crossed Macca off his list. Now that he thought about it, the poor guy just wasn't up to Laney's speed. She needed someone to push back, keep her honest. She was a passionate woman, and she needed someone to match that passion.

Sam resolutely stopped himself from thinking about exactly how passionate Delaney was as he tooled his car back to Charlie's beach house. The gravel driveway crackled beneath his tires as he pulled up, and his eyes grew unfocused as another prospect occurred: Charlie himself.

No problem with being a good provider—Charlie was raking it in with his job as an investment banker. And he owned property—witness the holiday house. He dressed well, and could handle himself in almost any situation. He didn't surf, true, but he did like to snowboard, so he was redeemable. He was funny, generous and very damned charming with the ladies, from what Sam had seen.

Pretty much perfect, really. Sam's jaw flexed and his fingers tightened on the steering wheel as he imagined setting Charlie and Delaney up on a date. Charlie could probably sweep her off her feet if he put his mind to it. His grip tightened even further on the steering wheel.

The two of them already knew each other, of course. So it wouldn't be too awkward. Sam frowned as a thought occurred. Maybe they knew each other too well? Maybe there'd be no excitement between them? Because if Charlie had been at all interested in Delaney, he would have made a move before now, wouldn't he?

Although Charlie hadn't seen Delaney lately, of course. Not since her makeover. Sam suddenly had an image of Charlie getting an eyeful of Delaney in her new skin-tight jeans and tiny tops. He could just imagine his friend's reaction.

Lips thinning, he crossed Charlie off the list as well. Any man who needed to see Delaney in skin-tight jeans to appreciate her just was not up to scratch.

Obviously it wasn't going to be easy finding someone who was Delaney's perfect match. And why should it be? She was a special, amazing woman. The man who wound up marrying her would be the luckiest sod on the planet, and then some. There wasn't a doubt in his mind that she'd make a great mother, either. She doted on her sister's kids, but he'd also seen her handle their tantrums with confident aplomb. She'd be a natural, no doubt about it.

Sam found himself in the living room, staring at Charlie's

seen-better-days sofa and ratty old black-and-white television. It was time to go back. He'd stalled his return for as long as he could, having left a message on Delaney's office voice mail on Sunday night explaining he'd be taking a few days off work. There was always a brief lull in between issues, so he'd known he wasn't placing too much of a burden on her by sloping off for a couple of days.

But it was Wednesday, and his time was more than up. He'd achieved what he'd set out to do. He'd got his head on straight where Delaney was concerned, gained himself some much-needed perspective. He had a game plan, a strategy to move forward with.

He whiled away the hours on the drive back to Melbourne reviewing more possible candidates for Delaney's future husband. By the time he was turning into the street housing their apartment block, it was after six in the evening and he'd come up with a shortlist of three prospects.

He was feeling quietly pleased with himself when he saw the sign. Six feet tall and almost as wide, it was fixed to the side of their apartment block and featured a big, splashy For Sale across the top, along with a high-gloss photo of the interior of a modern, funky warehouse apartment.

Sam almost drove into a tree as he slammed the brakes on and stared at the living room of Delaney's place.

What in the hell was going on?

7

DELANEY STUDIED the blueprints spread out on her dining room table.

"So, Steve, what did you think?" she asked hopefully.

"It needs a little work, but it's got good bones. At the right price, I think it's got a lot of promise," Steve said.

Steve was her sister's friend, an architect who'd done Delaney the favor of inspecting a house she'd found in the southeastern Melbourne suburb of Camberwell. She'd gone through the house for the first time on Monday night, spoken to a real estate agent about putting her apartment on the market the following morning, and watched as the sign went up the very next day. Working in publishing, she was familiar with fast turnaround digital printing, but she'd been somewhat breathless at the speed with which her agent had moved.

The plans in front of her depicted a classic California bungalow, with a deep, wide porch along the front of the house, and two sets of diamond-paned windows on either side of central double doors. The rooms inside were spacious, if a little dated with their seventies wallpaper and dingy nylon carpet. But she and Steve had pulled up a corner of the carpet to confirm there was a genuine Baltic pine floor underneath, just waiting to be rediscovered, and the wallpaper was a pretty easy fix.

As Steve said, it had a lot of potential. Delaney glanced

around her apartment, feeling distinctly wistful about saying goodbye to its gracious high ceilings and exposed timber beams.

"It's a great space," Steve said, as though he could read her mind.

Delaney summoned a smile. "But it's not really a family home," she said firmly.

The sound of her front door slamming open interrupted further conversation, and she swung around to see Sam striding toward her, six foot two of indignant, outraged male.

"What the hell is going on?" he demanded, his voice a fierce growl.

Steve shot Delaney a worried look. "Do you know this guy?" he asked.

Delaney nodded. "He's my neighbor."

"Neighbor?" Sam all but howled "Try again."

Steve kept his eyes on Delaney. "Do you want me to…?"

Delaney had a sudden flash of how quickly this situation could get out of hand.

"It's fine. But maybe we can talk about the house later, yeah?" she suggested.

"Not a problem," Steve said.

Rolling up the house plans, Steve shot a look at a glowering Sam before nodding briefly at Delaney and heading for the door.

Sam didn't bother waiting till the door had shut behind him before he started up again.

"When did you decide to sell your apartment?" he asked, his voice deceptively calm.

"While I was on holidays," she answered boldly. Sam actually flinched, and she realized that it wasn't the answer he'd expected.

"So it had nothing to do with what happened the other night?" Sam asked disbelievingly.

"No," she said.

She could see Sam didn't quite know where to go with either of her answers.

"Why didn't you tell me you were going to sell your place? Didn't you think I might be a tiny little bit interested?" Sam said. She could hear the hurt under the anger in his voice, and her stomach tightened.

"You weren't here, Sam. What was I supposed to do, hunt you down wherever you'd gone so I could let you know what was happening?"

Sam flushed a dull red and his gaze slid away for a few seconds. Then he was back on the attack.

"I can't believe you're doing this. Selling out of the business, moving apartments. And you never even bothered to sit down and talk to me about any of it."

"I'm just doing what I have to do," Delaney said flatly. Inside, she felt sick. Sam was right. She never made major life choices without talking it over with him. It felt wrong and weird and incomplete, somehow. But she couldn't tell him the real reason for all the changes. The man had hightailed it out of her life for nearly five days because they'd had sex. She loved him unbearably, but he was not someone she could pin her hopes and dreams on.

"I don't understand what any of this has to do with starting a family. Why can't you meet some guy and get married and have kids while you live here and work with me?" Sam demanded.

Delaney stared at him, the truth on the tip of her tongue. But there was no way she could lay herself open to that much rejection. She'd had two huge helpings of it over the past week, and it hurt too much.

"You wouldn't understand," she said instead.

Sam's eyes nearly bugged out of his head. "At least give me a shot at it! My God, Laney, how many years have we been friends?"

"A long time. Long enough that I would have expected you to hang around, or at least make a real live phone call after what happened between us the other night," Delaney said.

That stopped him in his tracks. He opened and shut his mouth a few times before he finally spoke.

"I needed to clear my head," he said, which made her so angry she cut across the rest of his words.

"What about protection, Sam? Didn't it even cross your mind that I might be pregnant? Or that I might be feeling a little confused as well?" she said.

He stared at her. "Pregnant?" A peculiar expression raced across his face. "Really? Could you be?"

Delaney grabbed either side of her head and held on tight, just in case her brain really did explode.

"No! I am not. Because I am on the Pill. Something you didn't even bother to ask about. I bloody hope you're not this reckless with the other legions of women you sleep with."

"I always use condoms. Always!" Sam said indignantly.

"Except with me."

"Well it wasn't as though I was planning on jumping my best friend," Sam yelled. "It wasn't exactly something I had on my list of things to do."

She tried not to flinch from the absolute certainty and outrage in his tone. It wasn't a surprise to her that Sam didn't think of her in that way. She had sixteen years of evidence to back up that belief. So why did it hurt every time he proved it to her over and over?

"Yeah, I got that, Sam. And the feeling is mutual," she said, hurt pride driving her now.

A taut silence fell between them as they glared at each other. Delaney tried not to notice that he was looking particularly delicious in an old pair of board shorts and a stretched-out muscle top. His biceps were golden and sculpted, his calves equally tanned and shapely. His face was all angles and planes, his eyes an intense, deep blue against his skin.

Suddenly all the fight went out of her as she realized exactly what she was sacrificing in the hope of finding future happiness. The last few days had given her a taste of what it would be like when she and Sam were no longer close friends. It had been lonely and hollow and empty. She'd picked up the phone to call him a dozen times before she'd remembered that not only was he not home, but she wasn't talking to him for a whole host of reasons. The problem was, her mind automatically defaulted to loving Sam, to wanting to be near him. She craved the sound of his laughter, and the way he always had of making everything assume its rightful perspective. Only this time he couldn't help her do that, because the problem she was tackling was him.

As if he sensed her sudden fragility, the heat seemed to drain out of Sam as well.

"I don't want to fight with you, Laney," he said.

Before she could brace herself, he'd crossed the space between them and was enveloping her in a hard embrace.

Despite her better instincts, she found herself clutching him, holding him as close as she could, pressing her face into his shoulder. God, she loved him. She loved him so much. And she was going to miss him more than anything in the whole world.

They stood holding one another for a long time, and slowly Delaney became aware that the desperate hurt that had fueled her was morphing into something much hotter and more undeniable. She inhaled deeply, taking in the scent of sea and salt

An Important Message from the Editors

Dear Reader,

If you'd enjoy reading romance novels with larger print that's easier on your eyes, let us send you TWO FREE HARLEQUIN PRESENTS® NOVELS in our LARGER PRINT EDITION. These books are complete and unabridged, but the type is set about 20% bigger to make it easier to read. Look inside for an actual-size sample.

By the way, you'll also get a surprise gift with your two free books!

Pam Powers

Peel off Seal and Place Inside...

LARGER PRINT
FREE BOOKS
EDITION

84

THE RIGHT WOMAN

she'd thought she was fine. It took Daniel's words and Brooke's question to make her realize she was far from a full recovery.

She'd made a start with her sister's help and she intended to go forward now. Sarah felt as if she'd been living in a darkened room and some-one had suddenly opened a door, letting in the fresh air and sunshine. She could feel its warmth slowly seeping into the coldest part of her. The feeling was liberating. She realized it was only a small step and she had a long way to go, but she was ready to face life again with Serena and her family behind her.

All too soon, they were saying goodbye and arah experienced a moment of sadness for all e years she and Serena had missed. But they d each other now and th t's what

She held

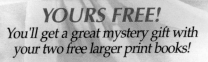

YOURS FREE!
*You'll get a great mystery gift with
your two free larger print books!*

GET TWO FREE LARGER PRINT BOOKS!

YES! Please send me two free Harlequin Presents® novels in the larger print edition, and my free mystery gift, too. I understand that I am under no obligation to purchase anything, as explained on the back of this insert.

PLACE FREE GIFTS SEAL HERE

106 HDL EFVU

306 HDL EFV6

FIRST NAME

LAST NAME

ADDRESS

APT.#

CITY

STATE/PROV.

ZIP/POSTAL CODE

**Are you a current Harlequin Presents® subscriber and
want to receive the larger print edition?
Call 1-800-221-5011 today!**

▲ **DETACH AND MAIL CARD TODAY!** ▲

(H-PLPO-09/06) © 2004 Harlequin Enterprises Ltd.

The Harlequin Reader Service™ — Here's How It Works:

Accepting your 2 free Harlequin Presents® larger print books and gift places you under no obligation to buy anything. You may keep the books and gift and return the shipping statement marked "cancel." If you do not cancel, about a month later we'll send you 6 additional Harlequin Presents larger print books and bill you just $4.05 each in the U.S., or $4.72 each in Canada, plus 25¢ shipping & handling per book and applicable taxes if any.* That's the complete price and — compared to cover prices of $4.75 each in the U.S. and $5.50 each in Canada — it's quite a bargain! You may cancel at any time, but if you choose to continue, every month we'll send you 6 more books, which you may either purchase at the discount price or return to us and cancel your subscription.

*Terms and prices subject to change without notice. Sales tax applicable in N.Y. Canadian residents will be charged applicable provincial taxes and GST.

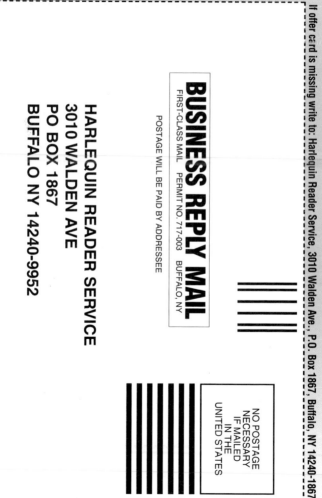

If offer card is missing write to: Harlequin Reader Service, 3010 Walden Ave., P.O. Box 1867, Buffalo, NY 14240-1867

BUSINESS REPLY MAIL
FIRST-CLASS MAIL   PERMIT NO. 717-003   BUFFALO, NY

POSTAGE WILL BE PAID BY ADDRESSEE

HARLEQUIN READER SERVICE
3010 WALDEN AVE
PO BOX 1867
BUFFALO NY 14240-9952

NO POSTAGE
NECESSARY
IF MAILED
IN THE
UNITED STATES

off his warm, hard body. Suddenly she was gripped with the urge to taste him, to press her lips against the strong column of his throat. Her breasts felt heavy and full, and warmth was spreading between her thighs. She wanted him again.

As soon as the thought coalesced in her mind, she stiffened and pushed herself away from him. She dared a quick darting glance up at his face as she moved away. His expression was shuttered, his feelings hidden from her. She reminded herself that, unlike her, Sam did not have control issues around bodily contact with his best friend.

"I'm sorry for fighting, too, Sam," she said in a muffled tone.

"Let's just forget it, all right?" he suggested. "We'll draw a line under the past week and call it moon craziness or whatever and never look back. You're too valuable to me to stuff it up for something as stupid and pointless as sex."

Delaney carefully picked a piece of lint off her jeans, desperately needing a few seconds to control her emotions. He'd called what had happened between them pointless, and he wanted to write last week off as though it had never happened. Again, it shouldn't have come as a surprise to her. She already knew that what had happened between them meant far more to her than to him.

"Yeah," was all she could manage to say, however. She simply wasn't that good a liar.

It seemed to be enough for Sam. Crossing to the dining table, he propped a hip against it.

"So who was the guy with the plans?" he asked.

"He's a friend of Claire's, an architect. I found a house I'm interested in in Camberwell," she explained dully. For some reason, all the color seemed to have leached out of the room. She felt brittle and tired and grey.

Sam's face was a picture of confusion. "I just don't get why you're moving, Laney," he said. She could tell he was making a mammoth effort to remain calm and rational. "You love this place. And you've never said a word about wanting to sell."

"It's not very practical, though, is it?" she said. "There's only one bedroom. Anyway, I saw this house and I just fell in love with it."

Sam's face lightened as she fed him her latest lie. She saw the way forward—all she had to do was convince him that she was obsessed with the new house, and he would think he understood why she was moving away from him. At some stage he was going to work out that the common factor in both leaving the business and selling her place was his proximity to her, but she was counting on his famed emotional blind ness to give her a bit of breathing room for a while yet. Besides, he had no reason to suspect that his best friend was about to cut him loose. Why would he? As far as he knew, nothing had changed between them. Despite their two sessions of desperate, greedy sex.

"Do you have any pictures?" Sam asked. He was doing his best to be supportive, she knew.

"Um, sure. It's on the Net," she said. He trailed her over to the corner alcove where her computer was hooked up to broadband Internet twenty-four hours a day. Another thing she'd have to set up from scratch in her new home.

She could feel the heat off Sam's body as he stood behind her while she keyed in the property's address. Her traitorous nipples hardened, pressing upward, hoping to gain his atten- tion. She crossed her arms and squeezed them tightly against her body, willing her breasts to behave.

"Looks great from the outside," Sam said as the first pictures came on screen.

Delaney clicked the mouse to bring up the internal shots,

and she could feel Sam's bewilderment as he took in the dark, dingy-looking rooms with their hideous floral wallpaper and virulent purple-brown carpet.

"Needs a bit of work," he said doubtfully.

"But it's a great floor plan, and there's plenty of land out the back for extending. Steve is going to draw up plans for a new kitchen and family room," Delaney forced an enthusiasm she didn't feel into her voice. It wasn't that she didn't like the house—she did. It had a lot of potential. But it was a sad, second-rate replacement for her old life. She had a feeling that everything was going to feel like that for a while.

"Once we've pulled down that wallpaper and ripped the carpet up, it'll look better," Sam said. Her heart twisted as she heard him automatically include himself in her plans.

"Yeah," she said. "The floorboards are good—Baltic pine—and the ceilings are great, lots of Art Deco features. It's got the potential to be a great family home."

There was a moment of awkward silence after she'd said this, and she could feel the tension radiating off Sam in waves.

"I've been thinking about all that stuff you said about family and everything," Sam said, clearing his throat a little as though he were choking on his words a little. "I want to help."

"Help?" Delaney made the mistake of twisting in her chair, her cheek nearly brushing against the fly of Sam's board shorts, he was standing so close behind her. He sprang backward as though she'd electrocuted him, and she felt her face flush warmly.

"Yeah, help. I mean, I know heaps of guys. I've been kind of mentally sorting through them over the past day or so, and I think I've come up with a couple of potentials for you."

Delaney frowned. "Potential what?"

"Husbands. Partners. Whatever you want to call them. So you can get stuck into this whole family thing," Sam said.

For a moment she couldn't breathe, couldn't think, couldn't do anything except hurt. Sam wanted to hook her up with his friends. He wanted to matchmake for her.

It was the ultimate rejection, the mother of all brush-offs. She put a hand to her stomach, worried she was going to lose the light dinner she'd had before Steve arrived.

Completely oblivious to her reaction, Sam continued arguing his case. "Don't worry, I won't hook you up with any losers. I know you better than anyone, so just think of it as a pre-screening program."

"I don't need your help to find someone, Sam," she said quietly.

He looked hurt. The big idiot. She couldn't believe he was so blind and misguided.

"But I want to help. I know I've been a shit lately, and I know this is really important to you. It's the least I can do."

She had no more words. She simply stared at him. Perhaps he saw the pain in her eyes because he reached for her hand. Stroking her fingers absently, he held her eyes steadily.

"I love you more than anything in the world, and if you want a family, you're going to get one," he said, deeply sincere. "You deserve the best, Laney. A husband who adores you, kids for you to nurture. I know you'll make a great mom. And I've been thinking—these kids of yours are going to need an uncle to teach them how to do stuff. Skate and surf, whatever. So I'm signing up in advance, Uncle Sam, ready to go."

Delaney pulled her hand free from his and stood. She couldn't look at him, she was so angry. How dare he stand there and offer her half a loaf? He was so thick! She wanted to hit him on the side of the head with something large and heavy.

Deep inside, she knew it wasn't his fault. She was the one changing the rules after all these years. But she was aching so much, and he was standing there, rubbing salt into her wounds.

"I'm only going to say this once—I can find my own husband," she said coolly.

Sam's eyebrows shot up toward his hairline. "What's wrong now, for Pete's sake? I'm trying to be nice here!"

"I'm not a bloody charity case, Sam. Men do find me attractive without having to be corralled into a date by my best friend."

"I'm not saying that! Did I say that? I just want to help!"

"Well, you can't. This is between me and my future husband. Ever heard the saying three's a crowd?"

Sam puffed his cheeks out as though he wanted to say something extremely rude but was restraining himself through sheer dint of will.

"Fine. I was just trying to be a good guy. More fool me," he said, stalking toward the door.

Delaney beat him to it, swinging it open to speed him on his way.

"You want to spend your time thinking about someone's personal life, why don't you concentrate on your own?" she said.

This surprised Sam so much that he froze on the threshold.

"You're not getting any younger yourself, you know, Sam," Delaney said, pleased to see the look of consternation creasing his face. "Can't be an overgrown kid all your life."

With that she pushed the door shut, forcing Sam to skip forward or risk barking his heels.

Guilt kicked in about twenty seconds later. She was such a *bitch!* The only thing Sam had done wrong was not return her feelings. Which he didn't even know she had! Offering to help her find a life partner wasn't a deliberate, malicious act on his behalf. She had no doubt that if she told him how she felt, he'd bend over backward to try to feel the same way. The very thought of which made her skin crawl and her toes curl in her shoes—Sam *trying* to love her would be ten times worse than Sam oblivious to her love.

The poor, unknowing man had just come to offer his help and support. And she'd thrown it back in his face.

She strode around her apartment a little, wondering what had happened to the calm, easygoing, rational woman she used to pride herself on being. She felt as if she were on a roller coaster, never knowing when to expect the next dip or rise in her emotional state.

But there was no reason for Sam to keep copping the fallout from her meltdown.

Guilt driving her, she grabbed her house keys and slipped out the door. The stairwell was just to the left of her apartment, and she took the steps two at a time as she made her way to Sam's place. She'd apologize for going off-tap. She'd thank him for his thoughtfulness in wanting to help her get a head start on building a family. And then she'd tell him in a much nicer, calmer fashion that she could handle the quest for a husband on her own.

Finding herself facing Sam's front door, she paused to take a deep breath before knocking briskly. Tucking her hands into the back pockets of her jeans, she ducked her head and waited for the familiar sound of Sam approaching his door. After a few moments, she realized he wasn't coming. Frowning, she rapped on the door again. Again, nothing. Her frown deepened. God, had she pissed him off so much that he was refusing to let her in now?

"Sam. I'm sorry. Okay?" she called.

Nothing but silence. Delaney chewed her lip. Sure, she could keep yelling her apology through the door. But she didn't exactly relish all their neighbors being in on the conversation.

Making a decision, she selected Sam's spare key from the collection on her key ring and slid it into the lock.

"I'm coming in, Sam. I just want to say I'm sorry," she called as she twisted the key in the lock.

To her surprise, Sam wasn't waiting on the other side of the door. The apartment seemed deserted, and she guessed that he must have gone out after their big fight. She was turning back toward the door when she registered the sound of the shower running.

Right. That was why he hadn't heard her. She hovered uncertainly, unsure about whether to go or stay. Then she shrugged. She and Sam had always treated each other's apartments as extensions of their own. Probably a couple of arguments and some incidental sex on the side weren't cause to change their unspoken arrangement.

Having decided to wait, she glanced around Sam's living space, looking for a diversion to keep her overactive mind busy. His living area was dominated by large, bright red leather furniture, modular and very practical for the way Sam lived—neither food nor drink could stain it, and sand brushed off easily. Modern paintings covered most of the wall—big, bright, bold exercises in color and form. They reminded her of Sam, somehow—full of energy and life, yet chaotic and unfocused. And incredibly compelling as a result.

Pressing her lips together, she turned toward the balcony and gravitated to her favorite seat in Sam's place—a squishy, formless-looking armchair made by a local furniture designer. Covered in a dark navy cord, it was incredibly comfortable and Delaney sank into it with a sigh. Staring glumly at the blue sky outside, she dropped her chin into her hands and tried to think ahead to a time when she wouldn't have to endure the wrenching, aching pain around her heart. It had to happen. Once she'd made the break, the awful, tight feeling had to go away. *Please, God,* she prayed. *Let it go away as soon as possible.*

She was so lost in her own thoughts that she didn't note the sound of the shower finishing, and she was completely off guard when Sam padded out past her, his naked body still half-wet as he headed for the kitchen.

Delaney froze, eyes widening as she scanned the back of his body from head to toe. She'd had sex with him twice now, but both times she'd been too busy grabbing him and holding on for dear life to truly appreciate his remarkable body.

His shoulders were broad and his back well-muscled from years of surfing and skiing and swimming. Despite all the atrocious junk food he consumed, his torso still narrowed athletically down to his hips. His butt deserved an hour of appreciation all to itself—pert and tight and rounded, it was the epitome of a sexy male ass. And now she knew exactly how firm and *right* it felt in her hands as she urged him to go harder, deeper, faster….

Swallowing a surge of lust, she finished her visual catalogue, eyes running down his long, muscular thighs and calves.

She should say something. This was like spying, with him not realizing she was there. She opened her mouth to speak, then Sam turned around. She forgot whatever it was she'd been about to say. He had such a good chest—the firm, masculine mounds of his pecs covered in a light sprinkling of hair that tapered down to an arrow as it moved south of his navel. The hair blossomed more thickly again at his groin, the perfect showcase for his *pièce de résistance.* Sam was a man who would never have to feel inadequate in the men's change room, that was for sure. She squirmed in her seat a little as her eyes found his penis and stayed there. Just looking at him brought back the memory of how hot and hard he'd been as he slid inside her.

The very vividness of her thoughts were enough to launch her to her feet as she belatedly realized that Sam had at last registered her presence.

"Sam, I'm sorry—I used my spare key. I was just waiting, I didn't mean to intrude...." she said, already striding toward the door.

She deliberately didn't make eye contact with him, instead keeping her eye on her goal—the door, and freedom from her own desires.

But Sam moved faster, darting across to catch her before she reached the exit.

"Delaney, wait!" he said, grabbing a hold of her arm.

Delaney stiffened and froze, terrified that if he looked into her face he would see exactly how much she longed for him.

"I wanted to say I'm sorry. That's all. I'll come back. Or you can come down to my place. Or we can talk about this at work tomorrow," she babbled mindlessly, eyes glued to the door.

"I'm sorry, too," Sam said. She could feel his breath warm on her face. "And you're right—finding a husband is your business, not mine. Hell, what do I know about relationships, right?" he said.

Delaney managed a tight little nod. She was trembling, inside and out. He was standing mere inches from her, his whole amazing body gloriously naked. Her knees felt weak, and she almost couldn't hear her own thoughts over the frantic beating of her heart.

"I have to go, Sam," she choked, trying to pull her arm from his grasp.

"Why?"

She couldn't answer him, and he wouldn't release her. In the end Delaney was forced to lift her face and make eye contact with him.

His irises were the darkest blue she'd ever seen them, and he scanned her face intently as she pleaded with him with her eyes. Surely he could see how tortured she was? How much she wanted him, needed him?

"Laney," he said, his voice harsh.

She gave a little gasping hiccup, a last attempt at resistance, and then she couldn't help it, she was leaning toward him and he was leaning toward her and her hands were sliding around his strong, muscular shoulders, her fingers splaying as she gloried in the feel of him under her hands.

His mouth angled over hers and she met the hot rush of his kiss with her own desire, forgetting to breathe or think or even stand she was so lost in the moment.

Sam's arms flexed to take her weight, his grip firming on her torso as he held her close. She could feel his erection hardening between them, and the greedy, hungry part of her wanted everything, all of it, right then and there.

As her blood thrummed through her veins, moment melted into moment: the delicious unfurling of sensation as Sam pressed his open mouth against her neck, his tongue whirling swirls against her sensitive skin; the sweet pain of her breasts pressed against the hardness of his chest; the dull ache of desire as she rode Sam's thigh where he'd pressed it between her legs.

Sam murmured his appreciation of it all as he slid her top down over her shoulder, exposing her bra. She let her head drop back up as she felt the rasp of his whisker-stubbled face against her skin. She wanted him so much. Too much.

The realization made her stiffen in his arms. Unless she was a glutton for punishment, now was her chance to step back from making yet another mistake. She closed her eyes, biting her lip as Sam's mouth at last found her nipple through the satin of her bra. Her hands reached for his head, and while she still had the strength she gently but firmly pushed him away. Sam at last seemed to register the tension in her body, and he lifted his head and locked eyes with her again.

"Not again, Sam," she said.

Frustration and anger crossed his face like clouds scudding across the sun. His body tensed as he made to move forward, ready to use everything in his sensual arsenal, no doubt, to win her round to his point of view. Which he could do, very easily, she knew.

She shook her head, stepping backward, pushing his hands away.

"I can't keep doing this," she said weakly.

She didn't dare even glance at the stunning erection standing out proudly from his body. She knew she didn't have enough willpower to resist that much enticement. Instead, she lunged for the door. Within seconds she was on the other side and heading for the staircase. She heard it open after her, then Sam called down the stairwell for her to wait.

The shocked squeal of Sam's neighbor stepping out of the lift took care of any pursuit he might have been planning, and Delaney scurried down the remaining stairs and into her own apartment.

Her top was still off her shoulder, her bra exposed, and she straightened her clothes with shaking hands. Wrapping her arms around her torso, she paced in front of the door, seriously shaken by what had just happened. She had no control where Sam was concerned. She had to face that fact now, and do something about it.

Reaching for the phone, she pressed a well-worn speed-dial number. Her sister answered on the first ring.

"I need help," she said desperately.

To her sister's credit, she remained steadfastly calm. "Where are you? Do you need me to come get you?"

"No. But can I stay the night?" Delaney heard herself ask. Until the words had come out of her mouth, she hadn't known what she wanted. But now she was clear—she needed to be somewhere safe and grounded and real. And she knew her sister's family could provide that for her.

"I'm making up the spare bed as we speak," Claire said calmly.

"I'll see you soon, then."

Delaney ended the call and went into her bedroom. Shoveling clothes randomly into her overnight bag, she turned toward the door just as Sam walked in. He'd stopped to pull on a pair of jeans and nothing else, and he looked ready to spit fire at her.

"Please, Sam," she said, stopping in her tracks.

Spotting her overnight bag, Sam looked startled.

"Where are you going?"

"To Claire's. I don't know when I'll be back," she said.

They stood for a moment in thick, heavy silence, then Sam stepped to one side. Delaney's shoulders slumped a little as some of the tension left her and tears filled her eyes. She didn't have the strength to resist him again. If he hadn't let her go, she would have been powerless. She shot him a small, grateful look as she moved past him.

"Thank you," she whispered. And then she was past him and moving away, determined not to look back.

8

HER SISTER, GOD BLESS HER, greeted her with a glass of wine and a box of tissues. Delaney allowed herself to be steered past the excited greetings of her nephews and niece and into the spare bedroom.

"Okay. Tell me what's going on," Claire said as she plonked herself cross-legged in front of the bed while Delaney slumped onto the bed itself.

Delaney shrugged her shoulders to indicate how helpless she felt in the face of the mess she'd made of her life.

"I don't know where to start," she said.

"Let me help you narrow it down. Is it about work?"

"No. Well, some, I guess."

Her sister nodded as if this made perfect sense to her. "Is it about work, and Sam?" she asked next.

Delaney nodded, holding the wineglass so tightly that her sister obviously feared for its safety. Uncurling Delaney's fingers from the stem, Claire slid the glass onto the bedside table.

"Perhaps now's a good time for me to let on that I know you love Sam, and that you have for years," her sister began prosaically.

As absurd as it was after everything that had happened over the past few days, Delaney buried her head in her hands with embarrassment.

"God. Is it that obvious?"

"It's okay. I only know because I'm your sister. To the independent observer, you and Sam are just great buddies. Although one or two of my friends have asked if you have any idea how hot Sam is."

"Am I blind?" Delaney said, choking on a half laugh, half sob.

"So, what's happened? Don't tell me Sam's finally met the girl of his dreams?" Claire guessed.

Just the thought of it made Delaney's stomach clench. "No. No, he's still footloose and fancy free, sleeping his way through the phone book as usual." She snuck a glance at her sister and decided to go for broke. "I guess he must be up to the Ds," she said, then winced as she anticipated her sister's response.

"Oh!" Claire said. Then, *"Riiiiight."*

Delaney felt she'd better explain.

"It just kind of happened. And then it kind of happened again. It's insane, because as soon as I came back from holidays with you guys, I told Sam that I was going to leave the business, and then all this just…happened."

Claire was nodding, but Delaney could tell her sister's mind was elsewhere.

"What?"

"Well, to be honest, I always kind of thought you and Sam had already slept with each other. I figured you were bed buddies, sleeping with each other on and off. I mean, he's pretty hot. And you're pretty hot. It seemed…natural that you'd have done it before now."

"Really?" Delaney was genuinely stunned by her sister's observation. And by the fact that her sister's married-mother-of-three sensibility acknowledged concepts like bed buddies.

"Yeah. I guess I have to reassess my opinion of Sam a

little. One of the reasons I don't invite him over here so much is because I don't like the idea of him using you like that."

"But he wasn't. He's never laid a hand on me until recently."

"No. I know. I get that now." Claire shook her head, a bemused expression on her face. "All I can say is, you must have self-control to spare."

Delaney pictured Sam's naked body again. "Yeah. And forearms like Popeye," she said before she could stop herself. To her surprise, Claire threw her head back and laughed.

Delaney felt a small smile curving her own lips. She and Claire had always been close, but never this intimate. Most of their talk was oriented around family and friends, and Delaney couldn't remember ever having a conversation that strayed into territory as revealing as jokes about self-gratification and sex. It was a relief to realize that her sister had a robust sense of humor about this sort of thing, as well as a much more worldly viewpoint than Delaney had previously given her credit for. She was beginning to think that coming here had been the smartest thing she'd done in a long time.

"So you and Sam have just caved after sixteen years of foreplay," Claire said, shaking her head in amazement. "Did the sheets catch fire?"

"We didn't make it to a bed. Both times," Delaney said, taking a big sip of wine.

Claire huffed out a laugh. "Go, girl!"

Delaney managed a small smile, but the reality of her situation was starting to weigh down on her again. Claire seemed to sense this. Reaching for the wineglass, she took a sip, then eyed Delaney carefully.

"So what went wrong? Obviously the sex was good, or you wouldn't have gone back for seconds."

"The sex is—I mean was—off-the-planet good," Delaney said.

"Right."

Claire waited patiently while Delaney picked at the hem of her tank top.

"It doesn't mean anything, though. We had sex, sure, but that just means I get to join the Sam Kirk Hall of Fame. He has no idea how I feel. And I know he doesn't feel the same way about me because there's no way he would have taken off like he did if he did."

"Whoa, slow down there for a second," Claire said, passing the wineglass back across and signaling for Delaney to have a drink. Delaney took a big mouthful and blinked away the tears that had rushed to her eyes. Ordering her thoughts, she tried again.

By the time she'd finished filling her sister in, they were on their third shared glass of wine and halfway through a jumbo jar of olives.

"I almost feel sorry for him," Claire said, shaking her head as she contemplated the ruin of Delaney's life.

"Thanks a lot."

"I didn't mean it like that. But you're going to be okay, Laney. You're going to move on with your life and finally get over him and meet someone else and have the family that you want. And when it's too late, Sam's going to understand exactly what he's missed out on. I think that's very sad."

"I would, too, if I ever thought it was going to happen. He has a pretty good time just hanging around doing his guy thing. He's not like me—it's not like he's going to wake up one day and realize that his dream of having a family is going to disappear in a puff of smoke if he doesn't do something about it."

Claire eyed her shrewdly. "Is that what happened when you were on holidays with us?" she asked.

Delaney nodded. "How did you know?"

"You went very quiet after that day with Callum on the beach," her sister said, referring to her four-year-old middle child.

Delaney smiled faintly. She could still remember the exact moment that she understood she was in danger of missing out on one of life's most amazing experiences. Some idiot had ignored the prominent notices along the beach that warned visitors about the safe disposal of glass, and Callum had stepped on a shattered beer bottle and let out a howl of pain and fright.

Her sister had been busy dragging Alana from the shallows, and she'd looked up instantly, alarm writ large on her face.

"Could you…?" she'd asked, her hands full of squirming two year old.

Delaney had already been racing to Callum's side. She'd lifted him to her hip and held him tightly.

"It's okay, hush, it's okay," she'd said soothingly.

Callum's face had been streaked with tears and he'd already managed to somehow transfer a fine coating of sand to his cheeks. But it was the way he held her that inspired her epiphany. Reverting to pure baby status, he'd wrapped his arms and legs around her torso and clung on for dear life, pressing his head to her chest as though she was the only thing in the world that could comfort him. His small, podgy limbs had been warm and soft around her, and his hair had smelled of salt and sand and little boy. Her heart had squeezed in her chest, touched by his faith in her, and low in her midriff, her long-ignored ovaries had sprung to life as though they'd been waiting for just this cue before making their presence felt.

"It was that hug," Delaney said fondly after a long moment of reflection. "Just for a second, I got a tiny taste of what it must feel like to be a mom. And I swear my ovaries just went crazy."

Claire smiled a little smugly. "I knew if I kept throwing you at the kids you'd work it out for yourself."

Delaney opened her mouth in shock, amazed to hear that her sister had had a secret agenda all these years. Claire shrugged unapologetically.

"I want my kids to have cousins," she said. "And if Sam isn't up for the job, then we'll find someone else who is."

Delaney nodded her agreement, but it didn't take the weight of sadness off her chest.

"For what it's worth, I think you're doing the right thing, selling out from the business and moving away from the apartment. For all his faults, Sam is bloody charming, and I can imagine how hard it must have been for you to pull away from him like this."

"Yeah."

"It *will* get better, Laney."

"I know. But it has to get worse first. Why did I sleep with him?" she wailed. "I was almost home free, and then I had to go and taste what I'd only imagined all those years…."

"That good, huh?" Claire asked a little wistfully.

Delaney uncrossed her arms from where she'd instinctively covered her breasts, revealing her erect nipples. "Just from talking about him," she said wearily.

"Wow. That *is* good."

Delaney nodded sadly. Claire's face wrinkled as she thought hard.

"Okay, here's what you're going to do. Cold turkey is not going to work in this situation. You've tried that, and I gather it's not really a happening thing."

Delaney thought back over the past week. "No, abstinence doesn't seem to work where Sam is concerned."

"So what you have to do is burn it out," Claire announced decisively.

Delaney raised a questioning eyebrow. "Which means?"

"Remember when Todd insisted that I give up smoking before we got married? And how I tried and I tried and I just couldn't kick it? A few nights before the wedding, I sat down in my room and I smoked a whole packet of cigarettes, one after the other. I was as sick as a dog the next day, but I have never touched one since. Can't even stand the smell of smoke."

Delaney was still frowning. "So you're suggesting I take up smoking?" she asked, not quite grasping the full concept.

"No, my sweet idiot. I'm suggesting you bonk Sam's brains out and keep on bonking until you can bonk no more. That, or until you've worn him down to a nubbin. Either way should do it for you."

Delaney stared at her sister, then glanced at the bottle of wine they'd been drinking. It was still a quarter full, so her sister couldn't be that drunk.

"You seriously think having more sex with Sam is the way to get him out of my system?" she asked incredulously.

"Yep. Look at it this way, if it doesn't work, you'll have some great snaps for the mental photo album."

Delaney turned the idea over in her head. It couldn't work. It was too attractive, for starters. And, besides, she had no guarantee that Sam would want to bonk until he could bonk no more. Even if there had been some heartening indications in that direction, there was no guarantee it would last. After all, Sam had hankerings for women all the time, and they never lasted longer than a few weeks.

"Think about it at least," Claire said, then she hiccupped loudly.

Delaney took the wineglass from her hand. "We still have bedtime to get through," she reminded her sister.

Claire pulled a face, then grabbed Delaney's hand. "Promise me you'll think about it. What have you got to lose, anyway? Believe me—anything, no matter how good it is, loses its luster after repeated viewings. If you know what I mean."

Delaney eyed her sister warily. "Please tell me you're not about to start talking about suburban sex parties," she said.

"God, things aren't as desperate as that," Claire said. Then she winked broadly. "We still do okay, don't you worry."

A knock sounded on the door, and Todd stuck his head in. "The kids want their aunt Delaney to read their bedtime stories."

Delaney stood with alacrity. "I'm on it."

As she slipped past Todd and out into the hallway, she heard her sister speaking behind her.

"Why don't you shut the door for a minute?" she suggested to her husband meaningfully.

Delaney gathered by the way the door promptly clicked shut that Todd wasn't about to look a slightly drunk gift-horse in the mouth.

She paused in the hallway for a moment. She wanted all of this. The domesticity, the familiarity, the belonging. And she was never going to get it until Sam was out of her heart.

Maybe her sister's advice wasn't so silly after all.

SAM ENTERED HIS OFFICE the next day and blinked in surprise at the expanse of polished wood that greeted him. Someone had cleaned his desk while he was away. He bristled instantly. He hated it when anyone cleaned his office. It was his mess, he knew exactly where to find things in it, and anyone who had half a brain cell knew that to rearrange a single piece of paper on his desk was to invite a reprimand. He guessed immediately who would have taken it upon themselves to do it—Debbie. She was new, so it was conceivable that she hadn't been warned about his no-touching-the-desk rule, and she'd been sending out signals that he'd been trying to ignore for a while now. Why was it that chicks thought that cleaning up a man's personal space was the way to impress him? In his book, it was about as hot and sexy as them spitting on a handkerchief and wiping something off his face.

He strode back to reception and waited for Debbie to finish taking a phone call before he tackled her.

"Yes, Sam?" she asked, batting her eyelashes at him.

"I'm going to cut you some slack, since you're new around here and you probably didn't know, but my desk is sacred. No one cleans it, moves anything on it, touches it. Got that?" he said, aware that his tone was probably a little more terse than it should be, thanks to the two hours sleep he'd had in between tossing and turning, worrying about what was going on with Delaney.

"I don't know what you're talking about, Sam," Debbie said, big brown eyes wide.

"Is there a problem?"

They both turned to find Delaney standing there. Sam's stomach lurched nervously and he tried not to notice how great she looked in a short denim skirt and fitted candy-striped blouse. It was hard to ignore the way her legs seemed to go on and on forever, however, thanks to the wedge-heeled sandals she was wearing. He settled for smiling moronically and tucking his hands into his pockets, something he'd been doing a lot of lately since his self-control seem to have gone out the window.

"I was just telling Debbie that I'm not keen on anyone

cleaning my desk while I'm not around," he explained, searching Delaney's face for any clue as to how she was feeling or what she was thinking after last night's debacle. Between the multiple visits to each other's apartments and his unintentional striptease for his neighbor, they'd put on a fair imitation of a French farce. Except Delaney hadn't looked amused when she left her apartment—she'd looked heartbroken. And it was his fault for not being able to keep his hands to himself.

"But I didn't touch it!" Debbie said, appealing to Delaney now instead of Sam. "I swear I didn't."

"Well, somebody did. I don't really care who—just as long as it doesn't happen again," Sam said, trying to be reasonable about it.

Delaney gave him a pointed look. "Could I see you in your office for a moment?" she asked.

"Sure."

Sam followed her, eyes glued to her swaying hips and butt. He was only human, after all. As long as his hands stayed in his pockets, he figured he could look but not touch.

Delaney waited until they were in his office before turning to face him.

"Sam, is there any chance that you sustained a head injury over the past few days? No knocks on the head or blackouts or anything?" she asked, her voice deceptively sweet and dulcet.

Sam knew her too well to buy it. "No. Why?" he asked cautiously.

Delaney shook her head at him. "I can't believe you actually accused Debbie of cleaning your desk, after what happened on Friday night," she said.

Sam's eyes widened as a full-color replay flashed across his brain—him carrying Delaney into the room and clearing his desk with one arm so he could get down to the very important business of having his way with her. He walked around his desk to confirm the memory. Sure enough, an enormous pile of paper, magazines, stationery and other rubble lay hidden on the other side.

"Oh. Right," he said stupidly.

"Nice to know it was such a memorable experience for you," she said coolly, walking out of his office stiff-backed.

Sam thunked his open palm against his forehead. He was such a lamebrain. No wonder Delaney was so angry with him. Gathering his courage, he went after her.

She was in the kitchenette, making herself a coffee. He studied the sleek line of her bent head for a beat before speaking.

"I didn't forget," he said. "I haven't been able to think of anything else."

Her head shot up, and he could see the surprise and wariness in her face. He was a little surprised, too. He hadn't known he was going to say anything like that until it popped out his mouth. But it was true, even if he was deeply uncertain about saying it to Delaney, given all that he stood to lose. But he figured it must be pretty obvious that he was hot for her, since he'd jumped her at almost every given opportunity lately. Anyway, she was probably so disgusted by his hit-and-run behavior that she'd cheerfully punch him in the face if he didn't offer some explanation for what had been happening between them. And Delaney had a mean punch—he'd been on the receiving end of it more than once over the years.

"Then how come you forgot about the desk?" she asked him, her expression shuttered now.

"Because I wasn't really thinking about the desk at the time. I had other, more pressing issues on my mind," Sam said. "Find me a guy who could think about a piece of furniture when he had you in his arms, and I will eat my bloody desk, legs and all."

Delaney didn't even crack a smile. She just stared at him, then turned back to her coffee mug.

"Where did you go last night?" he asked when she didn't speak again.

"To Claire's."

Not so good—he had a pretty fair idea that Claire wasn't his number-one fan. Something that probably hadn't improved much in the past twenty-four hours.

"I'm sorry about last night," he began, but Delaney held up a hand, her face creased into an expression of pained exhaustion.

"Please—I don't want to hear again how sorry you are about having sex with me, Sam. Or how you don't understand why it happened. Or that you wish you could take it back," she said.

"You said that, not me," Sam interjected. "After the first time, you said if you could take it back you would."

"Right. So you wouldn't take it back, then?" she asked, disbelief dripping from every word.

Sam held her eye and slowly shook his head. "No."

He realized it was the truth, too. How could he regret the hottest, most abandoned moments of his life? The fact that he'd shared them with Delaney only made them more precious, despite how much it had screwed up their friendship.

Delaney went back to stirring her coffee. Since she didn't take sugar, he figured she was feeling about as comfortable as he was. Which was not very.

"I don't want to lose you, Laney," he said very softly.

She nodded, her head still down. "I know. I'm just a little confused right now," she said.

Sam wanted to reach out to comfort her, but he knew he'd

lost that prerogative the first time he'd laid hands on her with nonplatonic intentions.

"Maybe it's because of you leaving the business," he offered. "Maybe we're both unsettled."

Delaney nodded again. "Yeah, probably that's it," she said.

She looked so sad, pressed up against the sink as though she didn't want to be there. He couldn't help himself.

"Stuff it," he said, reaching for her and pulling her close. He couldn't just stand by and watch her hurt, not when he was the cause.

The instant he felt the press of her body against his, he knew it had been a mistake. Desire pooled in his groin as his hands caressed the familiar-yet-enticing planes of her back. He inhaled deeply, unable to get enough of her smell—part perfume, part Delaney, completely sensual and inviting.

"Sam," she said, her voice muffled from where he'd pressed her head against his shoulder.

"Yes," he said, trying valiantly to will Little Sam back to sleep.

"Do you have an erection?" she asked.

Sam closed his eyes, mortified. "Yes," he admitted in a strangled tone.

There was a pause, then Delaney slid a hand between their bodies to grab the thick, heavy length of his erection through his jeans. He realized she was breathing hard and trembling a little.

"Oh God. Sorry!" someone exclaimed from behind them, and they both leaped apart like scalded cats.

"I totally didn't mean to intrude. I'll come back later, no problems," their layout artist Rudy said, eyes averted as he backed away.

Delaney made a low, pained sound and hid her face in her

hands as Sam shot his eyes toward the ceiling, hoping his boner wasn't as obvious as it felt.

Delaney waited a few seconds after Rudy's departure before grabbing her coffee off the sink. Then she brushed past him, face set.

Sam thunked himself on the forehead with the palm of his hand again.

Way to fix things, moron.

DELANEY PUT HER COFFEE DOWN very carefully in the middle of her desk, then extended her hands in front of her. They were shaking as though she had low blood sugar or had just had the shock of a lifetime. Or as though she were waging a war of wills inside herself—a battle between slutty Delaney who wanted nothing but Sam, hard and hot inside her, and sensible, goal-oriented Delaney who was determined to move on from her old love and find herself a new one.

Unfortunately, slutty Delaney had been in charge when Rudy walked into the kitchenette and caught her with a handful of Sam's crotch. Delaney closed her eyes. It was too, too embarrassing.

But it had proven something to her, above and beyond a doubt. For good or for ill, she and Sam were having some kind of mating season right now. They only had to be in the same room, and sex shot to the top of the agenda. She felt out of control, and more than a little obsessed. And very, very horny.

So maybe her sister's theory was worth giving a whirl. At this stage, Delaney was ready to try anything. She was already selling out of the business, and she was in the process of moving house. Which would safely remove Sam's physical presence from her life, but would still leave him firmly entrenched in her subconscious, the memory of his knowing hands returning to haunt her every time she let her guard down. It was so good between them, she knew it was ridiculous to expect herself to get over it anytime soon.

That meant drastic measures were called for. Delaney's breath hitched in her throat as she considered what she was about to do: offer Sam a weekend of untrammeled hedonism, just the two of them, no clothes, no distractions. She crossed her legs, pressing her inner thighs together to try and relieve the instant ache of desire that throbbed there. Probably she shouldn't kid herself that this was going to be a chore. In fact, in many ways it would be the fulfillment of a fantasy. It was the other end of the weekend that was going to be hard yards—drawing a line under the whole experience and walking away. If her sister was on the money, she'd be sick of the sight of Sam by that time. Delaney smiled grimly to herself. Fat chance. But, at the very least, she might gain herself a grace period, a safe zone for the remainder of her time with *X-Pro* and in the apartment. As her sister said, nothing retained its luster after repeated viewings. If she could just dull some of the magic, surely it would help her move on?

Delaney reached for her computer mouse and found a tourism Web site, despite not being entirely convinced by her own arguments. She suspected that the real reason she was going through with her sister's mad plan was because she wanted to bonk Sam as much as was physically possible. No higher calling, or rational motivation there. Sadly, the realization wasn't going to stop her from doing it, either.

After she'd found a suitable setting for her plan on the Net and made a couple of phone calls, she went to the bathroom to run some cold water over her wrists. Just thinking about a hot weekend away with Sam was driving her wild. And making her feel a little nauseous. What if he said no? She hadn't really factored that into her grand plan.

Fluffing her hair, she made a decision. She wouldn't tell him. It was cowardly, she knew, but she figured she was entitled to a few face-saving measures at the moment, given how exposed and vulnerable she was. She'd tell him it was just a platonic weekend away, between friends. To get things back on their old footing. Knowing Sam, he'd jump at the opportunity—anything to save himself from further awkward kitchen conversations.

Decision made, Delaney sought him out in his office. He'd restored his desk to its usual haphazard disorder by the simple expedient of lifting everything off the floor and dumping it back on his desk. She found herself smiling wryly despite everything. He was such a pig.

His blue eyes lit up when he glanced up and saw her standing there, and she corrected herself—a handsome, charming, irresistible pig. And, if things went according to plan, all hers for two whole decadent days.

"You up to anything on the weekend?" she asked idly as she propped a hip against Sam's desk. One of the teetering piles of paper shifted dangerously, and she stepped away hastily. Sam rested a hand on the rogue pile before it could turn into a paper avalanche.

"Nope. You?" he asked.

Delaney winced at how awkward and stilted they both sounded.

"Um, sort of. I was wondering if you'd like to come away to Daylesford for the weekend. There's a bush retreat there, really relaxing and peaceful, apparently."

"Oh," Sam said, studying her face intently. "That sounds pretty cool."

"I thought it might give us a chance to get things back on the old footing. You know," Delaney said. It was only a little fib in that it was partly true—*afterward* they could go back to their old footing, once she'd ravished him all weekend.

"Right," Sam said brightly, straightening in his seat. She knew exactly what he was thinking—they could brush the recent past under the rug of history, and never have to speak of it again. Wasn't that what he'd pretty much suggested already?

"Maybe we could do a bit of fishing," he said, getting into the spirit of things. "Go hiking or something."

"Yeah," Delaney said, thinking *Fat chance, pal. You won't be leaving the bedroom.*

"When do you want to leave?" Sam asked, completely committed to the idea now.

Delaney felt a surge of unease. Was she coercing him too much, doing it this way? But the thought of coming right out with her agenda and laying her cards on the table so blatantly made her knees turn to water. So, maybe she was a sneak. But she was a desperate sneak, with mostly good motives. And it wasn't like she was conning Sam into two days in the salt mines of Siberia.

"Um, how about we ditch work early tomorrow. Maybe around four?" she suggested.

"Great. It's a date," Sam said.

Immediately he seemed to regret the inadvertent connotation of what he'd said, because he shifted uneasily in his chair. "I mean, it's not a date. But you're on," he said awkwardly.

She just smiled at him.

Don't give yourself too hard a time, Sam, she thought as she walked away. *You're more on the money than you know.*

SAM SQUINTED THROUGH the windshield at the rusty road sign coming up on their left.

"Is this it?" he asked.

They'd been trawling through the unsealed back roads of Daylesford—about an hour's drive north of Melbourne—for the past twenty minutes. Getting to the small country town itself had been easy—it was a popular tourist destination thanks to the large gay population that had adopted the town, ushering in a new era of funky restaurants and great food, and the roads were excellent. But they'd left the township behind long ago, and were now thick in the bush, driving up rutted dirt road after rutted dirt road, following the instructions Delaney had been given by the real estate agent.

"Yes!" Delaney said, punching the air. "Turn left here."

Sam spun the wheel, the SUV's tires slipping on the gravel road. Delaney hung on and gave a little whoop of excitement. He couldn't help smiling himself, even though he'd been feeling increasingly tense the closer they got to their destination.

What had he been thinking, committing to spending a whole weekend away with Delaney to renew the bonds of their platonic friendship? Was he certifiably insane? He'd fooled himself into thinking that it was a smart idea for the bulk of Thursday and Friday, then he'd come downstairs from his apartment to pick Delaney up this afternoon to find her wearing a pair of short shorts, a tiny tank top and a pair of strappy sandals. Instantly he'd understood that getting their friendship back onto its proper footing was going to require a Ghandi-like display of moral fiber. That he didn't possess that kind of self-control did not surprise Sam—and it didn't bode well for a successful weekend, either. What was Delaney going to think of him when he was walking around with a permanent hard-on for two days running?

And there was no doubt in his mind that she was utterly

convinced that this weekend was going to cure whatever ailed their friendship. She'd been positively beaming since he'd committed to coming, the old bounce back in her step as she went about her business in the office. Although, now that he thought about it, she'd been a little quieter since they'd started driving. Maybe she, too, was beginning to realize that the weekend might pose some pitfalls in terms of willpower? He shot a sideways look at her as she stared pensively out the side window. It was obvious to him that she wasn't exactly unmoved by him on a sexual level. It had definitely taken two to tango every time they'd come together. In fact, that time in his apartment, when she'd caught him unexpectedly naked, it had been the raw lust in her eyes that had driven his own desire beyond the bounds of self-control.

So this was a two-way street, this thing between them. But he also had no doubt that Delaney wanted to erect a road-block. She had plans, and they didn't include him in her bed. Hence this weekend away.

"Here's the driveway," Delaney said, and he turned left into yet another rutted, gravel road.

Gum trees lined either side of the road, and then they rounded a curve and found their weekend hideaway—a charming mud-brick house set on a natural step in the hillside. It had a stone-built chimney on the outside, and a large claw foot bathtub occupying pride of place on the front deck.

It looked just about perfect—for a weekend of pure, una-dulterated torture. He shot Delaney another sideways look. Did she have any idea how romantic this place was?

She got out of the car first, pausing for a moment to tug her shorts into place. Sam groaned low in the back of his throat as he stared at her ass. He was such a goner.

Delaney looked back at him over her shoulder. Her toffee-brown eyes were unreadable as she offered a small, nervous smile.

"Looks pretty nice, yeah?"

"Oh, yeah," he agreed dryly.

Sighing heavily, he levered himself out of the car and grabbed their luggage from the back hatch. Delaney took her own overnight bag—she never let him carry her gear—and he scooped up his backpack and the bags of groceries Delaney had brought with her.

She led the way to the front door, and within seconds they were walking into a large room with a high, open-beamed ceiling. To one side, a sink and small counter denoted the kitchen, and in the corner was a door that he guessed must lead to the bathroom. The rest of the room was dominated by the open fireplace and an enormous bed. Frowning, Sam dumped his load and put his hands on his hips.

"This is it? There's no more?" he asked.

Delaney smoothed her hands down the sides of her legs, clearly as unsettled as he was by the fact that there was only one bed.

"The real estate agent must have made a mistake," he said, pulling his mobile phone out of his back pocket. He had no idea if they could get service out here in the bush, but he had to give it a shot because there was no way he could share a bed with Delaney for a whole weekend and keep the promise he'd made to himself.

"Um, it's not a mistake," Delaney said quietly.

Sam froze in the act of dialing the number. "Sorry?"

"I said it's not a mistake. I picked it deliberately."

Sam just stood there, immobilized by the many and varied thoughts rampaging through his brain.

"Sam, the past few weeks, we seem to keep…you know…"

she said, indicating with her hand that she was referring to them having jumped on each other's bodies at every given opportunity. "So there's obviously something going on between us. Don't you think?"

Sam could only nod. For some reason, he was finding it very difficult to breathe.

"And you know I have plans to find a husband and start a family. At the moment, this thing between us is kind of muddying the water. And it's making us fight all the time. So I figured that maybe we should just…get it out of our systems," Delaney finished in a rush.

She was flushed, and he watched, fascinated, as she lifted the hair from the back of her neck nervously.

"What do you think?" she asked when he'd been silent for too long.

"What exactly are you suggesting?" he asked carefully, keeping a very tight rein on himself until he heard what he needed to hear.

"That we have this weekend. No holds barred. Just you and me and that big bed. And then we draw a line under it, and it's done. Finished, out of the way," she said boldly.

The nervousness had left her now, he saw. In fact, if he was any guess, she was pretty damn excited. Which was good, because he was just about to explode he was so turned on.

"What do you say, Sam?" she asked, her eyes daring him to accept.

"Get your clothes off, you won't be needing them for a while."

9

DELANEY FELT all her nervousness and uncertainty fall away as she and Sam moved toward one another. The weight of Sam's mouth on hers was becoming a sweet, familiar torture, and she opened to him completely, inviting his invasion. She loved the way he kissed her as though he couldn't get enough. It was the ultimate turn-on. That, and his hard male body pressed against hers.

Determined to take things slowly this time, she slid her hands across his shoulders, measuring their width, adoring their strength. Hands mapping each sexy centimeter, she slid her palms down his back, pressing against his firm muscles as Sam began kissing her neck.

"I love it when you do that," she moaned, and Sam pulled her closer still, pressing his hips against hers.

He was as hard as a rock, and she tilted her hips to let him know that he wasn't the only one who was seriously aroused. He grunted his approval, his hands sliding down her back and under her waistband. He stilled for a second, pulling back to look down into her face.

"No underwear?" he asked, his expression one of comic disbelief.

"Nope."

"For how long? All day? Please don't tell me you were commando all day and I didn't notice," Sam groaned.

"Only since I changed after work," she said, laughing at his chagrin.

His big hands curled over her bare butt inside her shorts, pulling her against him even more firmly.

"This caboose should be registered as the eighth wonder of the world," he said as he massaged her sensually.

Delaney slid her hands to his rear, grabbing a tight male butt cheek in each hand.

"You're not so bad yourself," she murmured, scattering kisses down the tanned column of his throat. Opening her mouth, she swirled her tongue against his skin and he shuddered.

"You're right, that is good," he said, then she let out a whoop of surprise as he bent down to scoop her up in his arms. Taking two impatient strides to the bed, he threw her on it unceremoniously and started tearing his clothes off.

"I really want to go slow. Taste every part of you. Make it last for hours. But not just now," he said as he shoved his jeans down his legs.

Delaney was already wriggling out of her shorts and tugging her tank top over her head. "Couldn't agree more," she said.

Then Sam was on the bed, pressing the full length of his naked body against hers. It was the first time they'd made it to a bed, and she gloried in the heady feel of his skin on hers.

"Good, huh?" Sam said, echoing her thoughts.

"The best," Delaney murmured, pulling his head down for a kiss.

The rest was a blur. Both of them were so hot for it, foreplay was virtually nonexistent as Sam entered her with a single, powerful stroke. She almost came just from having him inside her, and from then on it was a fierce, wild ride as they both raced to the finish line. They found it simultaneously, Sam's hips shuddering into hers even as she cried out in climax.

It seemed to get better and better between them. And the best part was that afterward, neither of them felt the need to run away. This time, Sam lay on his belly beside her, one hand still wrapped around her waist, his fingers drawing idle circles on the tender skin of her belly.

She wanted to revel in the feeling, but she felt so content, so replete, that her eyelids were soon drooping down toward her cheeks. She could feel Sam's body relaxing beside her, too, and she snuggled into the pillow.

"Sleepy," she murmured as Sam opened his eyes and smiled faintly at her.

"Me, too. Haven't exactly been getting a solid eight hours lately," he said.

"Me either," she said without thinking.

Sam's smile broadened into a grin, and the hand on her waist spread wider as he pulled her to him possessively.

"Tell me it was because you were thinking about me," he said.

Delaney didn't know what to say. Admit the truth and risk Sam guessing her secret? Or lie, and break the spell they seemed to have fallen under since they walked in the door?

"Tell me, Delaney," Sam said mock-sternly. "Tell me you were thinking about me doing this."

He ducked his head to take one of her nipples in his mouth. Dancing his tongue across it firmly, he nipped her lightly.

"And this," he murmured sexily as his hand smoothed its way down her belly and into the moist curls between her thighs. Delaney bit her lip as one of his fingers delved into her sensitive folds to find her clitoris.

Eyes intent on her face, Sam slicked a finger across the sensitive bud. Unbelievably, given the incredible orgasm she'd just had, Delaney felt the familiar tension rising inside her again.

Eyes dropping to half-mast, she spread her thighs wider, hungry for more of his touch.

Sam seemed happy to oblige. Lavishing attention on her breasts with his mouth, he drove her wild with his deft stroking between her legs. Only when she was shivering and shifting needfully on the sheets did he stop, rousing her from the sensual haze she'd fallen into.

"Say it, Delaney," Sam ordered again, and Delaney was so close, so desperate for release, that she confessed the truth.

"Yes, I was thinking about you. About this," she breathed.

Sam looked so smug and self-satisfied that she couldn't help but add a rider. "And I thought about Jake. And that guy I was seeing last year, Tim," she said lightly. "And there was this photo of Eric Bana in the latest issue of *Cosmo...*"

Sam froze for a breath, then his hand began to move between her legs with renewed intent.

"You're lying," he said as Delaney began to gasp with need. "Tell me it was only me."

She nearly rocketed off the bed as Sam pressed the whole of his palm against her clitoris and mons, rocking it skillfully. Fulfillment was on the horizon, just a few seconds away, when Sam stopped again, his hand curving till it was doing nothing but cupping her heat.

"Sam! Please!" she begged, wriggling her hips desperately.

"Say the magic words, Delaney," Sam instructed.

Delaney looked up into his laughing face, desperate for what he'd promised, knowing somehow that this was a joke but also very serious.

"Only you, Sam," she finally whispered. A look of fierce satisfaction crossed his face, and he dropped his head to begin ravishing her breasts again, his mouth firm and delicious on her nipples. Between her legs, his palm began to rock again, and Delaney was powerless to stop her hips thrusting off the mattress as desire coalesced within her.

"Yes, Sam, yes! Yes!" she cried out, one hand fisted in the sheets, the other clasping his shoulder fervently.

Sam waited until she'd ridden it out before removing his hand from between her legs. She was boneless and exhausted, and she could see that Sam was feeling very proud of himself.

"Sleep with one eye open, Kirk," she warned him.

"Excellent. I look forward to a counterassault," Sam said cockily.

"You say that now. Wait until I've got you in my mouth, just about to explode," she threatened.

Sam's eyes darkened. "Tell me more."

Delaney smiled, realizing that she had him hooked already. Too easy!

"Not just yet. I might take a little nap. Then maybe we can discuss it some more," she said, rolling onto her belly and punching the pillow into a more comfortable shape.

Sam swore under his breath.

"Pace yourself, Sam. I haven't even started yet," she said, smiling into her pillow.

They had all weekend. Two nights and nearly two glorious days to tease and taunt each other as much as they liked. More than enough time to purge herself of sixteen years of fantasizing and obsessing, leaving her free to move on, at last, and build her new life.

Must remember to thank Claire for giving such good advice, she thought as she drifted off to sleep.

SAM WOKE FROM A DOZE to find that Delaney had pulled on her tank top and shorts and was searching through the bags of food.

His eyes widened as he saw her remove a punnet of dip and a long, flat loaf of Turkish bread from one of the bags.

"Tell me that is not from Golden Towers," he said, naming their favorite Turkish restaurant in the inner-west Melbourne suburb of Brunswick.

"There is no substitute," she said as she added a container of stuffed olives to the selection, along with a serving of tabouli.

Sam gave her an appreciative look. "Your future husband is the luckiest bastard on the planet," he said lightly.

"When I find him, your job is to keep telling him that for the next fifty years," she said after a small pause.

Sam felt his guts twist at her words. He hated the future Mr. Delaney Michaels, and he hadn't even met him yet. The SOB was scoring the sexiest, funniest, coolest woman around, and he probably wouldn't even understand what a prize he'd landed.

"What else have you got in those bags?" Sam asked, not liking the dark alleyway his thoughts were veering down. It was such a joke, anyway, him daring to critique another man's relationship—even if the other guy was purely theoretical at this point. The longest he'd ever dated one woman had been four whole months, a bold experiment he'd tried in his early twenties. Sasha had hated Delaney with a passion, and he'd swiftly gotten sick of fighting with her over her pathological jealousy of his best friend. He didn't do fights, and in his experience, most relationships eventually deteriorated into animosity as people's needs clashed. Either someone caved and became a doormat, or the relationship became a battleground. And Sam refused to live in either state.

That was why he'd hated these past few weeks with Delaney so much. The two of them never fought. Not seriously, anyway. Sometimes Delaney might take a shot at him over something, and he might fire back. But he'd never gone to sleep angry with her. Another reason why he'd found rest so elusive lately.

"There's cheese, some cold meats, and a couple of bottles of red wine. I also got champagne, but that needs chilling so we can save that for tomorrow," Delaney was saying as she rummaged through the bags. "Oh—and I got dessert. But that's a secret."

"Let me guess—chocolate something," Sam said, knowing her sweet tooth.

"You don't know everything about me, Sam Kirk," Delaney said a little huffily.

Sam just grinned. He might not know everything, but he knew her better than anyone else—and his knowledge was getting more thorough and more detailed every second.

They ate dinner sitting cross-legged in bed, the food spread out on a large chopping board Delaney had found in the kitchen. Sam loved the way Delaney enjoyed her food—her repertoire of delighted noises had always amused him, but now he took extra pleasure in watching her close her eyes over a particularly good stuffed olive, or moan with appreciation over the creaminess of the camembert. He was a little surprised to think that he hadn't noticed what a sensual person she was before. He frowned as he realized that all the clues had been there if he'd been willing to look—like her love of textured fabrics, as evidenced by the very tactile suede-like couch in her apartment. He could still remember her rubbing her hands along the seat cushions when it had arrived and purring like a cat.

The thought of it was enough to give him a hard-on.

And the great thing was, he didn't have to pretend he didn't have one anymore. He could sit across from her and devour her with his eyes and imagine what he was going to touch or taste next, building his anticipation and hers every time their glances brushed, each exchange becoming more and more loaded until finally he collected the remnants of their meal and strode across to dump them unceremoniously in the sink. After that, it was perfectly legitimate for him to saunter back to the bed, enjoying the way her eyes dropped to his erection. Some might say it was even incumbent on him to leap onto the bed, ruthlessly stripping her until every inch of her delectable, unforgettable body was completely naked.

"You drive me crazy," he said as he licked his way down her belly.

"You ain't seen nothing yet," she said, lithely twisting out from underneath him and using an old wrestling trick he'd taught her to force him onto his back.

"Nice," Sam said, appreciating both her skill and the fact that with her on top he had a spectacular view of her small but perfect breasts.

Delaney just raised an eyebrow at him, then lowered her head to his chest. First, she circled one of his nipples with her tongue while her hand stroked the other, pinching and teasing and sucking until they were both tight and hard—not unlike other parts of his body. Then she began to kiss and lick her way down his belly. He knew what was coming next— he hoped he knew what was coming next, anyway—and just the thought of Delaney licking and sucking and stroking him so intimately was almost enough to send him off on its own. At last she reached his crotch, her hands wrapping firmly around his shaft. She shot him a vastly knowing look from under her eyelashes, and then he was in her mouth, her tongue firm and hot and wet against his erection.

"*Ohhhhhh,* Laney," he sighed, giving himself up to the experience.

She was amazing. He'd never had a woman lavish so much attention on him before. A lot of women, in his experience, went down as though it were a duty, offering a few token bobs of the head to get things rolling. But Delaney seemed to really be getting off on his pleasure. By the time he was grabbing at the headboard to hang on for dear life, she was panting almost as much as him. After he'd come, a release that left him sagging with fatigue, she turned molten-toffee eyes to him and wiped the corners of her mouth delicately like a very pleased cat.

"In case you were wondering, that was dessert," she said.

It was the last thing he'd expected her to say, and he threw back his head and let out a crack of laughter. Her face crumpled with mirth, too, and for a moment they clutched at their stomachs and hooted and giggled together.

Sam realized that he felt great. Infinitely turned on, even if he wasn't about to do anything about it at the moment, completely comfortable and excited about what else lay in store on this weekend of discovery.

By the time they were ready to pack up and head home on Sunday, he had no doubt that he and Delaney would have resolved all the wrongness that had been between them lately. The fact that he'd have had the best sex of his life while doing it was just a big, fat bonus.

DELANEY WOKE FIRST the following morning. She lay very still as she registered the fact that she was pressed against Sam's back, her hand snaked over his waist and across his chest. The smell of him filled her senses, and she pressed her cheek against his warm back. She loved him so much. Last night had been so freeing, being able to touch him with passion and desire without having to hide her true feelings.

Although there had been moments when she'd thought she'd given too much away.

It was only after she'd gone down on Sam that she'd understood how lost in the experience she'd been. For starters, she'd intended to work him to a fever pitch, then hold off at the last minute and tease him in the same way that he had teased her. But she'd imagined pleasuring him with her mouth for so long. She'd fantasized about how he'd taste, how he'd feel, how long and firm he'd be in her hands. It had been absolute wish fulfillment to be able to have her way with him at last, and she'd gotten too caught up to remember her revenge. Next time she would have to be more careful.

She smiled as she registered her own thoughts. *Next time.* For a short while, she lived in a world where there were next times. And she was going to make the most of each and every one of them.

Sam stirred, rolling around to face her. His eyes were the soft, dreamy blue of a clear summer's day.

"Good morning," he said softly.

"Good morning," she said back.

For a moment they lay there, staring into each other's eyes. Delaney felt a wellspring of emotion rising up inside her. This man meant so much to her.

As though he sensed the tumult within her, Sam pulled her close and pressed a kiss to her forehead. He held her that way for a long moment, then leaned back so he could look into her face properly.

"So what are you cooking me for breakfast?" he asked cheekily.

Delaney smiled. Just like Sam to go for the light option. "Wrong question. What are you buying *me* for breakfast?"

They showered together, an overlong session that involved

lots of pressing each other up against the tiled wall and much dexterous work with slippery, soapy hands. Finally they were dressed and on the road back to Daylesford. They quickly discovered they were spoiled for choice for breakfast, and they opted for a café with lots of outdoor tables so they could watch the passing parade. They divided up a newspaper someone else had left behind, she taking business and arts, him the sports pages. They both ordered scrambled eggs on whole grain toast with freshly squeezed orange juice, then sat back to enjoy the morning sun.

Feeling too contented to concentrate on the newspaper, Delaney tilted her head back and enjoyed the play of sunshine on her closed eyelids. The sound of the people around them became amplified, and she smiled to herself as she relished the fact that she was here with Sam, that she'd woken in his arms, and that even though several women in the café had turned to stare at him when they entered, she was the woman he would be taking home to bed tonight. Or this afternoon, if she played her cards right.

She felt a gentle touch on her cheek and she opened her eyes to find Sam leaning close to her, his expression intent.

"You look very beautiful in the sunlight, Laney," he said softly. "Have I told you how much I like your new hair?"

"No."

"I do. I like it a lot." Sam had a mischievous glint in his eye as he shot her a conspiratorial look. "I like it this much," he said, lifting the newspaper from his lap to reveal a significant bulge in his jeans.

Delaney's mouth went dry as she stared at his crotch, wishing she'd opted to cook him breakfast in their cabin after all.

"Don't worry, it'll keep," Sam said confidently, reading her chagrin.

Further conversation was stymied by the arrival of their food. Once her meal was in front of her, Delaney was surprised to realize she was starving. She tucked in with gusto, and Sam gave an approving nod.

"Good. Keep up your strength. You're going to need it," he said.

"So are you, so eat up yourself," she warned him.

They grinned at each other. Delaney felt a rush of pleasure at the fact that the friendly teasing and rivalry that had characterized their friendship seemed to have transferred so readily to this new—if temporary—dynamic.

It's only because this is exactly how Sam likes it, an evil little voice whispered in her mind. *No strings, no tomorrows. Just fun and games with no consequences.*

Delaney banished the thought as soon as it had entered her mind. She was the one who had issued the invitation for this weekend. They were her rules. She had no right to start sulking over Sam's attitude when she was getting exactly what she'd asked for.

After breakfast, they wandered down the main street and discovered that the local church was having a trash and treasure sale. Delaney cast Sam a hopeful look—although she hated shopping in general, trash and treasure sales were a sentimental favorite of hers. Something to do with the fact that she and Sam had manned the lamington stand at their school fete when they were thirteen and had the time of their lives eating the leftovers. Her mouth watered as she thought about getting her hands on a home-baked lamington. There was something so simple and perfect about the fresh sponge squares rolled in chocolate frosting, then dipped in coconut. If they were really lucky, someone would have made them with jam in the middle.

"There's probably a cake stall," she wheedled when Sam rolled his eyes. "There might be lamingtons."

Making a big show of being magnanimous, Sam gestured for her to go ahead. Walking amongst the rows of trestle tables, she tried not to look too surprised when he casually slung his arm around her shoulders and pulled her close to walk alongside him. Sex was one thing, but this was a whole other ball game. Her heart seemed to expand inside her rib cage as they browsed slowly amongst the flotsam and jetsam from other people's lives, Sam's arm a warm, reassuring-yet-exciting weight across her shoulders.

At last they came to the food section, staffed as always by an array of elderly ladies. Delaney hid a smile as they all sat a little straighter, primping their hair and tweaking their dresses as she and Sam approached. Within minutes Sam was the center of a circle of elderly female admirers, and she was shaking her head at his apparently universal charm.

"Here, try my preserves," said a stick-thin old woman with the name Mabel embroidered on a homemade badge on her bony chest.

"He looks more like a marmalade man to me," a tiny, plump woman interjected. "Something with a bit of bite in it." The look she gave Sam was positively carnal.

Delaney wasn't sure at exactly what point Sam began to fear for his personal safety, if not his virtue. It didn't take the old dears long to segue from offering him samples of their culinary wares to asking how he stayed so fit and strong, and then reaching out to pat a muscle here and there.

Sam shot her a worried look as Mabel edged around behind him to check out his rear.

"As I suspected—not a saggy bit of denim in sight," she said approvingly. "Back in my salad days I had a boyfriend who was a surfer. Reginald. Excellent buttocks. Just like yours," she said.

Sam got a peculiar expression on his face, and insisted on buying one of each lady's offerings before ushering Delaney away.

"I still can't believe there were no lamingtons," she said whimsically as they arranged their jams, pickles, slices and fudges in the back of Sam's car.

"Just as bloody well. God only knows what the lamington lady would have done to me," Sam said.

"Sam!" Delaney said, choking on a laugh.

"I'm serious. That skinny little one—Mabel—she pinched me on the butt when she thought I wasn't looking," Sam said, his face a picture of outrage.

"Serves you right for being such a flirt."

Sam shot her a speculative look. "Don't tell me you were jealous, Laney," he teased.

Delaney puffed her cheeks out. "Jealous! Hardly," she said. She would never, ever admit to him that she'd had to staunchly resist the impulse to claim him by giving him a big pash in front of his elderly harem. *Not* her finest moment.

Sam wasn't buying, however, and he pushed her up against the side of the car and kissed her until she was mindless.

"Don't worry, Laney. They weren't even in with a chance," he said when he finally broke away.

She stared at him, unable to form coherent thoughts, let alone speak.

"Time to go back to the cabin," he said decisively.

Since it was exactly what she wanted to do, she nodded compliantly.

The journey back seemed to take far longer than it had going the other way, and she crossed and recrossed her legs, already so hot for him she could feel her pulse throbbing dully between her thighs. Sam kept shooting her hungry glances, and by the time they were pulling up next to the cabin Delaney was feeling well and truly breathless with need.

Sam strode into the cabin like a man on a mission and immediately began shucking his clothes.

She followed suit, kicking off her shoes, stripping off her jeans and panties in one smooth move, then leaning down to peel off her socks. When she straightened, Sam was lying on his back on the bed, stark naked and magnificently erect, his eyes glued to her body. Maybe it was the way he was looking at her, his gaze avid and intent and completely focused, or maybe it was something to do with the weekend being a time-out from their usual lives, or her newfound confidence since her minimakeover, but a heady rush of power swept over her. Slowing everything down, she reached languidly for the top button on her shirt, sliding it loose oh-so-casually before letting her hand fall to the next button, and then the next.

"Laney," Sam growled warningly. "Don't make me come and get you."

She just smiled, grasping the edges of her shirt and flipping first one side and then the other open, offering him fleeting glimpses of her breasts in her sexy, red push-up bra.

"I'm going to count to ten, then you're in big trouble."

Delaney just waggled her eyebrows at him and slowly pulled the shirt off one arm.

"One. Two. Three," Sam counted, eyes narrowed.

Delaney pulled her other arm free of the shirt, throwing it toward the bed so that it landed in the middle of Sam's chest.

"Four. Five. Six," Sam said, brushing her shirt aside impatiently.

Stealing a move from a Madonna video clip, Delaney

shimmied her hips and bent forward at the waist, reaching behind herself to unclip her bra. As the fabric fell slack around her ribs, she caught the cups of her bra in her hands and slowly peeled them away from her breasts while still bending forward. She knew it was a position that gave her the most possible cleavage, and she jiggled her shoulders a little as she dropped the bra completely.

"Seven," Sam said very slowly, his eyes glued to her breasts as she slid a hand down to touch her own nipples.

As they pebbled and thrust forward, Sam made an impatient noise and tensed as though he were about to jump off the bed and come get her. Determined to keep the initiative, Delaney beat him to it, striding toward the bed and stepping up onto the mattress in a long bound. Sam half smiled and reclined again, a look on his face that said he was more than prepared to sit back and enjoy the show now that she'd added a bit of audience participation into the mix.

Loving teasing him, Delaney boldly stepped over him so that she stood straddling his torso, looking down at his hard male body. Holding his eye, she slid a finger into her mouth, then slowly trailed it down her cleavage, over the erect, highly sensitive nipple of her left breast and down onto her belly. Sam's mouth opened a little as she headed south, sliding her hand between her thighs to touch herself. Positioned where he was, he had a box seat—so to speak—and she loved the way his breath hitched as he watched her pleasure herself.

When she figured he'd had enough, she bent her knees, preparing to lower herself over him and straddle him more traditionally, taking them both for the wildest of rides. But Sam had other ideas. As she started to kneel, he hooked a hand behind each knee and hauled her forward. Before she knew what was happening, she was off balance and falling forward, her bent knees landing just above his shoulders. His eyes locked to hers, Sam slid his hands up onto her rear, silently urging her farther forward still, and Delaney realized with a shock what he intended.

She was by no means a novice where oral sex was concerned, but to press herself against his mouth like that from above seemed so…decadent that she hesitated. Sam took the decision out of her hands by scooting down on the bed, and the next thing she knew, his mouth was closing over her and his tongue was dancing over her clitoris, at first fast and firm, then slow and gentle, then fast and firm again. Delaney's whole body shuddered and her thighs tensed as the most incredible sensations shot through her. Sam's mouth felt so hot, so wet, so right against her, she could do nothing but lean forward, grab the headboard and let it happen.

Within minutes she was writhing, on the verge, and Sam seemed to know exactly what she needed to push her over the edge. While he continued to caress her with his tongue, he slid a hand up her inside thigh and slipped a finger inside her. She came instantly, clenching around him, unable to contain her very vocal cries of ecstasy. Afterward, she slid off him and collapsed on her back, one hand falling across her face in a vain attempt to feel less exposed.

Sam allowed her a moment's respite before she felt the mattress dip as he moved to position himself beside her.

She felt the delicious pressure of his lips beneath her ear, and she slowly lowered her arm.

"You are the sexiest woman I have ever met," Sam said, his expression very intent.

All her self-consciousness left her. This was Sam. He'd held her hair when she was sick after too many cocktails when she was seventeen. He'd seen her throw temper tantrums when her laptop failed. He'd always been around to pick her up and dust her off when she'd fallen over. He'd just performed an incredibly intimate act on her, and she'd lost her mind for a moment—and she'd been safe the whole time, because she was with him.

She nodded minutely, letting him know that she understood what he was saying. Sam nodded back, and started kissing her neck again, right where he knew it got her the most. She almost protested, sure that she couldn't possibly even think about more sex after what had just happened.

But amazingly, her hands were already reaching for Sam, one hand grasping the thick length of him, the other dragging his hips toward her own. When Sam slid into her, she sighed and wrapped her legs around his hips and rocked her pelvis forward and closed her eyes. Heaven. She could never get sick of this. Ever.

Somewhere in the back of her mind, she knew that she'd just made a very dangerous admission to herself.

But Sam was inside her, and his hands and mouth were on her breasts, and there was no way she could think right now. Closing her eyes, she gave herself up to the moment.

10

SAM CLOSED HIS EYES and tilted his head back to rest it against the rim of the bathtub. At the other end of the tub, Delaney shifted her leg a little, and he felt the silky brush of her thigh against his in the water. He smiled wryly to himself. The idea of having a relaxing soak in the tub together was great in theory. In practice, there was no question of him ever being able to relax while Delaney was naked and in the near vicinity. In fact, he was beginning to wonder how he'd lasted all these years having her sleeping just below him. Even though their apartment bedrooms were separated by many, many inches of steel and concrete and floorboards, he knew that he would never again be able to lie in his own bed and not think of her lying below. And wonder if she were alone, and what she might be doing, and most importantly of all, if she were thinking of him…

Sam derailed that particular train of thought before it could go anywhere. He'd been telling himself all weekend that everything would resolve itself once they returned to Melbourne. This incredible sensual time-out would be over. Hell, their friendship would probably be even stronger because of it.

On a good day, with the wind blowing in the right direction and all the fates aligned, he almost believed his own bull.

"This French champagne is so good. I know it's unpatriotic to say it, but Australian champagne never tastes like this," Delaney said.

Sam opened his eyes. It didn't help with the relaxing thing, but it seemed nothing would while his body was tangled with hers.

They were soaking in the outdoor tub on the cabin's front deck, and Delaney's face was flushed pink from the heat. He could see the rosy tips of her breasts where they broke the surface of the water, but the rest of her was hidden by sudsy bubbles. Behind her, the bush was pitch-black, the darkness kept at bay by a circle of fat candles they'd placed around the decking.

She held a champagne flute in one languid hand, and her expression was dreamy as she savored a mouthful.

"Australia doesn't make champagne. It's sparkling wine now, remember?" he said.

Delaney wrinkled her nose. "I still think that was a bit mean of the French. Kind of stopped everyone being able to fool themselves," she said.

"Very cruel," Sam agreed, mock-solemnly. He sent a questing hand out to see what interesting things it might encounter. A smile curved Delaney's lips as he found her inner thigh.

"Hello, sailor," she said in her best Mae West impersonation.

He pinched her gently, and she sent a splash his way. Deciding she could keep, Sam reached for his own champagne glass.

She was right, it was good. In fact, this whole weekend was just about perfect. The only wrong element was that it had to end.

He frowned. Why was his mind constantly circling back to the same thought? He never dwelt on problems. He wasn't a worrier. Life happened, he dealt with it, he moved on. Simple. But it hadn't escaped his notice that lately he'd been spending

Anything for You

a lot of his time thinking about Delaney, about what she meant to him, and how much he didn't want things to change.

But they *had* changed. They'd slept with each other. And Delaney was leaving the business and moving house. Things would never be the same again.

Anxiety stabbed at his belly, and he took a hearty sip of champagne to try and dull it.

"It's so beautiful here," Delaney said dreamily. She shifted, lifting a leg from the water to prop an ankle on the edge of the tub.

Immediately his brain set to work imagining what was happening under the water, how her thighs would be parted, and the heart of her exposed.

"Yeah," he said distractedly, leaning down to place his champagne flute on the deck, the better to free up both hands.

"Thanks for coming away, Sam" she said suddenly. "I really appreciate it."

The distance inherent in her statement caught his attention.

"You don't have to thank me, Laney. I'd do anything for you, you know that."

She eyed him enigmatically for a beat before nodding. "Yes, I know that."

"And it's not like I'm not having the time of my life here," he said. Although, in truth, every great moment was increasingly tinged with thoughts about what would happen once they went home again.

"That's nice."

She looked sad all of a sudden. Sam sat up and patted the surface of the water in front of him.

"I think you need to come up this end where there's more company," he said.

She smiled, standing obediently. The candlelight reflected

off her wet, lean body as she towered above him, and his breath caught in his throat as he realized how beautiful she was on the outside as well as the inside. His Laney.

Turning away from him, she bent down and eased herself into the water so that she was sitting between his bent knees, her back leaning into his chest. He slid his arms around her torso and spread them possessively over her belly, holding her close. Her head dropped back against his chest and he felt her let out a deep sigh.

Pressing his cheek against her head, Sam stared off into the darkness. He felt so close to her right now—closer than they'd ever been in some ways. But for the first time in their relationship, he felt scared, too. It wasn't an emotion he associated with Delaney.

She'd always been his touchstone, his stalwart, the one immutable thing that anchored his life. Ever since he'd been a kid and he'd found comfort and warmth and normality in her family's home, she'd been a fundamental part of his world.

And now things were changing between them. As though she could sense his thoughts, Delaney wrapped her arms on top of his and squeezed him tightly.

"You're the best, Sam," she said. "I'll never forget this. No matter what."

Sam felt a deep certainty chiming inside himself, and suddenly he knew, beyond a doubt, that everything was going to be okay. He pressed a kiss to her head.

"It's okay, Laney. I'm not going anywhere," he said reassuringly.

And he wasn't. Their relationship might be changing, evolving. But Delaney was a part of his life, always would be. They would get through this.

Delaney didn't say anything, she simply lifted one of his hands and pressed a kiss into his palm.

Sam looked up at the stars twinkling high above them. It was a beautiful night, and he was in a beautiful place, and there was no one else he'd rather be here with. Relaxing at last, he settled more deeply into the water.

"It's all going to be fine," he murmured reassuringly as he closed his eyes.

DELANEY FOLDED her last T-shirt and pushed it into her overnight bag. Tugging the zipper closed, she sat back on her haunches and let out a small sigh.

It was all over. In an hour's time they would be back in Melbourne, and the weekend would be nothing but a memory.

"Kitchen's clean," Sam said, and Delaney quickly schooled her expression into something that might pass as normal.

Inside she was dying. She was such a self-delusional fool. She'd known this was coming, too. Telling herself that she could shag Sam out of her system—had she ever really believed that was true?

But it had been the excuse she needed to have this weekend. To pretend, for just a few crazy days that he was hers, that he returned her feelings, that they had a future.

Now it was time to pack it all away and return to reality. Time to pay the price for her flight of fantasy.

Last night in the bath, Sam had assured her that he wasn't going anywhere. She'd been so glad she had her back to him and he couldn't see her face. She was sure her thoughts were written all over it, as plain as day for him to see: he wasn't going anywhere, but she was.

Soon she would no longer work with him, and once she'd sold her apartment, she would no longer live with him, either.

And then it would just be a matter of slowly easing away. Within a few months' time, Sam would be out of her life.

"I'll start loading up the car," Sam said, breaking into her introspection.

She watched him stoop to collect his backpack and their other belongings, and an impetuous urge shot her to her feet. Stepping close to him, she put a hand on his chest and looked up into his face.

"We've still got another hour before we have to hand the keys back," she said, hating herself for being the one to cling to the magic of their time together.

Sam dropped the bags with alacrity. "You are *so* a woman after my own heart," he said.

Delaney almost burst into tears at his words, but lust came to her rescue. He only had to touch her and she was lost. She'd learned that by now. A weekend of lying skin-to-skin hadn't cured her of her addiction—if anything, it was worse, now that they had taken the greedy edge off their mutual desire. After their bath on Saturday night, Sam had made long, slow love to her, kissing and licking and teasing every inch of her body until she was writhing with need. Even when he entered her, he took his sweet time, stretching the experience out as long as he could. She came twice, the second time a climax that was so deep, so all-encompassing that she'd lost all sense of time and place.

Now, Sam kissed her deeply, holding her body tightly to his even as he backed her toward the bed. She felt the mattress behind her knees and allowed herself to fall backward, Sam coming with her.

Just the feel of him resting between her spread legs was bliss. A torturous, need-inducing kind of bliss, but bliss nonetheless. Knowing full well that she was touching his beautiful body for the last time, Delaney took her time peeling his clothes off, her hands smoothing reverently over each newly exposed expanse of skin. He was in his prime, strong and tanned and full of life. She drank him in with her hands and her eyes, her feverish mind trying to store away memories for later—the smell of his skin, the way his eyes darkened when he was turned on, the giveaway twitch of his hips when he particularly liked something she was doing to him.

His hands were just as slow and thorough on her body, and she was soon quivering with the need to have him inside her. Pushing his shoulders down onto the bed, she slid on top of him and guided him inside her. They locked eyes as she rode him, the act a mirror of that first, frantic time they'd come together. This time, however, Delaney delayed the inevitable, trying to stop time, to steal just a little more of Sam for herself. But inevitably the delicious tension built within her, and she bit her lip to hold back her moans of pleasure.

Sam's hands slid up her torso to cup her breasts, and she couldn't help herself.

"Sam," she breathed, sliding along his hard length. "Sam."

He seemed to understand what she wanted. His hands slid to her hips and he gripped them firmly as he thrust up into her, never taking his eyes off hers. His face grew taut, and she felt the muscles of his belly tense beneath her hands. He was close, she knew, and so was she.

Their cries mingled together as Sam's hips pushed up against hers one last time, the slip and slide of their bodies too perfect to deny for long. Exhausted both emotionally and physically, Delaney flopped across his chest for a brief moment. She could feel his heart pounding in his chest, and hear the harsh sound of his breathing.

She experienced a fierce moment of pride. She had done

this to Sam—she had pushed him to the edge and over, sent his pulse sky rocketing, made him hard with need and now compliant and lazy with satisfaction. She had this, at least, to keep her warm on the long, lonely nights to come.

Carefully, methodically, she pulled her messy feelings together inside herself and wrapped them up nice and tight. Right now was where it had to end. There could be no more reprieves.

Pulling away from Sam, she began to dress. A dull weight was sitting in the bottom of her stomach. She had a feeling it was going to be there for a very long time.

SAM KEPT GLANCING across at Delaney as he tooled along the freeway back to Melbourne. The sun was just going down on the horizon, and her profile was limned with the rosy fire of the setting sun.

She looked infinitely sad, and he wanted to pull over and demand that she talk to him. She'd been very quiet since they left the cabin, and he'd respected her silence so far because he had assumed that it sprang from the same regret he felt that their special time together was over.

Seeing her face now, however, he wasn't quite so sure.

"You okay?" he asked, even though he felt that he'd somehow traded away the right to ask such things when he'd agreed to their weekend.

"Just thinking about the business," she said.

Sam's hands tightened on the steering wheel. "Haven't changed your mind, then?" he asked, keeping his tone purposefully light.

"No," she said flatly.

Silence fell between them for a few kilometers. Finally Sam spoke again.

"The bank's cool with everything. You know that. I just have to tell them when I need the funds. And then it's done."

He could see her nod in his peripheral vision.

"Okay."

"So the timing is up to you," Sam said, stating the obvious.

He knew in his bones that she didn't really want to go. Why else would she be so sad about the prospect? She'd built Mirk Publications up with him from nothing. There was no way she didn't feel as passionately about it as he did. He held his breath as he waited for her answer. He'd called her bluff, and now it was time for her to talk in terms of months, and long handover periods and other time-consuming, face-saving measures that confirmed his belief that she didn't really want to go through with this.

"I was thinking maybe three weeks. If you think we can find a replacement for me that quickly," she said.

Sam felt as though he'd been kicked in the belly. *Three weeks?* Three measly, cotton-picking weeks?

"What do you think?" she asked, and Sam realized that he hadn't responded to her suggestion, and that he'd pressed his foot down on the gas and was now speeding.

Easing back on the accelerator, he tried to sound casual.

"We'll have to advertise straight away. It probably depends on notice periods for the new person, how soon we can get them."

"Of course. I won't leave you high and dry, don't worry," she said.

Sam wanted to turn and tell her that that was exactly what she was doing. But he didn't. Belatedly he saw that perhaps their weekend together hadn't cleared up any of the problems between them at all. Maybe, in fact, it had made things worse.

"I was thinking that we—I mean, you, sorry—could start training Sukie up into an assistant sales role. You could assign her some of our smaller advertisers, start her up slowly. That will leave the new person plenty of time to build relationships with our major players," Delaney said.

Sam forced his mind away from the dark place that had opened in his soul and tried to concentrate on what she was saying.

"That's a good idea. Sukie's great on the phone," he said.

"That's what I thought. And I kind of get the feeling that she might be getting a little bored with admin work. If you train her and give her a pay rise, she'll stay with you for longer."

They talked about the magazine the rest of the trip—careful, emotionless conversation about future planning and things they'd been putting off that Sam would need to do on his own now. Every word seemed to hammer home to him just how much he didn't want things to change, how much he was going to miss Delaney.

But he was slowly beginning to understand that this was really happening. She was going. She wanted to go, worse. And there was nothing he could do to stop her.

They were both calm but a little withdrawn by the time he pulled into his parking spot beneath their apartment block.

"Thanks for driving," Delaney said, flashing him a small smile. "I should have offered to drive us back, since you took us out."

"I like driving, you know that." Sam shrugged, hating the awkwardness. Definitely things were worse now than when they'd left.

And it wasn't about sex or lust or desire or guilt. It was about their friendship. He could see that now. The certainty that he'd felt last night in the bathtub evaporated and he realized there was a very real possibility that they would never recover from this seismic shift in their relationship.

The thought of it made him dizzy, as though someone had just told him that gravity was a myth and he was suddenly floating free, with nothing or nobody to tie him to the earth.

The feeling only got worse when he followed her up to her apartment and stood beside her as she listened to her answering machine messages.

"Delaney, it's Harry from the real estate office. We've been trying you on your mobile but you've been out of range all weekend. You've had an offer on your apartment. Spot on your asking price. I think you'll be very happy. Call me as soon as you get in."

Sam felt as though his legs were made from solid granite as he crossed to the sofa and sat while Delaney made the call. She talked quietly and briefly for a few minutes, then put the phone down. The expression she turned to him was completely blank.

"Wow. That was fast."

"You're going to take it?" he asked flatly.

"It's right on the money. They don't even want to haggle. And they want a three-week settlement. It's like it was meant to be," she said.

"Yeah."

If he were a more generous person, he'd be leaping up now, offering to go buy champagne to celebrate her news. But he wasn't that generous. He'd just been delivered two stunning blows, one after the other—he had only three weeks left of Delaney in the business, and about the same before she moved out. Despite all the reassurances he'd been making to himself, change was coming like a freight train along the tracks, and he was standing squarely in its way, about to get squashed and shredded.

"I don't suppose it would do any good if I asked you not to go?" he heard himself ask. If he thought it would make him look any less pathetic, he would have punched himself in the face.

Delaney's hands found one another and she gripped them tightly at her waist.

"This is a good offer, Sam. And it's time to sell the apartment. Time to move on."

Sam stared at her, deeply, mortally afraid that there was a deeper message for him in her words.

"You'll just have to put up with me hanging out at your new place all the time. Better get that spare bedroom up and running," he joked weakly.

"Which reminds me—I can put an offer in on the place in Camberwell now," she said.

Sam brooded darkly as she made another phone call, only tuning in again when he noticed her checking her watch.

"In half an hour? That would be great," she said into the phone. "I'll see you then."

She ended the call and was about to make another one when Sam spoke up.

"What's going on?" He was starting to feel a teensy bit irritated at the way he seemed to have been shoved into the corner and forgotten. They *had* just spent the whole weekend away together, most of it lost in each others arms. He didn't expect a brass band and ticker tape parade, but a little bit of attention wouldn't have gone astray.

"What? Oh, sorry. The agent has offered to get me through the house again tonight. The owners are really keen to sell," she said vaguely, obviously itching to get back on the phone.

"Who are you calling now?" he asked, hating the fact that he sounded jealous. He wasn't. He was just…interested.

"Claire. I need a second opinion before I start seriously thinking about making an offer."

Sam flinched. A second opinion. What was he, chopped liver?

Maybe Delaney read that she'd hurt his feelings, because she seemed to hesitate a moment before putting the phone down.

"Would—would you like to come, Sam?" she asked.

Sam stared at her a long moment, wanting to ask why she hadn't thought of him off the bat. Hadn't he always been her second opinion? Wasn't that the way they'd always worked, each having the other's back?

"Sure. I'd love to come," he said, making an effort to sound normal.

"Cool," Delaney said, and for the life of him he couldn't work out if she meant it or not.

Scooping up her car keys, she led the way down to the underground parking garage. Sam sat silently beside her as she eased out into the twilight, her MINI zipping smoothly out into traffic.

Desperate for conversation, he scanned the interior of the car. "Still running well?" he asked, patting the dash.

"Like a dream. Best car in the world," Delaney said, echoing his gesture and patting the dash as well.

They promptly fell into awkward silence again. Sam wracked his brains for something to say, but he was too busy trying to work out what was going on with Delaney. Did their weekend away mean so little to her? She was seriously behaving as though they had been fishing or hiking, not devouring each other at every given opportunity.

In just fifteen minutes, they were turning into one of the

oak-lined streets that Camberwell was famous for. Dense green boughs reached over the street from either side, meeting in the middle to form a leafy archway. Delaney leaned forward with excitement as they came up on a house with a For Sale sign on its front fence.

"Here we are," she said brightly. "Isn't it nice?"

Sam glowered at the wide porch and the diamond-paned windows and the charming heritage color scheme. It *was* nice. He just didn't want to acknowledge it right now. This was the house that could potentially steal Delaney from him. He intended to hate it on principle.

They were exiting the car when a slick real estate type pulled up in a late model Porsche. Sam did a mental eye roll. Could the guy be more of a cliché? *And* he was wearing a suit at eight o'clock on a Sunday evening. What a slimy shark.

Sam was about to warn Delaney to tread carefully when she strode out across the road to shake Mr. Slick's hand.

"Thanks for this, Matt. I really appreciate it," she said.

"Not a problem. As you know, the owner has moved into a nursing home so I knew I could get you through easily enough."

Sam noted that there was a definite glint in the other man's eyes as he gazed at Delaney, despite the fact that he only looked like he had twenty-five years under his belt.

Not going to happen, pal, he felt like saying. *Never in a million years would you have a chance with a woman like Delaney.* Instead, he had to be satisfied with crossing to stand behind her and placing a territorial hand on her shoulder.

To his chagrin, Delaney shot him a surprised look and twitched her shoulder, indicating she wanted him to let go. Teeth gritted, Sam complied. But he wasn't happy.

He didn't get any happier as he followed Delaney and Matt up the cutesy-wutesy garden path. It was a clear night with a full moon, and he could see that flowering plants and shrubs framed the brick walkway, the epitome of a charming English garden.

"The owner was a keen gardener, as you can see. The gardens are very well established and give the house good street appeal," Matt said.

"Lots of maintenance," Sam said, keen to offset Captain Slicko's patter. "Probably get over-run really easily."

"The old lady's family are using a gardening service to maintain it at present. I believe they're very affordable," Matt countered.

"For a few weeks, maybe. But not on a long-term basis, I bet," Sam said repressively.

Delaney shot him a look that plainly told him to shut up. But he wasn't going to. He felt as if he were fighting for his life here, and he was going out with a bang, not a whimper.

The agent ignored his last comment as he opened up the house and started walking through, flicking on lights.

Sam found himself blinking in a wide entrance hall with a doorway on either side and another straight ahead. The walls were a dull putty color, the timberwork heavy in its original dark stain from the 1930s, and the floor was covered with a truly repellent speckled carpet in shades of purple and brown.

Sam pulled a face and relaxed a notch. There was no way Delaney was going to buy this place. Her apartment was perfect—state-of-the-art kitchen and bathroom, soaring ceilings, great views, all the mod cons. She couldn't go from such urban perfection to this suburban hell.

Delaney waited till the agent had moved off before she spoke. "Isn't it great?"

Sam did a double take and stared at her. "Great? It's

gloomy, it smells funky, and I'm expecting one of the Munsters to pop out of a cupboard any minute now," he said. "And this carpet? Do you have any idea how many nylons died to make this carpet?"

To prove his point, he rubbed his feet up and down until he'd generated a decent static charge, then touched his finger to Delaney's arm.

"Ow!" she squealed, jumping from the static shock she'd received. "When are you going to grow up, Sam?"

It was something she'd said to him about a thousand times over the years, but it had never sounded so dark and damning before.

"Just demonstrating," he said defensively.

"Well, I guess beauty is in the eye of the beholder," she said, moving away from him.

Feeling her slipping through his fingers, Sam grabbed her arm, desperate to understand.

"Tell me what *you* see, then," he asked.

She hesitated, then shrugged. "Okay. It's got great ceilings. Nice and high, and see the period detail?" she asked, craning her neck and studying the ceiling rose. Sam followed suit and grudgingly admitted to himself that it was a pretty cool Art Deco ceiling molding.

"So...the carpet comes up, the floorboards are polished. I get rid of that junky old 1970s light fitting and find a 1930s replica. Paint the walls a nice clean neutral to bring out the timber trim and the floorboards. It'll be lovely," she said.

Sam blinked, for a moment able to see what Delaney saw. And she was right—it would look great. The entry hall was wide and welcoming as it was, and with the few cosmetic improvements she was talking about, it would shine.

Loathe to give the house anything, however, Sam just

lifted a shoulder dismissively. Delaney moved toward the first door on the left.

"Come and see the living room," she said.

They walked into another high-ceilinged space, long and broad, with two diamond-paned windows along the side, and one looking onto the front of the house. It was empty of everything except the hideous carpet, dusty mud-colored drapes, and an Art Deco era fireplace.

His heart sank as he took in the rounded curves and fluted columns of the fireplace surround and mantle. This *was* a great house—despite his burning desire to find fault with it. It was a bit faded and curled around the edges at present, but Delaney would lick it into shape. She had great taste, and endless enthusiasm, and she would get stuck into it and have it the way it should be in no time.

"Isn't the fireplace amazing?" she breathed.

Sam could only nod. "Yeah, it's pretty great," he said dully.

This was really going to happen. If the owners accepted Delaney's offer, this would be her new home. Nearly twenty minutes drive from his apartment. Unless he got a taste for suburbia and moved out here, too. And that would be just too pathetic. Once Delaney and her yet-to-be-found husband settled down, he could guess how quickly his presence would become superfluous.

Feeling sick at heart, he followed Delaney as she outlined her plans for the rest of the house. He could see her vision very clearly. He could almost see her living in her newly renovated house, surrounded by beautiful things, building a life for herself that didn't seem to have a place in it for him anymore. And when he was standing in the smallest bedroom with her, and she explained that she would make it the nursery, he had a painful flash of her standing over a crib, a tiny baby held close to her breast.

"You don't like it, do you?" Delaney asked as they walked back toward the front hallway.

"It's got a lot of potential," he said honestly. "I think you can make it amazing."

Delaney's face softened and she put her hand on his arm. Even after a weekend of nonstop sex, his body still reacted favorably to the contact. It was so inappropriate, he didn't even bother sending his nether regions a reprimand. Little Sam knew when he was pushing the envelope.

"Thanks, Sam. It means a lot that you like it."

Standing on tip-toes, she pressed a kiss to his cheek, and quickly turned away. He bit his lip and stared at the carpet.

He should say something, he knew, to stop this avalanche. There had to be something he could say that would stop Delaney from moving away from him.

He opened his mouth, willing something to come to him. But before any of his jumbled thoughts and feelings could settle into something remotely coherent, Matt had rejoined them.

"Any thoughts?" he asked, professionally chirpy.

"I want to make an offer," Delaney said firmly.

That quickly, Sam's life changed forever.

11

A WEEK AND A DAY LATER, Delaney eyed the woman sitting across from her assessingly. In her late thirties, Karen was slim, intelligent-looking and confident. She had a good sense of humor, a down-to-earth style and she seemed to genuinely love extreme sports. She'd bungee-jumped off a bridge in New Zealand, loved skydiving and had just bought herself a motocross bike. She had an exceptional résumé, having worked for several major Australian publishing giants.

"Why do you want to sell advertising for a one-horse company like Mirk after working for those big-name magazines?" Delaney asked searchingly.

"I'm getting to the age where I've got all the stuff I need—house, car, whatever. I want a life now. Don't get me wrong—I like hard work. But I don't like working for some faceless fat cat who expects me to have a nervous breakdown to line his pockets. If I'm going to pull my hair out, I want to know who I'm doing it for," Karen said. "I started out working for a small publishing company. I guess this would feel like going back to my roots, getting more involved in the day-to-day thrust of things."

Delaney nodded and made a note on her pad. On paper and in person, Karen was pretty much the perfect advertising sales manager. Delaney could already see her taking their major clients out to lunch, laughing at bawdy jokes and chugging down beers with the boys, bitching about how hard it was to meet a decent man and sipping cosmopolitans with the girls. She ticked every single box.

So why was Delaney feeling so depressed?

"When can you come back to meet Sam, Karen?" she forced herself to say. "He will, of course, be the one making the final decision."

Karen checked her diary and they made a time for later in the week. Shaking the other woman's hand, Delaney forced a smile she didn't feel and escorted her to reception. Debbie kept up her professional facade until Karen's tall frame had disappeared from view, then her eyes narrowed and she shook her head unhappily.

"Nope. She's not the one," she said dismissively.

Delaney rested her elbows on the reception desk and pretended she was doing her best to be patient. Secretly, she was thrilled that Debbie and the other staff members had been so resistant to the idea of Sam hiring a sales manager to replace her. So far, none of the interviewees had won their approval. And that was exactly the way Delaney liked it.

Too perverse, Michaels, she chastised herself. *Either you want to go or you don't. Can't have it both ways.*

"She's very cool. You guys will love her," she said enthusiastically, trying to make up for her not-so-enthusiastic thoughts.

"I've only been here two months and even I know that you leaving is a disaster," Debbie said boldly. "You and Sam are the Dream Team. It doesn't get any better than you guys. This has been the best job I've ever had."

Delaney saw with alarm that Debbie's eyes were filling with tears. Delaney couldn't even deal with her own tears, let alone someone else's. Glancing around a little desperately, she caught Sukie's eye. The Vietnamese girl shook her head wryly as Delaney indicated for her to come over and offer Debbie a shoulder to cry on.

"You owe me," Sukie mouthed silently, but she put down her filing and approached the desk.

"You okay, Debs?" she asked, sliding a sympathetic arm around Debbie's shoulders. Debbie sniffed noisily, and Sukie reached for the tissue box.

Feeling completely inadequate, Delaney patted the receptionist's arm awkwardly a couple of times before slinking away.

Truth was, she was probably going to howl like a baby when she left. She didn't have the capacity to handle anyone else's misery on top of her own. Plus, as she'd owned to herself earlier, she wasn't so great with the whole girly tears thing. Although she had a feeling she'd be getting a lot of very personal practice in the near future.

"Yo. How'd the interview go?" Sam asked as he strode back into the office, fresh from an interview with a visiting U.S.-based BMX star.

Immediately Delaney's stomach tensed. "Really well. I've made a time for you to see her on Wednesday. I think you're going to like her a lot," she said.

Sam nodded as though he didn't agree with her but wasn't about to argue the toss. "Cool."

Then he simply stood there in her office doorway, not quite looking at her, his gaze focused just beyond her shoulder. She recognized the move because it was one she'd been employing lately whenever she had to deal with him, too. Yet another of the many splendid side effects of their weekend away. They might not be fighting with each other anymore, but the cool constraint between them was driving Delaney mad. She knew she had no right to complain. She was the author of all of this, after all. She was the one who had fallen in love with Sam all those years ago and never been able to get over it. And she was the one with the stupid biological clock counting down inside her like a time bomb. Hell, she'd even suggested the dirty weekend away. All of which had left them where they were now—Awkwardville, with no sign of a reprieve anywhere in sight.

"She's got everything you're looking for," Delaney said after a long, tense silence. "She's very experienced and qualified."

"Great," Sam said stiffly. "That's great."

Then he swivelled on his heel and moved next door to his office. Delaney's shoulders sagged once he was gone, and she rubbed a hand across the back of her neck where yet another tension headache was marshaling its forces.

In the week since Daylesford, she'd averaged three or four hours of decent sleep a night, and had been knocking back aspirin as though there were no tomorrow. As though an over-the-counter painkiller could stop the ache in her heart.

It'll be over soon, she reminded herself.

But of course, that was exactly what she was afraid of.

TWO DAYS LATER, Sam ushered Karen into his office for her second interview. It took under twenty seconds for Sam to decide he liked her. She was laid-back, switched on and she obviously knew her job. He thought she'd fit in with the rest of the team well, and the fact that she had a natural passion for the subject matter of the magazine was a major bonus.

Her one and only defect was that she wasn't Delaney— but that wasn't her fault.

"So, when do you think you'll be making a decision?" Karen asked as they wound up their interview.

"Already have. If you'd like it, the job is yours," Sam said.

A part of him was freaking even as the words came out his mouth. It felt wrong to be making such a major call for the business without Delaney beside him. But this was the way it would be from now on. Mirk Publications was essentially now Kirk Publications. He was a one-man show, a mini-media mogul.

"That's great. I'd love to come on board," Karen said, grinning broadly.

Sam held out his hand and they shook to seal the deal.

"So, when can you start?" he asked, hoping he looked at least slightly pleased to have a new employee. Privately, he was wondering when he was going to wake up from this nightmare.

"I've already given notice at my old job," Karen said "Decided I was leaving no matter what. You know how it is when it's time to go."

Sam nodded, his mind instantly applying Karen's words to Delaney's decision. Was that what had happened for her? Had she just woken up one day and realized that she didn't want to be at Mirk anymore? Because he still wasn't buying the whole I-need-space-so-I-can-find-a-husband-and-start-a-family excuse.

"Would you say that's a woman thing?" Sam blurted, desperate for some kind of insight into what was going on with Delaney.

Karen blinked in surprise at the turn the conversation seemed to have taken. "Um, I'm not sure. Maybe. Haven't you ever felt like that?"

Sam thought about it, and had to admit that while he'd never felt that way about a job, there had been plenty of girlfriends whom he'd had the same experience with. A couple of weeks of casual dating was usually enough for him to see the writing on the wall. With Coco, it had been the baby talk and the poodle-kissing. A no-brainer, really. With other women it had been a variety of things, from odd personal quirks to clashing political ideologies to massively incompatible ideas about where their relationship was headed. The only woman he'd ever been able to spend large, open-ended amounts of time with was Delaney.

"I guess," he said, realizing that it was borderline inappropriate to be using his newly minted sales manager as a sounding board for his emotional confusion.

The fact that he felt the need to discuss his emotions at all was scary enough.

"So when can we have you?" he said, cycling back to his original question before he asked Karen to explain why Delaney wouldn't make eye contact with him ever since they'd come home from their weekend-of-a-lifetime at Daylesford.

"How does next week sound?" Karen asked.

Sam tried to look thrilled even as his stomach dropped like a rock. With Karen starting so soon, Delaney could leave whenever she liked.

"Excellent. We'll see you then. I'll get you a formal letter of offer tomorrow, okay?" he said.

Karen was all smiles as he saw her to the door. He stood by the reception desk staring blankly at the carpet for a long time before Debbie spoke up.

"You're not really going to let her go, are you?" she said.

Sam felt a sudden surge of anger rip through him. He wasn't *letting* Delaney go anywhere. She was extracting herself from the business, and ripping its heart out while she was at it. He'd done everything he could to stop her, and she'd just held his eye and kept restating her position. And if Debbie thought that the sense of loss she was feeling was anything compared to the gaping hole Delaney's absence would leave in his life, she had another think coming.

Debbie actually shrank back in her chair as he turned to glare at her.

"Not. My. Idea," he said through gritted teeth. Then he stalked back to his office. Halfway there, he caught sight of Delaney's questioning face as she looked up from her paperwork. She was probably wondering what had happened with the interview.

All the fight drained out of Sam and he forced himself to schlep over to her office doorway.

"I offered her the job," he said simply.

"And?"

"She took it."

For a moment, he thought he saw a flash of pain and loss in Delaney's eyes. She swallowed noisily, and blinked her eyes rapidly a number of times.

"Well, that's that, then," she said.

Sam eyed her steadily. "Haven't given her a letter of offer yet. There's still time for you to change your mind," he said.

She went very still, and Sam's heart kicked into overdrive. He'd known she didn't really want to go! He felt a surge of triumph. At last—finally—he'd called her bluff.

Then she shook her head. "No going back, Sam," she said very quietly.

He clenched his jaw, his hands curling into fists by his side. There was nothing he could do. He'd already known that. He had no choice but to stand aside and let her walk away.

"Okay," he said.

Her eyes dropped to the carpet for a long beat, then she straightened as though she was shaking off a bad thought or reminding herself of something good that lay in the near future.

"I'd better get back to this," she said, indicating her paperwork.

"Sure," Sam said. But he stood watching her for a few more moments anyway.

I don't want to lose you, Laney. The thought echoed in his mind. In his heart, he knew he already had.

A WEEK AND A HALF LATER, Delaney packed the last of her personal belongings into a box and stood back to survey her office. Dusty outlines on the bookshelves betrayed where her photo frames and souvenirs had stood, and a couple of coffee rings marred the otherwise empty surface of her desk. In every other way, all signs of her presence had been removed. The following Monday, Karen would move from the open-plan corral where she'd been camping temporarily, and the office would be hers. She'd put her own pictures on the walls, and arrange her own personal mementoes on the bookshelf. It would be as though Delaney had never been there.

Rubbing her hands along her thighs fretfully, Delaney headed for the kitchen to get a cloth and some spray cleaner. She had to keep moving. That was the only way she was going to get through the next few days. Her apartment sale was final this weekend, also, and the movers were coming first thing tomorrow to take all her worldly goods to her new house in Camberwell. And then she would be free—free to stop loving Sam, once the heartbreak had faded.

She figured she'd be ready for action again around the year 2050.

As luck would have it, Sam was at the sink rinsing out his coffee cup when she entered the kitchen, and she hovered indecisively on the threshold, unsure whether to enter into the small space or not.

She knew he was angry with her. He'd been angry with her since she'd let him hire Karen. That had been the moment of no return, and they both knew it. The apartment had been one thing, but dissolving her business partnership with him had been the king hit. And she'd made it, no matter how much it had hurt her to watch another person step into her shoes in a company that she'd helped build from the ground up. She had to get away from Sam. If she didn't—and soon—she knew she would be selling herself short for the rest of her life. Because she still ached to run her hands up his strong arms. And she still couldn't stop her eyes from dropping to the telltale bulge in his jeans whenever she thought he wasn't looking. She still sniffed the air furtively when he left a room, trying to capture a hint of his special, unique fragrance. And when she couldn't sleep at night, it was still his name that she whispered into her pillow as she pleasured herself.

Like an addict, she had to first give up her drug of choice before she could begin to recover. Even though she knew the withdrawals were going to hurt like hell.

Too late, she realized she'd lost her chance to escape as Sam caught sight of her.

"How's it going?" he asked, his tone blank of all emotion.

"Almost done. Karen can probably move her stuff in now."

"She doesn't want to step on your toes. She wants to wait until Monday," Sam explained.

A little dart of jealousy burned its way through Delaney's belly. Karen hadn't told her that. But that shouldn't have surprised her, of course—she hadn't been privy to many of the closed-door discussions Karen and Sam had had toward the latter end of the week. It was only natural, given that they were the ones who would be taking the business forward, that they would start to work more and more closely together, gradually excluding her from their meetings. After all, today was her last day. What point was there for anyone to include her in anything?

Delaney did a mental eye roll at her own childishness. It seemed she really did want everything her own way.

"That's nice of her," she finally managed to say, offering a tight little bend of the lips that might pass as a smile in certain company.

Not with Sam, of course, who knew her so well. But she suspected he wasn't about to call her on it. Honesty wasn't a big part of their relationship right now.

"Just going to clean my desk a bit," she said brightly, more to stop herself from sinking into a trough of maudlin self-pity than anything else.

Sam stepped to one side to allow her access to the sink and the utility cupboard beneath it. Again, she hesitated. She hadn't stood within arm's reach of Sam for three weeks. For a pretty fundamental reason—she didn't trust herself. But he wasn't giving her much choice in the matter, the way he was standing to one side in the small space, clearly expecting her to squeeze in and help herself to the cleaning products.

Girding her loins, she stepped forward and opened the cupboard. The bottle of spray cleaner seemed to glow like the Holy Grail as she tried not to register the waves of heat coming off Sam's body. Her nipples sprang to life and her thighs quivered as she dived toward the cupboard, her hand clutching desperately around the plastic bottle. Sam must have moved while she wasn't looking, however, and when she straightened again she found herself almost brushing against his chest, her face just inches from his.

His blue eyes were utterly unreadable as he stared down into her face. Try as she might, she couldn't stop her gaze from dropping to his sexy mouth, the memory of his kisses making her melt inside.

Then Sam stepped back, and she saw that he was holding out the washcloth in one hand.

"There you go," he said.

She took the cloth with a trembling hand, hoping like hell that he hadn't seen how much he affected her. They were supposed to be over the sex thing. That had been the whole point of their weekend, after all. For her to still want him not only broke the rules—her rules—but it was also a pretty big giveaway about how she really felt about him.

"Thanks," she said, ordering her treacherous body to back away from his.

But he was so close, and so hard and so male and so hot….

She took a jerky step backward, like a puppet fighting the will of its master. With distance came a return of rational thought, and she took another step, then another. She felt the cool surface of the fridge door behind her back, and realized she'd backed herself right into the corner. She could only imagine how revealing her actions must be, and she turned toward the door.

"Laney," Sam said, and before she could react, he'd stepped close again.

Her breath caught as he leaned toward her. He was going to kiss her. She couldn't believe it. It was so not what they'd agreed to. And it was so what she wanted, more than anything. She swayed forward, every nerve ending in her body screaming for contact with his skin.

Then Sam reached out and plucked something from her hair. "Dust bunny," he said, displaying the ball of fuzz to her.

"Right. Thanks," she said, hating herself for the surge of disappointment racing through her.

Would she never learn?

With Sam, apparently not.

Muttering insults to herself all the way back to her office, she set to cleaning it with a vengeance, even going so far as to pull all the reference books out of the bookshelf and wash the shelves down.

Occasionally, Sukie or Debbie or Rudy would wander by, their faces creased with concern as she put all her pent up sexual frustration into cleaning.

When there was nothing left to wipe, dust, polish or scour, she sat on the carpet with her back against the wall and stared into space. Squeezing the washcloth rhythmically, she tried to prepare herself for what came next—her goodbye party. She was still wringing the life out of the cloth when Rudy tapped on her office door.

"Hey. If you've finished sterilizing the office, the rest of us would kind of like to get the party started," he said.

Delaney looked up at him. "I don't think I can do this," she said brokenly.

To her surprise, Rudy crouched in front of her and grabbed her hands.

"I don't know what's going on between you and Sam," he said, "but you are one of the strongest women I know. And you always do what you set out to do. So I figure that the reason you're leaving is pretty important, yeah?"

She nodded. "Yeah."

"Then let's go rock this party," Rudy said, surging backward and using his body weight to counterbalance hers and pull her to her feet.

Delaney's eye fell on one of the photos in her box as she moved toward the door. It was a picture of Travis, Callum and Alana, a lovely candid shot of them playing with each other and laughing, their eyes bright with delight.

Yes, she reminded herself, one hand moving instinctively to rest on her stomach. *Yes. Rudy is right. Stick to your guns.*

Pulling her shoulders back, she stepped out into the main office, a big smile on her face.

"Who's got some champagne for a thirsty lady?"

SAM HOVERED ON THE EDGE of the party all night, watching the others talk and laugh and reminisce, nursing one warm beer for hours on end. He didn't want to get drunk. He had a speech to make. And he was already pretty damned worried about getting through it without cracking up as it was—a skinful of beer wasn't going to help any.

He alternated between drinking in every move Delaney made to being unable to look at her, he was so gripped with anger and frustration. This wasn't supposed to happen. They were friends. Friendship lasted when romance died and marriage vows soured and love turned to acrimony and revenge. Friendship endured. Didn't it? So why was it suddenly as though he and Delaney were sitting at opposite ends of a too-long dining table, unable to hear each other, barely able to see each other any more?

Most of his anger was at himself. He had ruined their relationship when he'd been unable to keep his hands to himself. He'd broken the golden rule of their friendship and he'd jumped Delaney, and now he was reaping the reward.

Stirring from his glum preoccupation, he registered that Debbie was trying to get his attention over at the entrance to the kitchen. She mimed blowing out candles on a cake, and Sam nodded his acknowledgement. Cake and speeches time. Great.

Everyone started hooting and hollering as the cake came out. Sam wondered sourly what the candles were supposed to represent—the flaming mess he'd made of his life?

Delaney laughed and joked with the others before stepping up to blow out the candles. Debbie shot Sam another prompting look, and he cleared his throat.

"Right. Well, I guess it's time for me to say a few words," he said, awkwardly stating the obvious.

He'd thought long and hard about what he wanted to say, he'd even made some notes, but as Delaney lifted her eyes to his it all fell away from him.

"Delaney and I have been friends for more than half my life," he found himself saying. "We've been pretty much inseparable since we first met, so it only seemed natural to start up a business together eight years ago. To be honest, I think we both secretly thought it would never get beyond a few ideas jotted on the back of a napkin. But here we are, and it's largely thanks to Delaney keeping me on the straight and narrow. I think we all know that Delaney's departure is going to leave a big hole round here, not just from a business point of view, but because she's the heart and soul of this company. She's the one who remembers birthdays and makes sure people go home when they're sick. She tells the best jokes, makes the best coffee. She's always there—the most reliable, present, loyal person I know."

Sam couldn't take his gaze away from Delaney's.

"We're going to miss you too much for me to be able to put it into words," he said, then he had to clear his throat or risk giving into the tide of emotion rising within him. "We love you, Laney. Don't be a stranger," he finally managed to say.

Delaney's eyes welled with tears and she wiped at them self-consciously.

"Come on, Delaney, right of reply," Sukie said, nudging her gently.

"No fair! Not while I'm blubbering," Delaney said, but she

took a couple of deep breaths and Sam could see she was making a visible effort to recover.

"All right. This business has been incredibly important to me. It's a huge part of my life, the best part, really," she began. Sam stared at her, willing her to make eye contact with him again. After a few seconds, she did, and they held the contact as she continued.

"And I know I'm walking away before any of the really great stuff happens. There'll be more titles, I know, and more successes. And Sam will get fat and rich and lazy."

There were a few laughs at this, but Sam didn't crack a smile.

"None of you will ever understand how hard it was for me to make the decision to go," Delaney said. Sam felt as though she were speaking directly to him. "I love coming here. I love working with you all. I'm incredibly proud of everything we do. And I'm going to miss you all like crazy and wonder what the hell I was thinking once the dust settles. But it's time to go, so… Thank you, everyone, for being so kind," she said, tears spilling openly down her cheeks now.

Sam grit his teeth for the next bit.

"We wanted to get you something to remember us by," he said, fumbling awkwardly in his pocket.

Delaney went very still as he handed over the small gift-wrapped box. He watched as she tore the paper off with trembling hands, and he heard her quick intake of breath as she flipped the jeweller's box open.

"Sam…I don't know what to say. They're beautiful," she said.

He had to swallow a few times before he could trust himself to speak again.

"They match your eyes."

Everyone crowded around to admire the gold-and-topaz

drop earrings he'd bought for her. He'd spent a whole afternoon trawling the shops during the week, trying to find something that expressed how precious she was to him. Nothing came even close. Finally, he settled on the earrings, since the deep amber of their glowing topazes was the exact shade of Delaney's eyes.

The goodbyes began in earnest then as everyone crowded around to hug and kiss Delaney farewell. Sam drifted back to the same piece of wall he'd been propping up all night and brooded some more. It was like watching a horror film unfolding in slow motion. He knew that something horrible was coming, but he couldn't do anything about it.

Finally the last of the staff had wiped their tears and said their goodbyes. Debbie started to clear up the dirty glasses and plates, but Sam stopped her.

"I'll do that. Thanks, Debbie. You go home," he said.

She smiled her thanks and followed the others out the door. Sam didn't need to look to know that it was just the two of them left.

"I'll help you," Delaney said, reaching for some paper cups.

"You're not cleaning up after your own leaving party," Sam said, wincing at how harshly his voice came out.

Delaney let the paper cups drop back onto the table.

"All right. If that's what you want," she said. "You're the boss now, after all."

It was a lame joke, and neither of them laughed. Sam strode into the kitchen and grabbed the rubbish bin, afraid that if he lingered, he'd start begging and pleading with her not to go.

It wasn't that he was too proud to beg or plead—it was more that he knew it wouldn't make a difference.

He tossed paper cups and plates into the bin methodically for the next few minutes, throwing leftover food away without a hint of guilt. He couldn't imagine ever having an appetite again, so there was no point in saving food that would never get eaten.

Delaney had retreated to her office to sort out the last of her things, and he watched surreptitiously as she wrote some last minute notes for Karen

When she turned to heft the box of her personal things, he stopped what he was doing and moved to her office doorway.

"What if I gave you back your half of the magazine, no charge?" he asked.

Okay, maybe he hadn't quite exhausted the begging option just yet.

"Sam..." she said, her mouth quirking into a sad little smile. "This is hard enough as it is."

"Then don't go."

Her eyes filled with tears and she put the box down so she would wipe them away.

"Whatever it takes, Laney. Tell me, and it's yours. Just don't leave me like this," Sam said. It was a plea from the heart, the absolute truth of how he felt.

"It's not about you. It's about me," she said.

He screwed his face up with frustration. "What does that even mean? It sounds like something I've said about a million times to some girl I wanted to break up with."

Delaney's expression became shuttered, and she bent to grab the box again. Sam stepped forward, reaching for the carton in her arms.

"Talk to me. Tell me why you're really going," he insisted, trying to wrest the box from her.

Delaney held on, her jaw firming. "There's nothing to talk about," she said, her grip tightening on the box.

"Put the bloody thing down and talk to me," Sam insisted.

He didn't know what else he could say to her. He just knew that if he let her walk out the door, it would all be over.

"No."

For a moment they struggled, the box wavering back and forth between them. Delaney was strong, and she had a good grip on the corners of the carton, but Sam was no less determined. After a few drawn-out seconds, Delaney abruptly let go of the box, sending Sam reeling backward a few steps.

"Take it. Send it to me by courier," she said, moving toward the door.

He threw the box to one side and dodged into her path.

"Laney," he said warningly.

"There's nothing left to say, Sam," she said, her voice rising.

"Well, maybe I don't want to talk anyway," he said, reaching out to haul her against his body.

It was the closest they'd been since their weekend away, and his body reacted instantaneously as he pressed himself against her.

"I've missed you, Laney," he said as he peppered kisses on her neck, shamelessly taking advantage of the fact that he knew it was a particularly erotic zone for her.

She groaned low in her throat, half protest, half capitulation, and then she turned her face toward his questing lips and their mouths meshed. He had forgotten how hot he could get just from kissing her. Her tongue stroked his, and her lips were soft and full. Angling his head, he strove for deeper access.

His hands gravitated to her torso, smoothing up over the fabric of her tight T-shirt and cupping her breasts. She strained toward him as he rubbed her aroused nipples through her top, her hips bucking reflexively when he pinched the tight peaks gently.

"Yes," she moaned, her hands racing across his back, down

to his butt, and then around to the front of his jeans where his erection was throbbing with need.

He grit his teeth as she smoothed her hand against his length, her fingers curling around his shaft through the softness of the worn denim.

Hungry for her, he started walking Delaney back toward the desk. He had to have her. He needed her. He wanted her.

He'd forgotten about the box, however, and they stumbled to a halt as her heels connected with it. Dazed, Delaney stared down at the carton filled with photos and books and mementoes for a long, drawn out beat, and when she lifted her eyes back to his face he knew that he'd lost her.

"We made a deal, Sam," she said, reminding him of their agreement that their weekend away was the end of anything physical between them.

"You want it. I know you want it," he said, grinding his hips into hers. Her pupils dilated and she caught her breath, but still she shook her head.

"We drew a line, and we're sticking to it," she said, stepping away from him now.

"It was a stupid line, and I say we break it," he insisted, reaching for her again.

"We can't." Her tone was clipped and firm, indisputable.

Sam's temper flared as she stooped to pick up her stupid bloody carton of belongings again.

"What about what I want?" he said. "You've had everything your way since this whole thing started. What about what I want to happen?"

She eyed him carefully. "So what *do* you want, Sam? Apart from sex at the moment, and for everything to go back to the way it used to be?"

"And what's wrong with any of that?" he asked belligerently. "Haven't you been happy here for the past eight years? Because if you haven't been, you're the best damned actress I've ever met. Next you'll be telling me you faked all those orgasms I gave you."

"You just don't get it, do you?" Delaney shouted back. "You're happy as long as you have everything you need—the magazine ticking along nicely, me to keep you company whenever you feel like it and some handy hottie in your bed whenever you get a bit horny. Well, I want more than that from my life, Sam Kirk! I want someone to hold me at night and children to love. I want a family."

Her words resonated with something deep inside him, but he ignored it and continued to give vent to his hurt.

"Fine. Am I stopping you from getting it? I just don't understand why you have to leave the business and sell your apartment to have a family," he yelled, all the frustration of the past few months at last finding an outlet. "I feel as though I'm being punished or something. I'm your *friend,* Delaney."

All the fight went out of her then. Her shoulders slumped and she lost the feverish, angry glint in her eye.

"I'm doing you a favor, you just don't know it yet," she said quietly.

"Great. More goddamned riddles," he said, throwing his hands in the air.

"Sam, look at us. We've been friends for sixteen years. We live above each other. We work with each other. Why do you think none of your relationships last? Why do you think I've been single all these years?"

Sam stared at her. She nodded.

"You see what I mean? There is no *room* in our lives for anyone else."

Suddenly Sam got it.

"You're leaving because of me? Because of our friendship?" he asked, stunned.

"Because I want a family. And I will never have one while you and I fill the gaps in one another's lives," she said.

"And that's why you've sold your apartment. You're moving to get away from me," Sam stated flatly.

It was all painfully clear to him now. And he couldn't believe it—Delaney was choosing some unknown, yet-to-be formed family over their friendship.

"Yes. I am."

He felt as though he'd been sucker punched. It had all been there, of course. If he'd bothered to get his head out of his butt long enough to make the connections.

"So what was our weekend away about?" he asked, all the certainties in his world torn lose from their moorings.

"It was goodbye, Sam."

He stared at her, seeing the tremble in her lips, the moisture in her eyes, but for a split second hating her for what she was saying, what she was doing. She was the center of his world and she was dumping him like last season's designer fashions so she could make room for her new life.

He felt sick and angry and overwhelmed.

Silence sat thick and heavy between them, and finally Delaney swallowed audibly and moved toward the door.

"I'm sorry, Sam," she said.

And then she left him.

12

DELANEY'S SISTER opened the door after the third knock, her face creased into a frown of impatience over the lateness of the hour. The irritated look faded the moment she saw it was Delaney on the doorstep. Still clutching her stupid box of things from the office, Delaney just stared at her sister for a miserable couple of seconds, the tears sliding silently down her face.

"Come inside, you duffer," Claire said gently.

Delaney hiccupped noisily. "I was going to go home. But then I couldn't face being alone, so I told the taxi driver to come here," she sobbed. "I know it's late. I didn't wake the kids up, did I?"

"They sleep like little rocks once they drop off. They're fine," Claire assured her. "Come on, I'll make you a coffee."

"Okay," Delaney sniffed, happy to have her sister take charge for the moment.

"Are we drunk as well as heartbroken?" her sister asked conversationally as she set the kettle boiling.

"No. Just tragic. Same old same old."

"You're not tragic for loving Sam, Delaney."

Delaney made a face. "Feels like it from where I'm sitting."

"What happened to bonking him until you could bonk no more? I give you good advice, and you ignore it," Claire said wryly.

"I did not! Sam and I went away for the weekend three weeks ago, I'll have you know," Delaney said indignantly.

"And?"

"And we had the most amazing two days on record. Then it finished, and that was that. And no, it didn't burn anything out," Delaney reported heavily.

"Hmm," Claire said, looking a little guilty.

"What?" Delaney asked.

"Well…I didn't really have a lot of faith in the burning-out theory, to be honest," Claire said. "I was just kind of banking on Sam getting his act together and realizing that you're his dream woman."

Delaney stared at her sister. "You tricked me?"

"Hey, you still got a whole weekend of sensational sex as a consolation prize. Don't go feeling ripped off about it," Claire said defensively.

"What about all that stuff about things losing their luster, blah, blah?" Delaney asked.

"I know. I can really talk a load of horse-hooey when I want to, can't I?" Claire said proudly. "I think it's all those pretend tea parties with Alana. It's really cultivated my creative side."

Delaney couldn't help laughing ruefully. The truth was, she'd wanted that weekend for herself, all other ulterior motives aside. She couldn't regret it, even though it made leaving Sam so much more painful.

Claire slid a cup of coffee across the kitchen counter toward Delaney.

"You want me to make up the spare bed again?" she asked.

Delaney wrapped her hands around the mug and inhaled the fresh aroma. Just the promise of caffeine gave her strength.

"No. I'd better go home. The movers are coming first

thing, and I've still got to pack my books and DVDs." She said it flatly, as though she was talking about her imminent appearance before a shooting squad.

"You're moving into your new house, Laney. That's something to be excited about, isn't it?" Claire said, walking around the kitchen counter and sliding an arm over her shoulders.

"Yeah, I know."

"I predict that in a year's time you will be in love with someone else and on the way to being married and knocked up," Claire said brightly.

Making an effort, Delaney crossed her fingers. "Here's hoping."

The sound of small footsteps sounded in the hallway, and they both turned to see Travis easing his way into the room. At six years old, he was all eyes and teeth and hair, his toddler's body having well and truly morphed into a long, skinny little boy's frame. He was dressed in cartoon character shorty pyjamas, and he rubbed his eyes theatrically with his knuckles.

"I can't sleep, Mommy," he said. Then he saw Delaney, and he instantly put aside the playacting as his eyes lit up. "Aunty Delaney!" he said, racing across the room to give her a hug.

She hoisted him onto her lap, figuring that he wasn't too old to have a proper cuddle with his aunt.

"Hey there, big guy. Isn't it a bit late for you to be out of bed?" she said, pressing kisses onto his soft cheeks.

Travis pulled away, his face wrinkling into an expression of distaste.

"Ugh!"

"Mmm. Forgot to tell you. Kisses are out now that he's at school. Hugging is still cool, though," Claire informed her.

"Ah."

"Come on, mister, let's get you back to bed," Claire said,

lifting Travis out of Delaney's arms. "I won't be a tick," she said as she disappeared down the hallway toward the bedrooms.

Delaney took a contemplative sip of her coffee while she waited.

She'd just walked away from a man and a life that meant the world to her in the hope that she still had a chance at having a family of her own. Not for the first time, she wondered whether she was being greedy. Maybe she should have just been content to have a great job and a great apartment and a great friendship with Sam. Maybe she should have channeled all her frustrated maternal instincts into being the best, most amazing aunt in the world, and counted herself lucky that her life was rich and full and that, even if her love was secret, she was an important part of Sam's world.

"It's too late, Delaney," she told her coffee cup. "You've made your decision, you've jumped. Now you just have to fall until you hit the bottom."

And she had a horrible feeling that she was going to hit hard once the reality of a Sam-free world sank in.

SAM LOOKED UP from the copy he was editing to find Karen in his office doorway.

"Hey, Sam—have you got a moment?" she asked, uncharacteristically tentative.

In the two weeks since Delaney had moved on, he'd gotten to know his new advertising sales manager a lot better. He'd made the right decision as far as the team went. Despite their intense loyalty to Delaney, he could see that they were beginning to like and respect Karen on her own terms, which was as it should be. Now he just had to work on his own little hang-up where she was concerned.

"Sure. Grab a seat," Sam said.

Pushing his copy to one side, he put on his best grown-up professional face. It was strange being the sole owner of Mirk Publications. It wasn't until Delaney had gone that he understood that sharing the burden of management with her had made a huge difference to how he felt about the business. In the past two weeks, he'd had to deal with a number of issues solo, and he'd felt severely handicapped, like a newly separated Siamese twin. No one to bounce ideas off. No one to whinge or bitch to. No one to work late with. All the joy had gone out of the magazine, and he'd even found himself rifling through his desk drawers, looking for the file he'd kept of the offers they'd received over the years to buy the magazine. For the first time ever, he'd allowed himself to toy with the idea of selling out, too.

"So, what's up?" he said, forcing his mind to the matter at hand.

"I wanted to talk to you about us," Karen said a little awkwardly. "Our relationship."

Sam shifted uncomfortably in his chair as his man senses began to tingle. Where exactly was she going with this? As far as he knew, they didn't have a *relationship,* apart from employer and employee. A sudden thought occurred, and he tensed. Surely Karen wasn't one of those bunny-boiling women, the type who latched onto unsuspecting men and stalked them to death?

"Um. *Okaaaaayyyyy.* What exactly did you have in mind…?" he said cautiously, pushing his chair a little farther away from her.

She grinned. "You don't have to freak, Sam. I'm not about to wig out on you. I just wanted to clear the air, because Delaney's been gone a while now and you still seem to be having trouble spending more than five minutes in my company."

Sam blinked. "I don't think that's true," he said stiffly.

"Well, it is. I walk into a meeting, you walk out. Even with clients you find an excuse to go make a call or order coffee or something. So. What's going on?" Karen said.

Feeling cornered, he stood and moved behind his chair, resting his hands on top of it.

"See. You're trying to come up with an excuse to get me out of your office right now, aren't you?" Karen guessed shrewdly.

He twitched—he *had* been about to fob her off, claiming he had an interview to get to.

"I know you must miss her like crazy," Karen said gently. "But it's bad for office morale and it's bad for business and it's not much fun for me being the stinky kid all the time."

Sam stared at her for a moment, then he slumped back into his chair and put his head in his hands.

"I'm sorry. I'm just…I'm sorry. I didn't realize I was doing it."

"I know. For what it's worth, I wish that I'd had as much impact on a place where I worked as Delaney seems to have done here. I kind of wish I'd had a chance to work with her longer."

"Yeah. She gets you like that," Sam said, a smile tugging at the corners of his mouth. God, he missed her.

"But she *has* gone," Karen said. Her tone was firm but kind. "And we all need to move forward. Don't you agree?"

Sam nodded. "Yes, of course. Listen, why don't we organize some catering tomorrow, and we'll put on a lunch for the gang? Hang out for a while as a team," he suggested.

"Great idea. I'll talk to Sukie," Karen said.

Standing, she gave Sam a cheeky look. "New record—a whole fifteen minutes in the same room with me," she said.

Sam smiled guiltily. "I'm sorry," he said again.

She waved his apology off. "It's cool. Don't sweat it."

The smile dropped from Sam's mouth as soon as she was gone. He couldn't believe he'd been so unaware of his own behavior. Poor Karen, feeling like a leper for the past two weeks while he wallowed in his loss.

The truth was, he'd been reluctant to get to know and like Karen as his new colleague because then he would have felt as though he had truly replaced Delaney. It would have felt like the last step in letting her go.

He'd been so angry with her when she'd walked out on him that night after revealing that the reason she was leaving was because she didn't "have room" in her life for him *and* a family. He'd felt betrayed. Abandoned. Discarded. What about their years of friendship? All the memories, all the good times? No one knew her better—no one. And she suddenly didn't value that anymore? It had made his blood boil for the first few days and he'd stomped around and growled at staff and hit the skate park hard.

But slowly loneliness had risen up to swamp his anger. His apartment was an empty box, and he rattled around inside it pointlessly each night. Below, he could hear the sounds of the new owner moving around in Delaney's apartment. The muffled beat of music playing downstairs, or the sound of a door opening and closing had always meant that Delaney was there—where she was supposed to be, near him. But now she was gone, and the same sounds only seemed to accentuate his loneliness.

He missed her. His chest ached with it. He couldn't sleep, food tasted like cardboard, nothing could hold his attention for more than five or ten minutes. He was a wreck.

So many times he'd picked up the phone to call her, or

started to drive toward her new house. But each time he'd stopped himself. What was he going to say to her? She'd made her feelings more than clear. She wanted a family more than she valued her friendship with him. It was that simple.

He just had to get used to the idea that she was no longer a part of his world.

The phone ringing in the outer office snapped Sam out of his reverie. He'd been doing too much sitting around and moping lately. He'd become a pathetic TV dinner man, staring slack-jawed at the tube at night, or sitting numb and senseless at his desk during the day. Something had to give.

Reaching for the phone, he dialed a number from heart. Charlie was always good for a night out. Charlie answered on the third ring and Sam arranged to meet his mate for a beer after work.

He felt a ridiculous sense of satisfaction when he ended the call. He was going out into the world after two weeks of mourning. It could only be a good thing.

He wasn't so sure when he walked into the local pub after six that night. The smell of beer and fried food and the raucous sound of other people's laughter and conversation combined to present a seemingly impenetrable wall of activity. He didn't want to be around other people, he realized. This had been a mistake. He hesitated on the threshold, ready to retreat back to his monk's existence in his apartment. But Charlie had already spotted him, and he raised a hand and waved to get Sam's attention.

Gritting his teeth, Sam wove his way through the tables to join his friend at the bar.

"Kirk!" Charlie said affectionately, giving Sam the kind of half hug, half thump on the back that signaled they were old friends.

"Kenner. Nice to see you took your tie off at least," Sam said, trying to sound like his normal self. He always gave Charlie a hard time for being a corporate slave.

"Those of us who work for a living have to dress to impress. I'll explain it to you sometime," Charlie said, shoving a cold beer in Sam's direction.

Sam forced himself to take a mouthful of beer.

"So, how have things been?" Charlie asked.

"Great. Really good," Sam lied.

"Look like you've lost a bit of weight. Want to tell me the secret?" Charlie said, patting his own slightly paunchy belly.

Sam stared down into his beer. "Delaney left the business"

He hadn't meant to say that. This evening was supposed to be about forgetting Delaney, moving on, but suddenly he needed to talk about her desperately.

"She came back from holidays with her sister and announced that she wanted to sell me her half of the magazine. Just like that. No discussion, nothing."

"Wow. So you bought her out?"

"Had to. Had no choice," Sam said bitterly.

"And she never explained why the sudden change of heart?" Charlie asked.

"She wants to find a husband, have kids. Biological clock stuff."

Charlie raised his eyebrows. "Right. Can't argue with that."

"Sold her apartment, too. Moved out to Camberwell," Sam explained.

And I can't stop thinking about her, he wanted to add. *I dream about her every night. I imagine holding her, touching her, being inside her. I crave the sound of her voice, the smell of her perfume, the look she gets in her eye when she's about to have a go at me.*

"So you're the big boss now. How you liking that?" Charlie asked, reaching for some pretzels from the bowl on the bar.

"It's fine. Not that different, really," Sam lied. The office was a desert without her. He could barely stand to look in her office because he knew he'd see Karen sitting at Delaney's desk. It was wrong. The whole world was wrong.

"Guess we're all getting to that age, though, eh? Starting to think about the future, what it's all about. Not much point working like a dog when you've got no one to come home to and share it all with."

"Yeah."

Sam realized with a rush of mortification that he was dangerously close to losing it. He pushed his beer away. No more alcohol for him if it only took half a glass to reduce him to a gibbering wreck.

"I was seeing a woman recently," Charlie admitted after a long silence. "Did I tell you about Petra? Works in the office."

Charlie turned his beer glass in circles on the bar, staring at the wet marks it left behind.

"Started thinking about buying a ring, you know? Swapping the Porsche for a family wagon. Then she dumped me. Said she wasn't sure if she loved me or not."

Sam winced at the resentment and bewilderment in his friend's voice. He knew exactly how he was feeling.

"Just like Laney. One minute everything's cruisey, the next minute you're on your own, can't see them for dust," he said.

"Well, it's not quite the same. I mean, you and Delaney were never romantic. It's a bit different for me and Petra." Charlie gave a little huff of embarrassed laughter. "Haven't felt this shit about a woman since high school."

Sam was still stinging from Charlie's assumption that his pain over losing Petra trumped Sam's hurt over losing Delaney.

"Let me guess—can't sleep. Feels like there's sandpaper under your eyelids. Everything tastes like crap. You want to drink yourself stupid, but every time you have even a single beer you almost cry. You want to ring her half the time, the other half you want to write her off and never think about her again. How am I doing?" Sam asked a little belligerently.

Charlie blinked. "I didn't know you and Delaney were involved. I thought you were just mates," he said.

"We are. Were. I mean… We did cross the line recently, if you know what I mean. But it was just a stress thing," Sam explained awkwardly.

Charlie gave him a sceptical look. "So you and Delaney slept with each other, and she's gone and you're sitting here looking like a big sad sack, and you're just friends?"

"Yeah," Sam said uncertainly.

"And you don't love her? You're not sitting at home alone every night staring at the TV, eating frozen dinners?"

Sam stared at his friend, a frown forming as something shifted inside him. He missed Delaney. He wanted to spend all his time with her. He wanted to touch her, hold her. He wanted to make her laugh, and protect her from the world. Most of all, he wanted to be the most important person in her life, the one she turned to instinctively when she needed support.

He loved her!

Sam's eyes nearly bugged out of his head as the realization hit him. He loved Delaney. He adored her, worshipped her, craved her, was obsessed by her. He wanted to father her children. Be her husband and helpmate, the companion of her old age. He wanted everything, as much of her as she was willing to give him.

"I am *such* a moron," he said.

How long had he felt this way? He cast his mind back over

the years, remembering the way he'd always avoided talking about her love life, the way he'd never dared think of her as a woman. A long time. He'd felt this way for a long time.

A second realization hit him, and he slumped forward on his bar stool. He loved Delaney—and she'd left him. She'd left him to start a family. With some other man, some yet-to-be-decided man who would get to spend the rest of his life with the most amazing, stunning, sensual, clever, funny, brave woman he'd ever known.

"Shit," he said, reaching for his beer and downing the remaining half glass in one big mouthful. "Shit."

Charlie patted him on the pack reassuringly. "Don't worry. After a few months the pain becomes kind of bearable."

"Months?" Sam asked incredulously. It would take him years to get over Delaney.

If he was stupid enough to let her go. He stood, desperation spurring him on. He knew what he had to do.

"Here," he said, throwing a twenty on the bar.

Charlie looked confused. "You going somewhere or something?"

"Yeah. I think I am. I'm sorry—I'll explain later," Sam said over his shoulder, already heading for the door.

He was in his car and on the way to Delaney's place in under thirty seconds, his jaw set grimly as he dodged in and out of traffic, determined to get to Delaney without wasting another precious second.

He couldn't live without her. He needed her. He had to get her back.

He knew what she wanted—she'd been telling him exactly what she wanted for the past month. A family. Children. He had to convince her that she could have those things with him.

He gripped the steering wheel with steely resolve. He knew he'd never been a candidate for the role of husband in her mind. She'd never so much as hinted at it. Hell, she'd come back from holidays with her sister and neatly gone about excising him from her life—that was how much she didn't think of him like that. So he wouldn't scare her off with a declaration right off the bat. He could only imagine her reaction if he came clean about his feelings. They'd been friends for sixteen years. He couldn't just announce his realization to her and expect her to return his feelings. But he wouldn't sit back and let her marry someone else, either. If he could get her to marry him, he would spend the rest of his life bringing her around to his way of thinking. He already knew they were spectacular in bed. And they were the best of friends. Love would come. He was sure of it.

He just had to convince Delaney to take a chance on him, prove to her that friendship and sexual chemistry were great foundations for a marriage. If he had to, he'd seduce her down the aisle. Whatever it took.

Because he wasn't taking no for an answer.

DELANEY STEPPED BACK from the wall and tilted her head to one side. Wrinkling her nose, she made a disgusted noise. This was the sixth off-white paint sample she'd tried, and it still wasn't right. Turning back to the color chart, Delaney frowned. There had to be one color that didn't completely repel her.

Problem was, she was finding it difficult to make choices about lots of things lately. It was almost as though she'd used up all her strength of will in making the break from Sam. Now she was adrift in a sea of indecision. Soon, she knew, she would have to start looking for a new job. And the contractors were waiting for her to finalize her decisions about wall color and fittings and carpet.

And all she could think about was Sam.

Two weeks. It had only been two weeks since she'd left the magazine and her apartment. It felt like an eternity. She had no idea how she was going to survive without him.

The doorbell rang, and Delaney schlepped her way up the hallway to the front door. She didn't care that she was dressed in ragged cutoff jeans and a ratty old T-shirt with no bra. She didn't even care that her fancy new hair color was starting to grow out or that she hadn't styled it properly a single time since she'd left Mink. There was only one person who she wanted to impress, and he'd seen her at her best and her worst and passed on both versions.

Damn you, Sam Kirk, she thought as she twisted the front door lock open. *Damn your gorgeous eyes.*

"Laney."

She stared at Sam, her heart going from nought to a hundred in record time.

"Sam."

"Can I come in?"

Delaney mutely stood to one side, instantly aware that she looked like a refugee from a home makeover show with her shabby clothes and paint-spattered hands and forearms.

Feeling at a distinct disadvantage, she ushered Sam into the living room. Her couches were all covered with drop cloths, and she gestured around helplessly.

"I'm not really set up for visitors," she said.

Sam eyed her steadily. "I'm not a visitor."

There was something very determined and grave about him, and a flutter of nervousness raced up her spine. She'd wanted to come up with an excuse to make contact with him so many times over the past two weeks. But seeing him now, she realized why she hadn't— it was torture wanting to touch him and not being allowed to.

"Do you want coffee?" she asked, keen to buy some time to find her feet.

"Do you still want to have kids? And get married?"

As a rejoinder, it was something of an attention grabber.

"What? Why?"

"Just answer the questions."

She studied him a moment before nodding. "Yes. To all of the above."

"Then marry me," Sam said boldly.

It was so close to every dream that she'd ever had that for a moment she couldn't believe what she was hearing.

"I—I don't…" she stuttered, utterly bewildered, the beginning of hope starting to bloom in her belly.

Sam moved forward, taking one of her hands in his. Despite the fact that most of her was reeling, she still found time to marvel at the instant spark of desire that raced along her veins from that simple, casual contact.

"Don't make fun of me, Sam," she blurted tremulously.

"I'm not," he said, his fingers caressing hers as he stared into her face intently. "I had a beer with Charlie tonight, and we were talking about marriage and kids. And I realized that I could never imagine having any of those things without you."

She shook her head, trying to clear it. "I don't understand."

"I know you better than anyone else in the world, don't I?" he asked.

She nodded.

"And you know me better than I know myself. We work well with each other, we respect each other, we seem to be pretty damned compatible in bed. We make a great team,

Laney. You want kids. That's what this is all about, isn't it? I think we'd make great parents."

Delaney stared at him, hope shriveling once again inside her. This was what she'd always wanted—almost. It was picture-perfect, with one fatal blemish; Sam wasn't looking into her eyes and telling her how much he loved her. He wasn't telling her how he couldn't live without her and how he stayed awake at night thinking about her and how he wanted to spend the rest of his life with her. He was proposing a relationship based on compatibility, comfort, familiarity. Sure, there was love there. There had always been love. But not Love. Not the kind that rippled through every fiber of her being when Sam so much as glanced in her direction.

Unable to think clearly with Sam standing so close, Delaney tugged her hand free and walked over to stare out the window. She was trembling. And she knew why—she was tempted. She was so tempted, she didn't know if she had the strength of will to send Sam packing.

She loved him with all her heart. And he was offering her her dream—him in her bed, his children to nurture and love, a family. With just that one vital ingredient missing. But she'd lived so long on only the promise of Sam's love—sixteen years. Would it be so bad if she could have everything else? Would it matter that he didn't love her the way she loved him?

"Laney, I've missed you so much. Nothing is the same without you," Sam said from close behind her, and she felt the faint hush of his breath against her hair before his lips pressed against the tender skin of her neck. She shuddered, a wash of liquid heat instantly rushing to her core.

"We'd be happy, wouldn't we?" Sam murmured in her ear as he slid his arms around her body.

She groaned low in her throat as his hands came up to cover her breasts.

"We'd make great babies, Laney. A little girl who looks like you, a little troublemaker brother for her to keep in line. We can fix this place up, make it your dream home. Whatever you want. You name it, it's yours," he whispered in her ear.

She could feel how aroused he was, the length of his erection pushing against the curve of her bottom.

"Say yes, Laney," he said, his fingers plucking relentlessly at her breasts.

She couldn't think. She didn't want to think. She wasn't strong enough to hold out on principle. She loved him. She wanted him. If that meant she was accepting second best, then so be it.

"Yes," she said, turning in his arms. Reaching up to cup his face with her hands, she looked deeply into his eyes. "Yes. I'll marry you, Sam."

He swooped down, his mouth taking hers in a fiery, almost savage kiss. Then he bent and scooped her up in his arms.

"Which one's the bedroom?" he asked, already striding out into the hallway.

Delaney pointed at a doorway, too busy pressing hungry kisses to his throat to speak. Sam dropped her on the bed, quickly climbing on top to press his body against the length of hers.

"I've missed you so much," he murmured as he nuzzled his way into the neckline of her T-shirt.

"Me, too," she admitted.

Tears pricked at the back of her eyelids as Sam began to peel her top off. It was almost perfect, being with him like this. Almost.

But Sam's hands were already sliding beneath the waistband of her cutoffs, his clever fingers delving into the wet heat between her thighs. She had this much. She would have to learn to be content. School herself not to give away her feelings.

It was better than nothing, and a whole lot more of him than she'd ever thought she'd have.

Pushing away everything but her desire, she gave herself up to the fire growing inside her. It would be good…even if it wasn't everything.

THE BEDROOM WAS FILLED with the bright, clear light of morning when she awoke. It took a moment for memory to return, and she stiffened. Sam had come calling. He'd asked her to marry him, and she'd said yes. They'd rushed straight to the bedroom and raced each other to climax. Afterward, Sam had curled his body around hers and she'd told herself that a few stupid words were not worth giving up something so compelling and precious.

She frowned as she tried to work out whether she still held to that belief in the cold light of day. Without Sam's body pressed against hers, his breath in her ear, it was easier to think.

It wasn't her dream. Some people might think it fell far short of her dream. But she wasn't going to push Sam away; she loved him too much. And if that made her weak…then so be it.

For the first time, she allowed her imagination to quest forward into the future. Sam as her husband. Sam as father to her children. Sam coming home to her bed every night. A smile began to stretch her mouth. There was a lot to celebrate in all those thoughts. A hell of a lot.

Anticipating one particular attraction of the arrangement, she rolled over, determined to wake Sam in the best possible way. She stilled as she saw the other side of the bed was empty. Putting out a hand, she felt the sheets. They were cold.

Not even daring to think, she slid out of bed and grabbed her robe.

"Sam?" she called as she padded out into the hall.

Nothing. Her voice echoed hollowly off the newly stripped floorboards. A dread certainty growing inside her, Delaney checked the kitchen and the bathroom and even the backyard. Nothing. Sam was gone.

It didn't escape her attention that she'd played this game before—after she and Sam had slept with each other the first time.

She froze in the middle of the kitchen, all her fears rising up to flood her. She could see it like a movie in her mind—Sam had woken up, remembered his impulsive proposal of the night before, and quietly freaked out. Utilizing his years of experience as a sexual hit-and-runner, he'd slithered out of bed and let himself out of her house. No doubt he was now at the local skate park, or on his way to a surf beach somewhere to try and sort himself out.

Suddenly she was having trouble breathing. Curling her hands into fists, she pressed them against her too-hot eyes. She wasn't going to cry. Not over Sam. Not again. And, anyway, she was angry, not sad. He'd suckered her in with his vision of the future, and she'd allowed herself to believe in him.

But she'd known all along that she was buying a pipe dream. Sam didn't do commitment. He didn't want a family and a house in the suburbs. He wanted her—on his terms. She'd scared him with her abrupt withdrawal, and he'd talked himself into giving her what she wanted in order to regain the old footing of their relationship.

It was never going to work. And she was a deluded fool for even trying for a second. He was going to rip her heart out and smash it to a pulp day after day after day with his indifference and lack of understanding. Every time he had to go "clear his head" she'd be left wondering if he'd at last woken up and realized that he'd compromised too much and made a terrible mistake.

Pressing her hands against her stomach, Delaney opened her mouth on a silent cry of pain. She loved him so much. She couldn't take so little from him.

"Hey. You're up."

She swung around to see Sam in the doorway, a bag of groceries dangling from one finger. "I snuck out to get us some brekkie stuff. Bacon, eggs, avocadoes. I can whip up some hash browns if you want."

"I want you to go," she said, her voice low and throbbing.

Sam shook his head as though he'd misheard her. "Sorry?"

"I want you to get out. Forget everything that happened last night. Forget all of it. I don't want you coming around here anymore," she said.

Sam blanched, his face a picture of confusion. "Laney. What's going on?" he said, starting forward. "Has something happened?"

Delaney took a step backward, holding up her hand palm out. "Don't touch me."

She knew she couldn't do this if he laid a hand on her. That was how weak and foolish she was.

"I need you to just go, Sam," she said, striving for a more normal tone of voice.

"No way," Sam said. "You agreed to marry me last night, Delaney. We made a deal, and I am holding you to it."

"We can't get married. It wouldn't work," she said firmly.

"Why not? We've been friends for sixteen years. You think we can't make a marriage work?"

Delaney couldn't stand it any longer. She'd stuffed her feelings down inside herself for more than a decade. She'd cried and longed and sighed over Sam too many times to count. She'd walked away from her job and her apartment and the best man she'd ever known. She really, truly had nothing left to lose.

"Don't you get it, Sam? I have been in love with you since I was fourteen years old. I have watched you sleep with a cavalcade of bimbos, I have cried myself to sleep over wanting you, and I've given my body to you knowing that you don't feel the same way. I can't do it anymore. I certainly can't marry you because you miss me and you hate change and you want your old pal back. I want more. I want all of you, and I know I can never have it and I'd rather have bloody nothing than accept some…feeble half measure that would only make us both incredibly miserable," Delaney said, all her thoughts and feelings tumbling out of her. Tears were streaming down her face and she swiped at them ineffectually with the back of her hand.

Sam looked stricken. The grocery bag dropped from his fingers and hit the floor with a crack of breaking eggs as he stared at her.

"Say it again," he demanded, moving toward her with intent.

She wiped at her face some more and threw her hands up helplessly.

"I love you. I love you. I love you. Always have, probably always will. Happy?" she said.

He stopped when he was standing mere inches away. Reaching out, he captured her face in his hands and smoothed his thumbs across her cheekbones to clear her tears.

"You have no idea how relieved I am to hear you say that," he said.

And then he kissed her. A long, slow, infinitely tender kiss that filled Delaney with wonder and a breathless, terrifying hope. She pulled back to stare intently into his face.

"Sam?"

"I am an idiot. Laney…how can one man be so dumb? I love you. I love you so much that not having you in my life makes my chest ache."

He stared at her, his eyes a fierce, clear blue.

"All these years I've wasted, keeping you by my side but at arm's length. Can you forgive me? I promise to try and make it up to you each and every day. I'll be your slave. I'll be your whatever. Because I love you. I always have, and I always will. You're the first thing I think about when I wake up in the morning, and the last thing at night, I dream about touching you, making love to you. I can't live without you."

She was trembling, and she reached out a hand to cup his dear face in her hand. She couldn't believe this was happening, but inside her, the pain that had wrapped itself around her heart was dissolving.

"Sam. So long. I can't believe we've waited so long."

"Maybe we're just slow learners," Sam said. "I can't believe how close I came to losing you."

Her heart lurched in her chest as she saw tears shimmering on the ends of his lashes. She caught one on the tip of her finger.

"No more tears," she said.

"No. Not even at our wedding."

She smiled and leaned toward him, glorying in the love shining openly from his eyes and the fact that at last she could say all that she wanted to.

"I adore you," she whispered as she pressed her lips against his. "I absolutely adore you."

"The feeling is incredibly mutual," Sam said.

His hands slid around her, pulling her close. She could feel his heart pumping under her hand, a ragged rhythm that exactly matched her own.

And it did, she realized—at last, Sam's heart matched her own.

"Take me to bed," she said as she swayed toward him. "Take me to bed and let's start making up for lost time."

Sam grinned down at her.

"Mrs. Kirk, you are full of excellent ideas this morning," he said as he stooped to pick her up in his arms.

"Mrs. Kirk? No one said anything about giving up my name," she said teasingly as he strode through the house.

Sam tossed her onto the bed and covered her body with his. "You're mine, and everyone's going to know it. You got a problem with that?"

She stared up at the passion and determination and love in his face.

It seemed that sometimes you *could* have it all.

"No," she said. "No problem at all."

* * * * *

*Set in darkness beyond the ordinary world.
Passionate tales of life and death.
With characters' lives ruled by laws the everyday world
can't begin to imagine.*

Introducing NOCTURNE, *a spine-tingling new line from
Silhouette Books.*

*The thrills and chills begin with UNFORGIVEN
by Lindsay McKenna*

Plucked from the depths of hell, former military sharpshooter
Reno Manchahi was hired by the government to kill a thief,
but he had a mission of his own. Descended from a family of
shape-shifters, Reno vowed to get the revenge he'd thirsted
for all these years. But his mission went awry when his target
turned out to be a powerful seductress, Magdalena Calen
Hernandez, who risked everything to battle a potent evil.
Suddenly, Reno had to transform himself into a true hero and
fight the enemy that threatened them all. He had to become
a Warrior for the Light....

*Turn the page for a sneak preview of UNFORGIVEN
by Lindsay McKenna.
On sale September 26, wherever books are sold.*

Chapter 1

One shot...one kill.

The sixteen-pound sledgehammer came down with such fierce power that the granite boulder shattered instantly. A spray of glittering mica exploded into the air and sparkled momentarily around the man who wielded the tool as if it were a weapon. Sweat ran in rivulets down Reno Manchahi's drawn, intense face. Naked from the waist up, the hot July sun beating down on his back, he hefted the sledgehammer skyward once more. Muscles in his thick forearms leaped and biceps bulged. Even his breath was focused on the boulder. In his mind's eye, he pictured Army General Robert Hampton's fleshy, arrogant fifty-year-old features on the rock's surface. Air exploded from between his lips as he brought the avenging hammer down. The boulder pulverized beneath his funneled hatred.

One shot...one kill...

Nostrils flaring, he inhaled the dank, humid heat and drew it deep into his massive lungs. Revenge allowed Reno to endure his imprisonment at a U.S. Navy brig near San Diego, California. Drops of sweat were flung in all directions as the crack of his sledgehammer claimed a third stone victim. Mouth taut, Reno moved to the next boulder.

The other prisoners in the stone yard gave him a wide berth. They always did. They instinctively felt his simmering hatred, the palpable revenge in his cinnamon-colored eyes, was more than skin-deep.

And they whispered he was different.

Reno enjoyed being a loner for good reason. He came from a medicine family of shape-shifters. But even this secret power had not protected him—or his family. His wife, Ilona, and his three-year-old daughter, Sarah, were dead. Murdered by Army General Hampton in their former home on USMC base in Camp Pendleton, California. Bitterness thrummed through Reno as he savagely pushed the toe of his scarred leather boot against several smaller pieces of gray granite that were in his way.

The sun beat down upon Manchahi's naked shoulders, grown dark red over time, shouting his half-Apache heritage. With his straight black hair grazing his thick shoulders, copper skin and broad face with high cheekbones, everyone knew he was Indian. When he'd first arrived at the brig, some of the prisoners taunted him and called him Geronimo. Something strange happened to Reno during his fight with the name-calling prisoners. Leaning down after he'd won the scuffle, he'd snarled into each of their bloodied faces that if they were going to call him anything, they would call him *gan,* which was the Apache word for *devil.*

His attackers had been shocked by the wounds on their faces, the deep claw marks. Reno recalled doubling his fist as they'd attacked him en masse. In that split second, he'd gone into an altered state of consciousness. In times of danger, he transformed into a jaguar. A deep, growling sound had emitted from his throat as he defended himself in the three-against-one fracas. It all happened so fast that he thought he had imagined it. He'd seen his hands morph into a forearm and paw, claws extended. The slashes left on the three men's faces after the fight told him he'd begun to shapeshift. A fist made bruises and swelling; not four perfect, deep claw marks. Stunned and anxious, he hid the knowledge of what else he was from these prisoners. Reno's only defense was to make all the prisoners so damned scared of him and remain a loner.

Alone. Yeah, he was alone, all right. The steel hammer swept downward with hellish ferocity. As the granite groaned in protest, Reno shut his eyes for just a moment. Sweat dripped off his nose and square chin.

Straightening, he wiped his furrowed, wet brow and looked into the pale blue sky. What got his attention was the startling cry of a red-tailed hawk as it flew over the brig yard. Squinting, he watched the bird. Reno could make out the rust-colored tail on the hawk. As a kid growing up on the Apache reservation in Arizona, Reno knew that all animals that appeared before him were messengers.

Brother, what message do you bring me? Reno knew one had to ask in order to receive. Allowing the sledgehammer to drop to his side, he concentrated on the hawk who wheeled in tightening circles above him.

Freedom! the hawk cried in return.

Reno shook his head, his black hair moving against his broad, thickset shoulders. *Freedom? No way, Brother. No way.* Figuring that he was making up the hawk's shrill message, Reno turned away. Back to his rocks. Back to picturing Hampton's smug face.

Freedom!

* * * * *

Look for UNFORGIVEN by Lindsay McKenna,
the spine-tingling launch title from Silhouette Nocturne™.
Available September 26, wherever books are sold.

nocturne™

Save $1.⁰⁰ off

your purchase of any
Silhouette® Nocturne™ novel.

Silhouette

nocturne™

Save $1.⁰⁰ off

your purchase of any
Silhouette® Nocturne™ novel.

Receive $1.00 off

any Silhouette® Nocturne™ novel.

Available wherever books are sold, including most bookstores, supermarkets, drugstores and discount stores.

Coupon expires December 1, 2006. Redeemable at participating retail outlets in Canada only. Limit one coupon per customer.

RETAILER: Harlequin Enterprises Limited will pay the face value of this coupon plus 10.25 cents if submitted by the customer for this specified product only. Any other use constitutes fraud. Coupon is nonassignable. Void if taxed, prohibited or restricted by law. Consumer must pay any government taxes. Mail to Harlequin Enterprises Ltd., P.O. Box 3000, Saint John, New Brunswick E2L 4L3, Canada. Limit one coupon per customer. Valid in Canada only.

52607136

SNCOUPCDN

If you enjoyed what you just read,
then we've got an offer you can't resist!

Take 2 bestselling love stories FREE!

Plus get a FREE surprise gift!

Clip this page and mail it to Harlequin Reader Service®

IN U.S.A.	IN CANADA
3010 Walden Ave.	P.O. Box 609
P.O. Box 1867	Fort Erie, Ontario
Buffalo, N.Y. 14240-1867	L2A 5X3

YES! Please send me 2 free Harlequin® Blaze™ novels and my free surprise gift. After receiving them, if I don't wish to receive anymore, I can return the shipping statement marked cancel. If I don't cancel, I will receive 6 brand-new novels each month, before they're available in stores! In the U.S.A., bill me at the bargain price of $3.99 plus 25¢ shipping and handling per book and applicable sales tax, if any*. In Canada, bill me at the bargain price of $4.47 plus 25¢ shipping and handling per book and applicable taxes**. That's the complete price and a savings of at least 10% off the cover prices—what a great deal! I understand that accepting the 2 free books and gift places me under no obligation ever to buy any books. I can always return a shipment and cancel at any time. Even if I never buy another book from Harlequin, the 2 free books and gift are mine to keep forever.

151 HDN D7ZZ
351 HDN D72D

Name	(PLEASE PRINT)	
Address		Apt.#
City	State/Prov.	Zip/Postal Code

Not valid to current Harlequin® Blaze™ subscribers.

Want to try two free books from another series?
Call 1-800-873-8635 or visit www.morefreebooks.com.

* Terms and prices subject to change without notice. Sales tax applicable in N.Y.
** Canadian residents will be charged applicable provincial taxes and GST.
   All orders subject to approval. Offer limited to one per household.
   ® and ™ are registered trademarks owned and used by the trademark owner and/or its licensee.

BLZ05   ©2005 Harlequin Enterprises Limited.

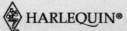

HARLEQUIN®

Blaze™

COMING NEXT MONTH

#279 THE MIGHTY QUINNS: MARCUS Kate Hoffmann
The Mighty Quinns, Bk. 1
With her sex video scandal about to hit the tabloids, Eden Ross just wants to hide out on her daddy's boat for a while. Then she finds scrumptious Marcus Quinn working on board, and can't deny herself a little fun. After all, if Marcus thinks she's some serial sexpot out to use him for his body, she'll just have to prove him…right.

#280 ASKING FOR TROUBLE Leslie Kelly
It Was a Dark and Sexy Night…, Bk. 2
Budding journalist Lottie Santori is dying to escape her overprotective family and experience a little sexual adventure. And her upcoming—out of town—job, researching scary old Seaton House, offers definite possibilities…. Because her host—dark, sexy Simon Lebeau—looks as if he can give Lottie the thrill of a lifetime. If she lasts that long…

#281 THE PLEASURE CHEST Jule McBride
New York artist Tanya Taylor is amazed—and incredibly turned on—when real-life pirate Stede O'Flannery magically appears before her very eyes. But Stede has only one week to break a deadly curse. He's got to fall in love—and fast. Good thing Tanya, with her chestful of toys, knows the most *pleasurable* ways to a man's heart.

#282 JUST DARE ME… Stephanie Bond
Adrenaline Rush, Bk. 3
Marketing exec Gabrielle Flannery likes a challenge, but this one's something else! In order to win the account she deserves, she has to compete, head-to-head, with sexy Dell Kingston in a wilderness survival weekend. Little does she guess how many other body parts she and Dell will end up bumping together….

#283 THE MAVERICK Rhonda Nelson
Men Out of Uniform, Bk. 3
Former Ranger Guy McCann has built a reputation for pulling off the impossible. There's never been anyone who's dared more, done more…. Still, he's nervous when his former commander Colonel Garrett calls in his "favor." The last two guys who paid ended up married! But that's not about to happen to this Guy…is it?

#284 A WHISPER OF WANTING Jamie Sobrato
Lust Potion #9, Bk. 1
Could spontaneous lust be blamed on a potion? There's no other logical reason Nicole Arroyo just tangled with Ethan Ramsey…again…in his backseat! While the potion might explain the first time, what explains all those other sexy interludes?

HBCNM0906